M000312226

To my husband, Chadley.

Also by Mia Thompson

Stalking Sapphire

Diversion Books
A Division of Diversion Publishing Corp.
443 Park Avenue South, Suite 1004
New York, New York 10016
www.DiversionBooks.com

Copyright © 2013 by Mia Thompson

All rights reserved, including the right to reproduce this book or portions thereof in any form whatsoever.

For more information, email info@diversionbooks.com

First Diversion Books edition October 2013.

Print ISBN: 978-1-62681-213-0
eBook ISBN: 978-1-62681-067-9

SILENCING SAPPHIRE

A Sapphire Dubois Thriller

MIA THOMPSON

DIVERSIONBOOKS

CHAPTER 1

There were two people in the garage that night and only one of them was going to make it out alive.

The light bulbs in the staircase were dying. They flickered on and off as if the building was trying to warn her. *Run. He's coming for you.*

In the darkness he felt superhuman. The strobe effect moved him from one place to the next in the blink of an eye. She was three flights above him and every time the light flashed back on, he was that much closer to her.

How? was the only question running though his mind. *How will she die?*

Unlike his fellow murderers, who seemed to have one set M.O., he refused to be redundant. The girl's personality mattered to him, but other than that, he lived his life not day by day, but moment to moment. He ate when he wanted to, killed when he wanted to, and worked only when he wanted to. Unless, of course, he was with his mother, then he did everything *she* wanted to.

That wasn't the only thing that separated him from the others with a thrill for a kill. He never kept track of how many he slayed. There were only two kills that mattered to him, his *first* and his *next*.

The first time he killed was accidental. He was raping a young woman in the alley by a crowded downtown street when it happened.

With tears in her eyes, she reached toward the bustling masses only five yards away. She screamed and he squeezed his hand hard over her lips and nose, drowning her voice with pressure. It took him awhile to realize that the reason her body stopped trembling wasn't because she gave into him, but because he stole her breath.

He would never forget how that last tear trickled down her cheek. Her lifeless eyes and hand still reached to the busy crowd, as if they could save her from death.

Staring down at her, he realized that stealing life was power in its absolute form. He thought raping gave him control, but her death gave him something more. She was dead because *he* had the power to end her life. The feeling was indescribable. He wanted to repeat and relive that moment of death for the rest of his life.

Tonight was no different.

He flew up the staircase, two steps at a time, chasing after her. She was one level above him now. He could feel the urge to kill rising within him. Hot, black, and overpowering, it poured out of him. He prepared to become her God.

Though she pretended otherwise, he knew she was sacred. Her steps were short and fast because she was tense. Like the others, she didn't want to run because, in her mind, the person following her was not a deranged serial killer, but simply someone who had parked on the same level as her.

But the man following her was, in fact, a deranged serial killer. She was getting the warning signals, but years of social training—don't make a fool of yourself—overrode her survival instincts.

So many girls could have gotten away from him had they listened to their instincts and ran. Honestly, he wasn't that fast.

He leaned over the railing, catching a glimpse of her brown hair and petite frame before she got off on her level.

Her name, which he loved, was that of a gemstone. Then again, weren't all their names gems, sweets, or months of the year?

He took his time with the last steps, grateful that she decided to take the stairs instead of the old elevator. The chase allowed him the time he needed to figure out how she would die.

In order to repeat the feeling of surprise from his first kill, he kept his options open. He might decide on throat-cutting, for instance, then change his mind and rip her esophagus out with his bare hands instead.

For this gem, he already passed on the usual kills. Stabbing felt cliché. Strangling too boring. Decapitation overrated.

The bulb flashes grew faint, their life coming to an end. Like hers.

He sped up and the rapid beats of his steps bounced between the thick cement walls of the garage. He knew she heard him coming. When he reached the last steps, he saw her run.

The bulbs burned out and the staircase turned black. He stared at her from a blanket of darkness. She was exposed and her sprint reminded him of a terrified rabbit.

He knew what he wanted.

He wouldn't kill her in the garage. He would bring her to the woods. There, she would be strung upside down in a tree and skinned alive. He would take his time peeling the skin away from her red flesh like he'd done with rabbits when he was a kid.

His gaze drew to the humming metal box next to the garage's elevator and a smirk spread across his face. He grabbed his knife and stabbed it into the generator.

The overhead lights shut off in a domino effect that ended at the girl. As the last overhead went out she stopped. After a moment, she moved again. Her pace was fast and focused now, the sound of a woman running for her life.

He moved toward her in the shadows, traveling fast and on light feet. He hid behind a wall divider and peered at her as she scrambled through her purse for the keys. She looked over her shoulder every second, her senses yelling that she wasn't alone.

He waited until she found her keys and got into her car. Just as she exhaled, believing she was out of harm's way, he lunged for her.

He ripped the door open and reached for her. She let out a sharp scream and grabbed his arm. She fought back.

He knew she wouldn't go down without a battle. She was a tough one, which is why he liked her. He just didn't expect her to be *so* strong.

Trapped by her twisting grip, his knees buckled under him

and it looked as though he was losing. It caught him off guard. He was supposed to be Zeus, *not* her.

He let his free hand search for something, anything. His fingers wrapped around the base of her side mirror and ripped it off.

He swung the back of the mirror and smashed it into her face. Again and again, he heard her bones crack and her skull shatter. He bashed until there was nothing left to bash. He didn't stop until his face was covered in her blood.

As her lights went out, the overheads burst back on; the backup generator had kicked in.

He looked down at her and his adrenaline pumped, filling him with life. Her pretty face was gone. Bloody flesh and fragments of her nose remained.

He headed for the elevator, grinning. The bashing was wonderful, just as unexpected and fulfilling as his *first*. He killed for fun, and she—his gem—was just that.

The elevator doors closed, and his smile faded on cue. This always happened when the moment was over. She, who had just meant everything to him, now meant nothing. She was in the past, just as forgotten as the others.

He sighed, knowing he would have to walk around with the hollowness as he waited for the only thing that mattered: his *next*.

The elevator dinged and the doors opened.

Then again, he thought, trying to be optimistic as he looked at his blood splattered watch, *the night is young*.

And his curfew wasn't until 11:30.

CHAPTER 2

Run.

She smiled over the ocean of rich and famous.

The Beverly Hills Country Club was filled with people laughing, drinking, and swapping bodily fluids with those other than their spouses in the coatroom.

On the outside, Sapphire Dubois looked the part. From the Jimmy Choos and Dior dress, to the man holding her hand, she gave the impression of the typical Beverly Hills heiress.

It was a lie.

On the inside, Sapphire was screaming for only two things: to hunt *them* and to be with *him*.

Run. Her legs were unresponsive, crossed at the ankles in proper Beverly Hills fashion.

A sharp *ding ding ding* came from a 0.15 karat diamond wine glass held by Mrs. Vanderpilt, her fiancé John's mother. Next to John's mother sat Mr. Vanderpilt, wearing the expression of a man surrounded by cockroaches. The Dubois' 250 million worth was trailer trash compared to Vanderpilt's multi-billion-dollar empire.

"Good evening, dear friends and family. I'm so pleased you all could join us for the pre-rehearsal dinner tonight."

Only in Beverly Hills did people rehearse a rehearsal.

Breathe, Sapphire, breathe. This is how big the mess had gotten.

"Through our years of marriage, my husband and I have traveled the world." The crowd held onto Mrs. Vanderpilt's every word. "Many times to help those who could not help themselves."

Beverly Hills Translation Guide (BHTG): "*Shipping jobs overseas, receiving substantial tax cuts.*"

"The poor villages in Africa, the starved children of Indonesia."

BHTG: *"Locating cheap child labor."*

"Saving the endangered baboons of the rain forest."

BHTG: *"Cutting down the rainforest and using its baboons for medical research."*

"And now, we welcome you, Sapphire, into our family." She raised her glass. "To young love!"

BHTG: *"May it end before the prenup kicks in."*

The family and friends seated around the U-shaped table raised their glasses along with the guests in the middle of the room. Everyone seemed oblivious to the fact that Mrs. Vanderpilt had just compared Sapphire joining the family to saving a baboon. To them, she was just another charity case.

Sapphire watched the crowd sip their Dom. She wanted to blame them for the wedding and for 18 years of making her feel like a caged animal, but she knew they weren't the problem. *Sapphire* was the black sheep disguised in Dior. *She* was the one who didn't belong and who wanted to be out hunting *them*.

The only other person around the U-shaped table who didn't seem to be enjoying herself was Petunia, her Uncle Gary's daughter. Petunia sat next to her boyfriend, dragging her finger around her water glass while keeping her narrowed eyes on Sapphire. Her thoughts were clear: *Why does* she *get to marry a Vanderpilt and not me? I'm* the actual Dubois, not her. *What does he even see in her?*

Good question, what did he see in her? Sapphire looked at him.

John Vanderpilt III stared at his reflection in the caviar bowl, making a series of faces.

"What are you doing?" Sapphire asked.

"Practicing for the wedding photos," John said, eyes still on himself. "I call this 'The Daniel Craig'. What do think?" He pouted, furrowed his eyebrows, and squinted.

Run.

Sapphire initiated a stare-down with her legs. Nothing, not even a twitch. Not that it mattered. Even if her legs obeyed,

John's iron grip on her hand would keep her trapped.

How had it even gotten to this point? How was she so close to marrying a man she couldn't stand?

"Aaa-ha-ha-haa!" Chrissy laughed next to Sapphire, throwing her head back.

Sapphire peered at her best friend. Christina Kraft, heiress of the Kraft industry, was deeply entertained by an anecdote that she, herself, had just told.

That's where it started, with Chrissy.

It was months ago, right after a killer had stalked her, tortured Shelly McCormick, and nearly drowned Julia, the Dubois' ex-housekeeper and the woman who had raised Sapphire.

John and Sapphire had been broken up when he burst into the middle of Julia and her husband, Antonio's reception. He stole the microphone from the band and got down on one knee, asking Sapphire to marry him.

The proposal was gladly accepted…by Chrissy on Sapphire's behalf. Sapphire had stood in shock, opening and closing her mouth like a fish.

This was nothing new. Chrissy always did things on her behalf. Like deciding to assign Sapphire a new wardrobe, or give her a pony. But a fiancé? That was a bit much, even for Chrissy.

Sapphire tried to hold a grudge against her friend, but it was like trying to stay mad at a puppy. Chrissy didn't know any better and her eyes were always big and full of innocence. Ever since last November, when they had that talk, Chrissy annoyed her less. There were even times when Sapphire enjoyed being around her now.

Sapphire had opted to not worry about the wedding; the Vanderpilts had threatened John with the loss of his inheritance if he married Sapphire. She had been confident he would dump her the second his beloved Porsche and allowance were taken away.

She was not prepared for the Vanderpilts to cave.

John was their *only* son, the one meant to carry on the family fortune. The bastards had been bluffing, hoping *he* would fold. But he hadn't, and Sapphire's problem had jumped from manageable to mayhem.

The Vanderpilts were high up on the social scale, right below the Sinclairs, Krafts, and Rockefellers. Not wanting to marry a Vanderpilt was as preposterous as avoiding air. If Sapphire broke it off, people in Beverly Hills would want to know why and the rumors would begin. *Was Sapphire Dubois abnormal? Insane?* She couldn't have that.

Sapphire had spent the last three years hunting and capturing *them*: Southern California's most-wanted serial killers. With eight under her belt, she was a vigilante known to the police as the Serial Catcher. She was hunted by a detective who had no idea that the Serial Catcher he was so hell-bent on tracking down had already shared his bed.

She couldn't raise suspicion, couldn't risk being known as anything other than a stereotypical heiress, someone who thought Ted Bundy was a character from *Married with Children*.

When Eloise—the wedding planner from Hell—was brought on board, everything spiraled out of control. Millions were spent on the preparations.

Sapphire knew the only way to stop the madness was a plan. A perfect plan that would make her emerge from the whole debacle blameless.

So far, she'd only come up with imperfect plans, like faking her own death, building a time machine, or joining the circus.

She would *not* marry John Vanderpilt.

"Pardon me. Pardon meee!" Sapphire's mother, Vivienne, elbowed her way to the microphone.

Oh God.

Sapphire used her hand to block her mother out of sight and searched for *him* instead, knowing he wouldn't be there. She turned him away months ago. He was a hunter and she, his target. Not a great foundation for a healthy relationship. She thought he would vanish from her mind with time and distance. Instead he grew like a tumor. A really *hot* tumor.

"Is this on?" Vivienne pounded the microphone. A series of high pitched squeals sounded.

The audience covered their ears, and Sapphire closed

her eyes wishing for two things. One: that her mother would be sober...ish. Completely sober was unrealistic. Two: that the country club would spontaneously combust and force the night to end.

The universe responded.

While over-explaining her joke, Vivienne gestured wildly, accidentally clocking Mrs. Vanderpilt in the face, who. fell into the thick curtains. The curtain pole couldn't hold the weight and came crashing down, knocking over a waiter who was just about to flambé the crepe suzette. Instead, he flambéed the whole table.

A mass panic broke out. Oblivious, Vivienne tried to save her joke. "*Skinny*, get it? John owns slaughterhouses and Sapphire's a vegetarian. What will she eat?"

In slow motion, Sapphire watched John's fingers unclench her hand. He took off into the chaos to help his mother.

"Aaa-ha-ha-haa!" Chrissy laughed, pointing at the waiter whose sleeve was on fire.

Not one eye was on Sapphire.

Run!

Sapphire's legs jerked and she reacted. She marched for the ceiling-high double doors and pushed them open. The cool evening breeze hit her, and she took her first true breath of the night, her body tingling with relief.

Sapphire made her way to the valet where she found John's friends and Justin Bieber cooing over someone's new Jaguar. They were blocking her only way out. Sapphire looked over at the wall on the other side of the golf course. In two swift moves, she kicked off her Jimmy Choos and left them for dead.

Hearing the seams of her tight Dior dress rip with every stride, Sapphire sprinted through the sea of sprinklers and across the wet grass. The farther she got from the Beverly Hills society, the better she felt.

One person ran through Sapphire's mind as she scaled the stone wall. *Him.* The one man she should be running from, not to.

Aston Ridder.

. . .

Detective Aston Ridder was in the middle of a threesome.

He stared up at the ceiling above his bed and shifted his nuts, placing his arm behind his neck for support. To the left of him lay a man, the Serial Catcher, and to the right of him a woman, Sapphire Dubois.

Neither of them were really there, but with the amount of space they always took up in Aston's mind they might as well have been.

"You've had months and I'm still free," the Serial Catcher boasted. *"Losing your touch, Ridder?"*

On his other side, Sapphire propped herself up on her elbow and smiled. *"No, there's someone on his mind who matters more than you. He just won't admit it."*

"Don't be ridiculous," the Serial Catcher said. *"We both know the only thing Aston Ridder truly cares about is himself. You're a temporary obsession at best. I'm the ticket to making his childhood dream a reality."*

When the trapped serial killers started showing up across Southern California three years ago, Aston was hooked. Sure, the cases intrigued him, but in the back of his mind he knew that bringing down the Serial Catcher could get him a foot in the door with the FBI.

They'd already turned him down twice, even before his leg got jacked. That damned leg was what took him out of action-packed downtown L.A. and landed him in Beverly Hills.

The FBI's excuse was Aston's supposed "lack of social skills." It didn't make sense; he had been on his best behavior. He only called the psychologist evaluating him a perverted mind-fucker *once*. Twice, tops.

If Aston bagged the Serial Catcher, they wouldn't be able to turn him down, bad leg or no.

He wasn't sure if news of the Serial Catcher had reached the FBI yet. The media knew nothing. The guy existed only by word of mouth. It was an embarrassment. A vigilante who caught murderers before the police even had suspects. If word got to the media before the Serial Catcher was caught, it would be a freak show of superhero fanatics and copycats, dying for their fifteen minutes of fame.

Bringing in the Serial Catcher would be a career boost to say the least, but Aston didn't give two shits about the media attention that was sure to come along. He just wanted to catch the fucker so that he could move out of Beverly Hills and into Quantico.

"Screw it," Aston said and lit a cigarette. He preferred to smoke by the window, but he was too sapped to roll off the bed.

It was one in the morning, and he had had a long-ass day. They had spent the day re-watching Rath's interrogation in Thousand Oaks and the night with beers at another one of Capelli's strip clubs, *Kitty's Cave*. He had gotten home, ready for a good night's sleep, but was still wide awake.

Aston puffed on his cigarette, trying to remember the last expression he'd seen on George Rath's face. The man had been a godsend to Aston and Capelli: a serial killer caught by the Serial Catcher himself at their full disposal. Rath had just started talking and then...

Somebody knocked on Aston's door.

He pulled on his jeans, leaving his upper body bare. Who was the idiot coming over at this hour? Aston yanked the door open.

"H-hey," he said, taken aback.

Sapphire stood in front of him in a short dress, wet hair clinging to the sides of her face, dark makeup smeared under her eyes and on her cheeks, her bare feet covered in grass strands and dirt. Needless to say, she looked *hot*!

"Hi…"

They stood in comfortable silence. He didn't want to look down, but he had to. His eyes drew to the big ugly diamond that was *still* on her fucking finger.

She followed his gaze and her hand clasped to cover the ring.

"Sapphire, what are you doing here?" he asked, acting as though he hadn't driven by her house at least thirty-six times in the past few months.

Looking down, she leaned into the door frame, her body inching closer to his. Involuntarily, Aston closed his eyes to take her in. She smelled *really* nice, but also like dirt and grass.

"I…"

"Aston?" A woman's voice called out.

Fuck.

Sapphire quickly looked up, surprised, her gaze landing on the woman Aston knew was standing behind him.

He had forgotten. It slipped his mind.

"Aren't you going to introduce me?" Officer Moore asked.

"Um," he tried, "this is Officer Moore."

"*Angelica.*" Moore leaned around Aston to shake Sapphire's hand. She was wearing panties and his old Dodgers t-shirt, her hair still wet from the shower.

Sapphire's eyes shot back to Aston. He knew he looked as guilty as he felt. Not that he had any reason to feel that way. *She* was the one who was engaged. He, by all means, was free to sleep with whomever he wanted.

"Ah…hi. Sapphire." Sapphire's face grew a few shades redder as she stared at Officer Moore's lack of attire. "I'm sorry for interrupting you guys…I didn't know."

"It's not—" Aston started the lie.

"No worries," Officer Moore cut in. "Just be glad you didn't come twenty minutes earlier. *Then* you would have interrupted something." She laughed and elbowed Aston playfully in the ribs. It kind of hurt.

There was a long uncomfortable silence.

"I should go," Sapphire said. "I should…go. Nice to meet you, Angelica."

"You too." Officer Moore smiled. She went back inside and Sapphire started walking down the hallway.

"Sapphire…" Aston called after her. She pretended she didn't hear him. She didn't stop or turn and was soon on her way down the stairs.

Aston stepped back inside, shooting Officer Moore a glare. She stood in the small kitchen of his studio, eating *his* All-Bran cereal from *his* breakfast bowl.

"She was nice. Who is she?" Moore asked and rubbed her eye hard.

"She's…no one," Aston answered, one hundred percent honest, convinced she was no one to someone.

He probably shouldn't have said that, he realized. He didn't want Moore to think their arrangement was leading somewhere it wasn't, like so many women before her.

They had slept together three times in the past month, not counting their quickie when he first transferred to Beverly Hills. He'd been working late, and Sapphire had been on his mind an excruciating amount. He realized there was only one thing he could do to smoke her out of the corner of his mind where she had nested.

Aston feared he'd never be able to stop thinking about Sapphire. He needed to move on. A palate cleanser. And Moore had assured him several times that she just wanted some fun. Nothing serious.

"She looks young. Wish I still had her skin." Officer Moore chuckled as she finished her bowl of cereal.

"Twenty-three…just turned," he said, pissed about Sapphire's surprise visit. So pissed that he thought about letting Officer Moore spend the night. Surely Sapphire would be running into the arms of her little rich boy. The imagery shot through Aston's mind like a repulsive slide show and settled any doubts he had. He *would* let Moore spend the night.

"Ooops." Officer Moore shook the cereal box over the bowl. "You're out of cereal."

"Get out."

CHAPTER 3

An elderly woman burst out of the confessional, bawling into her handkerchief. Sapphire looked after her and stepped into the booth, feeling her nerves settle by just being in his presence.

She should never have gone to Aston's. She went against her own rule and now the image of Beverly Hills' most attractive female cop in Aston's shirt was burned into her mind. It had sent Sapphire running to her confidant, to the only person who knew she collected serial killers like her contemporaries collected songs on their iPods.

"Holy crap! Did you go to town on the Hail Marys with that lady or what?" she asked Father O'Riley as she sat down.

"Can you try to make it five seconds before you fire off the blasphemy, Sapphire?" he responded. "I *may* have told her there was a chance she'd burn in hell for all eternity."

"For what?"

"You know I can't tell you that...but I wasn't really listening anyway. Same old stuff. Unclean thoughts about the mailman. Envy over the neighbor's award-winning peach cobbler...yada-yada-yada."

Sapphire frowned. She'd never heard him talk this way. He was one of the kindest people she knew and his congregation meant more to him than he meant to himself.

"So what's on your mind?" he asked. "No wait, let me guess. Unwanted marriage. Wanted cop. And, as always, the main course: serial killers."

"Well yeah, but do you have to be such a sourpuss about it?"

"I have problems, too. Does anyone care? No. Why am I always the one who has to listen to everybody else's problems?"

"I'd assume because of the whole priest thing." Sapphire

pushed her nose against the net. "What's up with you?"

He bowed his head, remaining silent.

"Tell me it doesn't involve *her* and more boning. You know what they say, bone me once shame on..."

"Please stop saying *bone*."

Father O'Riley had slept with a woman in his congregation the year before. He had broken it off but had been plagued by Catholic-priests-shall-not-bone guilt ever since.

"Sapphire, I'm curious. Why are you so compelled to capture these men?" Father O'Riley asked harshly, changing the subject.

"Would you ask a painter or a chef the same question?" Sapphire couldn't mask her defensiveness.

"Okay, let's put it this way," he offered. "What do you want most at this very moment?"

"Kind of want you to quit being rude. Other than that, I guess, my next killer."

"So, you can't break off the engagement with the man you don't want to be with because Beverly Hills will think you're a nutcase. And *because* you capture serial killers you can't have any negative attention aimed your way."

"Yeah?"

"You're pining for a cop, who you can't have because he's after the Serial Catcher. Which would be you."

She knew where this was heading. "Can we talk about something else? How 'bout them Dodgers, eh?"

"You do realize that all your problems can be solved by simply removing serial killers from your life, right? By *stopping*. But the only thing you can think about is finding your next catch."

Sapphire scoffed. "I can't just stop."

"Why?"

"Because someone needs to stop them, *that's* why!" Sapphire was getting flustered.

"The cops handled it long before you came along. Ever ask yourself why you're unable to stop doing something that is not only dangerous, but also the culprit of all the problems you whine about?"

Sapphire grabbed her purse and stormed out of the confessional, slamming the door behind her. She felt sick when she reached the parking lot. Having her trust turned against her was something Sapphire expected from the people in Beverly Hills, not Father O'Riley.

She gave the door to her old Volkswagen three kicks and a knee. It responded to the code, allowing her to open the door. She sat behind the wheel, the car's Febreze-resistant scent of decomposing Cheetos filling her nostrils. To Sapphire this stench was the calming aroma of independence; it barely made her gag anymore.

A knock made her jump. She rolled down the window, the lever coming off in her hand.

"What do you want?" She tossed the lever over her shoulder, where it joined the other dead parts in the backseat.

"I'm sorry, kid." Father O'Riley smiled. "I haven't been myself since the ordeal with the…you know…"

"Boning," Sapphire filled in.

"Woman," he corrected, then braced his elbow against the roof. "You know, I still meant what I said, but I shouldn't have pushed something I knew you weren't ready for."

Sapphire clenched the wheel.

He watched her for a moment, then waved his hand. "You know what, forget what I said. I have a solution for you."

"Oh yeah?" *Doubt it.*

"Why don't you leave? Beverly Hills, I mean. It's not what you want in life, and the whole serial killer bit is, so just go."

"Yeah right." Sapphire tilted her head. "I get a weekly allowance from my mom, all my actual money is tied up in Charles's will, and I have nowhere to go."

Father O'Riley mulled it over. "Why don't you come live with me until you get a job and place of your own?"

Sapphire looked at him, surprised. "Thanks, but…well, for starters I can't leave Charles alone with my mom. And, as much as I don't like it, being a Beverly Hills heiress has its benefits in the Serial Catcher department. I have the perfect cover. Why would I give that up?"

"I hear excuses," he said, softly. "I think the big bad Serial Catcher is scared to leave the comfort of a society she doesn't even like."

"I think the priest is so scared to deal with his own issues that he's pushing everybody else's. You're obviously not happy here anymore. If it's so easy, why don't *you* leave?"

Father O'Riley searched for words, conceding with a nod. "Well played."

"I learned from the best," she said, putting the car in drive. "See you next week?"

"Right..." Father O'Riley gazed off into the distance, lost in thought.

Once she was on the freeway, the news came on the radio. She turned up the volume using a screwdriver, hoping for a new killer.

"A series of car-nappings have been reported. The latest in Colorado..."

Sapphire smacked the radio off.

If it wasn't California, she couldn't do anything about it. Even before the wedding chaos started, Sapphire was never able to leave without people noticing. Not to mention the paper trail that would come from flights and hotel stays. She was as chained to California as she was to Beverly Hills.

She tried to focus on something else, but with the radio off, Father O'Riley's interrogation was ringing in her ears.

It wasn't the question of *why* Sapphire had the strong need to go after murderous men that turned her stomach; she had asked herself that more than a few times.

It was the answer that scared her.

• • •

"What do you think, will it rain today?" Richard Martin peered at the gloomy gray clouds through the windshield.

She remained silent.

The blood was everywhere. There were very few spots, besides from the windshield which he had wiped clean, that weren't covered in the dried red substance. It was even in the interior of the glove compartment; which was surprising considering it had been closed.

"I'm getting hungry; shall we stop for breakfast?" Richard asked.

The woman lay zombie-like in the passenger seat, her dead eyes staring at Richard.

It was nice to have someone to talk to, even if she was deceased. He knew she was dead; he wasn't crazy, just a bit on the lonesome side.

Before that predator ruined everything, Richard hadn't realized how much he'd enjoyed the human, non-killing, interactions in his life. Every Friday, he'd have lunch with his coworkers at *Smart Tec*; he needed them to stay sane.

It had been months now since that horrible night.

She had been sitting in one of the bars where Richard picked out his girls, dressed the way he liked. He had followed her out of the bar and into Garrison forest. She had run, pretending to be scared, then he had fallen into that godforsaken *pit* she'd made.

She'd stood over him with that look of superiority; then she had laughed. Yes, *she* had laughed at *him*. Richard still heard that acidic laugh sometimes, ringing in his ears like a fire alarm.

After she shredded his self-confidence to nothing, she called the cops anonymously and left. The police arrived minutes later.

When they had questioned him, he'd said nothing. It was the most humiliating experience of his life. To have his own victim turn on him was *sickening*.

After he was sentenced to San Quentin, he'd overheard two cops talking smack about him. They'd whispered *its* name: the Serial Catcher.

He wasn't her first. She had spent years fooling and trapping murderers like him. And worse yet, the cops had kept it quiet, perhaps too embarrassed as well. Had Richard had his say, a national warning would've gone out.

During the transport to California's number one maximum security prison, Richard managed to get loose. He had set the prison truck on fire, killing the guards, and escaped with a single goal in mind.

Her, the Serial Catcher.

He'd been traveling in and out of Los Angeles ever since, staying a week at a time. He always had to keep moving; he could *not* get caught before she was dead.

Richard pulled into the diner, insisting to his co-pilot that he should pay for breakfast. He took her dead silence as concurrence and pulled out the petty change that was left from the hooker he snuffed in Colorado.

Richard looked around. Was he in Utah today? A few months back all the states had started to blur together. Same ever-stretching roads, same monotonous gas stations, same neglected motels, wherever he was.

He took a window booth and pulled down his ball cap to hide his face.

Not because he was hunted. The fire Richard set had spread to the fuel tank and the prison truck exploded in the vacant desert. By the time it was discovered, the guards' bodies had been cremated into ash. Since he'd been chained inside, the police had assumed he was among them. Richard Martin was officially dead. But it was possible that someone would recognize him from the media circus of his trial. If they alerted the police that the Double Blade Killer was still alive, there would be a manhunt. Richard's revenge mission was already difficult enough. He couldn't allow any more obstacles.

He ordered his pancakes from a young waitress in a turtleneck. *Yuck. How does she expect people to want to kill her wearing that?* He gazed out the window, feeling blue.

How many times had he gone back without results? Searching for a young attractive woman without a name in Los Angeles was like searching for a single grain of sand in the Sahara desert.

Perhaps, a small voice in his head suggested, *it's time to give up and run to Mexico instead.* He could spend the rest of his days in peace, drinking margaritas, swimming in the ocean, killing unsuspecting senoritas.

A year ago that lifestyle would have sounded like a dream to

Richard. His kills nowadays had seemed dry, boring. Maybe he was just fed up with Americans.

He didn't want to give up. He wanted to demolish that cocky smile of hers and extinguish her ridiculing laugh, but he wasn't sure he'd even be able to, and Mexico was certainly looking tempting.

A woman in a deliciously short skirt stepped out of a Blue Chevy in the parking lot. A young, very much alive, woman who was much more beautiful than the dead ol' ball 'n' chain in the car.

Richard's eyes followed her as she walked in.

"Restrooms?" she asked the waitress, who gave her a key and directed her outside.

The girl pulled out her phone, rolling her eyes. "Dad, please stop calling. I'm almost there." She headed for the restroom. "You're such a worrywart. Nothing bad is going to happen."

When she turned, Richard saw the back of her tightly fitting hoodie, featuring the University of California, Los Angeles.

UCLA: Come, Your Future Awaits.

It was a sign. Destiny was telling him not to give up, urging him to continue on his mission.

"Pancakes," the waitress said, putting his plate down.

"On second thought, I'll take them to go," he said.

Richard Martin would head for California, to once again seek out the Serial Catcher. He smiled, filled with a strong comforting sense; this time he would find her.

He grabbed his pancakes and moved toward the restrooms with a renewed pep in his step, off to meet his new travel companion.

• • •

"A job?" Sapphire muttered as she pulled into the gas station. Who was Father O'Riley kidding? What could she possibly put on her resume? Rich, spoiled, bagged eight serial killers? Nobody would hire her.

She got out, slamming the door. She grabbed the nozzle

and stuck it in the Volkswagen as she watched the small TV above the pump.

"Thursday night," the female reporter stated. "A young woman was brutally murdered in a parking garage after leaving her shift from the downtown Los Angeles strip club, the Golden Mirage, around 9 p.m."

Sapphire was hooked.

"To her fans and coworkers, the exotic dancer was known as Amber," the reporter continued, "but her real name was Jennifer Stark and she is the third young dancer that has been killed from the establishment in the past few months. At the moment, the LAPD is not making any statement about the man dubbed the *Stripper Slayer…*"

Sapphire was absorbing every detail, photo, and image. This was it. The colors and sounds around her faded as she focused on the TV screen.

This man—this serial killer—was hers.

Her gaze shifted from the TV to a guy at the opposite pump. He was rudely gawking at her: mouth open, eyes popping.

Creep.

Sapphire gave him her best stink-eye, then looked down and realized what he was staring at. She hadn't let go of the handle and the gas was pooling around her feet.

"Crap!"

She yanked the nozzle out and clamored back into the car, mildly embarrassed but extremely excited.

Since she got stalked last year, Sapphire had, despite serious effort, caught no serial killers whatsoever. Zero. Zip. Zilch. Not even one little rapist.

Now Sapphire felt the familiar rush. Her senses sharpened. Her mind focused. The stress of the wedding faded, disappearing to that sector where less urgent matters went.

For the first time in months, she veered off toward Beverly Hills with a smile. Sapphire would do everything in her power to save the girls at the Golden Mirage. She would take his aim away from them and put it on herself. She would become his next target.

Sapphire had done a lot of things to get her killers: put on weird wigs, worn outlandish clothes, and faked accents.

Never had she gone this deep undercover.

Father O'Riley was onto something, after all.

Sapphire Dubois, the Beverly Hills heiress, was about to get her first job.

CHAPTER 4

"NEIN!!!"

Sapphire halted with one foot in midair at the entrance of the kitchen.

Berta Braun, their new housekeeper, was pointing down at the wet floor, then at Sapphire's feet. A slew of German curse words followed.

"Sorry-sorry-sorry," Sapphire pleaded, skipping to one of the stools.

Julia, the mother of all things good, had been replaced by this big-boned German woman who ate two pounds of cabbage a day, farted blatantly while mopping, and yelled *NEIN* whenever she disagreed with someone's behavior, which was most of the time.

Everybody was terrified of Berta, especially Sapphire's mother. So terrified, she didn't dare fire her.

Sapphire didn't care. Berta scared the living crap out of her, but she also made sure to take good care of Sapphire's paraplegic stepfather, Charles. Though Berta's tone was never sweet like Julia's, it wasn't as harsh when she spoke to him.

"Good morning, Charles." Sapphire gave her stepfather a habitual kiss on the forehead.

"Merk," he tried as Berta gave him a second helping of a weird-looking porridge made of cabbage.

Sapphire began hoarding the newspapers as Vivienne entered in her pink robe and high-heeled slippers. It was clear that she was not only hungover from the day before, but was still drunk. Vivienne had been "still drunk" for about four months.

Their already impaired relationship got worse *that* night, the night Vivienne went from classy alky trophy wife—a common breed in Beverly Hills—to incoherent drunk, whom the other trophy wives gossiped about.

"Who is my father?" Sapphire had asked that night, watching as Vivienne set down her cocktail glass on the deck's flat railing.

Her mother's hands had been shaking and her demeanor was full of angst. But it was as if she'd awaited the question for years.

"The first time I met your father," Vivienne had explained, closing her eyes, "I was nineteen. I left your grandmother's house to go make something better of my life, but the minute I met that man it was all out the window. He had no money, no stable job, and he lived in this nasty one bedroom in Oregon, but I fell so hard for him. I thought I could live in poverty forever as long as I got to be with him. We were happy for a long time."

There had been a peacefulness on her mother's face as she spoke that Sapphire had never seen before; real live emotion from the vodka-on-ice queen. Then her eyes had been overtaken in pain.

"He would go out of town on random jobs then come home to stay for a few weeks before he went back out. After you were born he would take you with him and you loved it." She had sighed. "You and him, two peas in a pod. If he moved, you followed."

Sapphire had mustered a smile, but it was hard to fathom being so close to someone who she couldn't remember.

"One night, when you had just turned four, you guys came back from one of his trips. He was his old charming self, but you were very quiet, which was unlike you because usually no one could shut you up. He kissed me and said that he came to drop you off because he got a new job opportunity and you couldn't go." Vivienne's eyes had filled with tears as she inhaled sharply through her nose. "And that was the last time I saw him."

"What happened?"

"The police searched but were never able to find a trace of him. I assumed he either left me or…died. I don't know which is worse."

"We could try again, Mom," Sapphire had urged. "Hire a

P.I. He could still be out there."

"No, it's over. He's in the past," Vivienne had snapped at her. "There were *things* with your father, Sapphire. Things you wouldn't understand. Things I didn't understand."

"Like?" Sapphire's heart had raced and her palms sweated as she processed her mother's implied accusations of something she didn't understand.

"It doesn't matter," Vivienne had said, but based on the look on her face, it mattered...a crap load. "A few months after he disappeared, I met Charles. He stuck around until I agreed to marry him. His lawyer did his magic and took care of my divorce within a year. I never looked back."

"What was my father's name?"

"Will. Will Green."

"So, my name was Sapphire Green. You named me *Blue Green*."

"Your father thought it was cute." Both sorrow and happiness had danced on Vivienne's face.

Sapphire had reached for her mother's hand. "I'm sorry you had to go through that, Mom." For the first time in her adult life, Sapphire was full of compassion for Vivienne. "It must've felt horrible to—"

"Would you look at that?" Vivienne had pulled her hand away, as if Sapphire's touch was tainted. Her eyes transformed back to empty, like her glass. "I need a refill."

Vivienne had gone to get another drink...then kept drinking for four months straight.

The conversation had left Sapphire feeling lost. For years she wondered who her father was and it was the hardest question she'd ever had to ask. Even when she finally got it out, she'd felt a resistance from some part of her.

After that night, Vivienne only spoke to Sapphire when necessary. Should they be in the same room for more than ten seconds, Vivienne would leave as she tossed an excuse over her shoulder.

Today was no different. She saw Sapphire in the kitchen and turned on her heel to escape.

"Nein!"

Vivienne stopped in her tracks.

"Sit!" Berta ordered.

Vivienne followed the command with reluctance and both she and Sapphire were rewarded with bowls of the strange porridge.

Charles enjoyed it, accepting a third helping with a lopsided smile, but his opinion was moot. The stroke he had seven years earlier left him lacking control over seventy percent of his body and at least half his taste buds.

An uncomfortable silence followed, interrupted only by Berta's farts, which in turn made the whole situation that much more uncomfortable.

Sapphire finished the bowl with a mild gag, then grabbed the newspapers and headed for her attic. She locked her bedroom door and climbed up through the flap, entering her sanctuary.

She opened a cabinet and slowly ran her fingers over her files: her pride. There were eight of them now, numbered in the order in which she had caught them. She stopped on number seven: Richard Martin. The last she'd read up on him, he had been sentenced to San Quentin. She was sure they'd fit like a glove: horrible place, horrible man.

File number eight was George Rath. She'd convinced herself that he was the man who had sent her the finger in a box. It turned out he wasn't, but at least she got the killer off the streets. She'd spotted a short article in the Thousand Oaks newspaper that said Rath had died of a heart attack before he even got to court. She wasn't surprised; she'd been in his apartment and knew his eating habits were atrocious.

She couldn't count the religious psycho from last year; he'd been the one stalking her. Plus, she didn't capture him, Aston shot him.

Sapphire closed the cabinet and grabbed the newspapers.

Immersed in her routine, she cut out every article she could find on the Stripper Slayer and his three victims. She put them up in the empty spot on the attic's wall; adding to her one-of-a-kind serial killer wallpaper.

The articles already on the wall were about unsolved cases, killers she hadn't been able to find, victims she couldn't connect. Once a case was closed, she'd take the articles off the wall, place them into a new folder, and number it. It was the best and worst part of her process. It was a surge of feelings of success followed by inexplicable disappointment. There was a part of her that felt like she hadn't gotten what she wanted, even when she got the very man she was supposed to. It was strange, even to her.

Sapphire studied her wall, unsure of how to start her transformation from Beverly Hills heiress to penniless downtown stripper. She couldn't just stroll into the Golden Mirage knowing nothing about stripping. She needed time for pole-dancing lessons and research.

As she flipped through the *L.A. Times*, she stopped short in the Classifieds.

The Golden Mirage seeks Exotic Dancers.

She searched for the date and time of the audition.

Sapphire had exactly twenty-four hours to master the art of stripping.

. . .

"The bar was crawling with broads," Capelli said in his thick New York accent. He held the pause button on the DVD player. "Guess what I came home with?"

"Five kinds of STDs," Aston said. "Would you push play?"

"No, this makeup artist named Diana. We go to her place, and I'm thinkin' this place is lookin' familiar. Which was weird because, you know me, I never forget a face…or a nice set of knockers, so I hadn't slept with her before."

"Push play."

"Turns out I had been there before, because in walks Diana's roommate, Stacy. *She* was the one I'd slept with…"

Aston zoned out.

When Capelli first moved from the East Coast to L.A., he and Aston became the dream team at the downtown station—

according to them, at least. Not only did they catch high grade pimps and murderers when they put their minds together, but they also got along on a personal level. After work, they'd go to the bar and bullshit about the Serial Catcher and play wingman for one another's lay-of-the-night. After a few months, Capelli transferred to Thousand Oaks and Aston partnered with Wilson, a vulgar son-of-a-bitch from Compton.

He and Capelli fell out of touch until Capelli called to let Aston know that he had a Serial Catcher victim in custody. Capelli convinced his chief that he needed Aston's expertise, and he was allowed onboard despite being from a different county.

Aston assumed they'd fall into their same pattern, but Capelli had changed during their time apart. The Serial Catcher was still priority, but he spent more time talking about tail than he did focusing on the task.

"So, long story short," Capelli continued. "Diana didn't want to sleep with me that night, so my balls still look like fat Smurfs."

"Just give me the remote!" Aston snatched it from Capelli and pushed play for the hundredth time.

On the screen George Rath stuffed his face with hamburgers and fries; his gigantic stomach folded over the edge of the table in front of him.

The Serial Catcher had caught Rath, a shoe salesman/serial killer, last year in Thousand Oaks, Capelli's district. The police received the anonymous call and found Rath hanging upside down above a meat grinder in the old slaughterhouse. Next to him lay a recording of Rath himself confessing to the murders.

He was the only serial killer caught by the Serial Catcher who'd been willing to talk. The McDonald's food was the only thing they were able to bribe Rath with to have a conversation without his ever-present lawyer. Junk food meant a lot to this guy, maybe even more than killing.

Aston sat in the opposite chair. Capelli stood behind him with crossed arms and a puffed chest like a bouncer. He was 250 pounds of Italian muscle and was the obvious choice for the intimidating, silent cop.

"Like I've told you and Rocky Balboa over there," Rath said, nodding to Capelli, "I'll tell you whatever you want to know if you can get me released."

"Mr. Rath, you admitted to murder on tape, and we found locks of hair belonging to all the victims in your apartment," Aston said. "You've repeatedly screwed the pooch and there's not a judge in the world that would set you free."

Rath rolled his eyes as if the women he had killed were inconveniencing him. "Fine, give me your best shot."

"Men like you," Aston said, "usually go somewhere like San Quentin where you'll be a prey to other inmates with soft spots for women, like their mothers and sisters." Aston got up as he always did when it came to negotiation. "We can try to persuade the judge to get you a spot at Pleasant Valley State Prison. A vacation resort compared to San Quentin."

Rath took a huge bite of his Big Mac, sucking in the dressing like the juice of a ripe pear.

"Ah-aaaah," he groaned, as if getting laid. He took another chunk off the defenseless burger.

Aston puked a little in his mouth.

"I also want In-N-Out. Double-Double, animal style. A large milk shake, half vanilla, half choc…why aren't you writing this down?"

Aston tapped his finger to his head. "Got it all right here."

There would be no Double-Doubles for George Rath. As soon as he spilled the beans, which Aston was convinced he would do, it would be bland chow at San Quentin.

"So you're basically saying my choices are shitty jail or shittier jail? No deal." Rath placed his blubbery arms over his even blubbier stomach. "Don't think I don't know how bad you want this. And trust me, what I got will blow your mind."

Rath grabbed the second Big Mac and opened his mouth. Aston snagged it and slapped him with it, leaving a blob of dressing across Rath's face.

"Let me tell you something, lard ass." Aston put his hand under the table. "If you think you're safe where you're sitting, you're wrong. I've manipulated the system before, and I can do it again. I will do everything in my power to make sure you and your triple XL ass get sent to Texas where they have less mercy. San Quentin would be a goddamned walk in the park compared to what the right wing will do to you." It was a lie. Aston had no ability to reshuffle the state-to-state system, but Rath didn't know that.

"Bullshit," Rath said.

Okay, maybe he did know it.

Aston let on the tiniest smile. "Right now, there's a Smith and Wesson forty cal' cocked at your crotch."

"You're lying."

"Yes I am," Aston said and pulled the hammer. "*Now*, it's cocked."

Beads of sweat accumulated above Rath's lip. "You can't shoot me. You'd get fired."

"I would," Aston agreed. "Luckily, the live feed will mysteriously skip right before you attack me and I'll be driven to use lethal force. Does that sound about right to you, Capelli?"

"Sure does," Capelli nodded.

Rath's already labored breathing grew thicker. "What about the Serial Catcher?"

"Meh." Aston shrugged. "If you're not going to talk, your life is worth shit to me. In fact, the way I see it, your death would benefit both the system and the hard working tax payers. Do you pay taxes, Capelli?"

"Sure do."

Rath was sweating everywhere. Even his pudgy earlobes were dripping.

Aston looked at his watch. "You have three seconds to talk before I shoot; no Mississippis. One-two-"

"I'll take it!" Rath shouted, holding his hands up. "I'll take Pleasant Valley State!"

"Okay, then let's try this again." Aston put the gun back in his brown shoulder holster and clasped his hands on top of the table, hiding his excitement. "Who is he? Who put you in that slaughterhouse?"

"It's not what you think," Rath started. "I didn't see it

coming." He shook his head. An odd expression overtook his face. "He is a sh…" Rath's voice broke off.

Aston and Capelli waited as he cleared his throat, trying again.

"Sh…sh-sh-sh-shhh," Rath stuttered. His face turned red. He clawed at his chest, then his head hit the table with a thump.

Aston and Capelli watched befuddled as George Rath lay dead, forehead down.

Aston turned to Capelli. "I told you not to give him two Big Macs."

The screen froze.

Capelli wailed with laugher, waving the stolen remote in his hand. "That's my favorite part, when you realize our star witness just kicked the bucket."

Aston stared at the image of George Rath's face planted on the table, pissed. Not because Rath was dead—it *was* tremendous for tax payers—but if the tubby fucker had the decency to die ten seconds later, it would have made Aston's life a lot easier.

"What the hell was he trying to say?" Aston said. "It's not who you think it is. He is a sh…what? Sheik? Sheriff? Shepherd?"

"The doc said we can't take his last word into account; it was the sound of a guy whose ticker went out."

Aston pulled his jacket on.

"Where're we going?" Capelli asked, then lit up. "Boobie-bar?"

"No, and stop calling it boobie-bar. It's embarrassing. Everybody knows the proper term is titty-tavern. You sound like a…"

After months of watching the same footage something finally clicked. Aston's memory melded with the footage and his brain went from fuzzy to high-def.

"Like a what?" Capelli asked in the distance. "Ridder?"

There was a flash of disdain in Rath's eyes when he said his knowledge of the Serial Catcher would blow Aston's mind. There was amazement in his voice paired with body language that showed embarrassment as he was about to reveal the Catcher's identity. It was just like the other killers. They'd lied through their teeth about who had trapped them.

"Blink once if you've had an aneurism, Ridder."

What would men who killed, raped, and slaughtered all be embarrassed about? It was a question Aston had asked himself countless times. These killers took satisfaction in being masters and in absolute control over the women they handpicked. What is the one thing that would humiliate them the most?

"RIDDER!" Capelli yelled. Aston blinked. "He's a *she*."

CHAPTER 5

The bar smelled of old liquor, sweat, and cologne from the establishment's regulars. It was dark, dead, and the only light that wasn't soft and red was a ray of sunshine that penetrated beneath the heavy black swing doors.

Sapphire stood in a line leading up to the stage behind girls dressed in brightly colored mini dresses and eight-inch platform heels.

She looked down at her too-small dress. Sapphire thought she had picked out a revealing outfit from her small secondary closet in the attic, but this was a whole other level of revealing.

She had a one-day intense striptease course at Madame Louvier's dance studio in Hollywood, hoping it would be enough.

Madam Louvier, an orange wig-wearing lady in her late 70s who chain-smoked cloves, had guaranteed Sapphire success at her audition in exchange for $500. Seeing the other girls' moves, Sapphire wasn't so sure.

The girl in front of Sapphire stepped up on the stage as the DJ swapped one shrill repetitive techno song for another.

Sapphire feared the techno and scowled at the DJ. He had to be at least 40. *A little too old to be a DJ*, she thought. But who was she to judge. Sapphire was a little too rich to be a stripper.

The girl on stage grabbed the pole, spun, humped, and swooshed as her clothes gracefully slid off her body.

The Golden Mirage was 21-and-up, as opposed to a 18-and-up joint where the dancers were fully nude. This meant no nipples and no down under exposure, which meant Happy Sapphire.

"Lovely! Lovely!" the club owner yelled in a strong British accent as the girl got off stage. "Not a dry seat in the house, or what do you say, Buddy?"

"Not a dry seat, Giles." The balding bartender nodded to his boss as he stocked beer in an oversized fridge behind the bar.

"Next!" Giles yelled.

Her turn.

Giles examined Sapphire's bare legs with narrow eyes.

The DJ put on—surprise—techno as Sapphire climbed on stage and tried to look more confident than she felt. She struggled to keep up with the tempo of the music as she grabbed the pole to do a basic Bunny Move. She got two more of Madame Louvier's moves in before Giles motioned the DJ to kill the music.

"I've seen enough!" he exclaimed.

Sapphire put her hand on her hip, waiting.

"That was brilliant. You're hired."

"Really?" Sapphire's neck pulled back in surprise.

"No! Of course not!" His forehead creased. "That was absolutely dreadful. I wasn't turned on at all! Not even the tiniest tingle in my bollocks. Did you fancy her, Buddy?"

"Nope, sorry," Buddy responded. His American accent sounded drawn out compared to Giles's. "You looked like you were in pain or something."

"Can I try again?" Sapphire pleaded. Waiting for another audition wasn't an option. Who knew how many girls could have died by then?

"If you force me to relive that, I will gouge my bloody eyes out. Please get off the stage and never get back on *any* stage, *ever* again."

Had Sapphire not been there to hunt a serial killer, she might've been embarrassed when Giles cupped his hands and yelled, *"Boo! Booo!"* until she got off the stage.

A sane person with dignity would have left the club. But lacking both sanity and dignity Sapphire headed for the other six girls waiting to find out if they had a new job. She plopped down next to a girl with pigtails who twisted her body away from Sapphire to make sure she would not be affiliated with the world's worst stripper.

Sapphire watched the last girl dance with grace and

precision, her mind racing for a way to change Giles's mind. Her eyes landed on the TV above the bar, which was playing another segment on the Stripper Slayer.

She smiled and leaned closer to the other girls. They were having a heated conversation on whether or not leather lingerie made their asses sweat. It seemed to be a unanimous yes.

"Isn't this the place," Sapphire asked loudly, "where all those dancers got killed?"

The group glanced at each other.

"Was that here? I did hear something about that," a brunette said, looking around. "I thought it was weird. Usually there's like twenty girls at these auditions."

On stage, the girl finished her dance with the splits. *Christ!*

"Ladies!" Giles yelled. "I will deliberate with my bartender and will let you know in a few minutes!"

"It's on the news right now." Sapphire motioned to the TV.

The girls' faces dropped as they watched the photographs of the dead girls pop up.

"I am so out of here," Pigtails said as she got up. Two other girls followed while the rest sat, unsure of what to do.

"Three girls," Sapphire prompted, shaking her head. "And there's what, fifteen working here? Three out of fifteen, that's like a twenty percent chance you'll be the next to die."

The remaining girls got up swiftly made their way to the exit.

Giles came around the bar just as they reached the doors. "Ladies, where are you going?! Star, I was going to put you on prime hours: Titty Tuesday and Free Shrimp Friday!"

"I want the job, but I want to stay alive more," Star, aka Pigtails, replied.

Giles stared after them, long after the doors had swung shut. "What am I going to do, Buddy? That bloody man is killing my girls *and* my business. I was lucky those dancers even showed up. We are understaffed as it is. I need girls *now*!"

"...There's one left," Buddy offered.

"Oh?" Giles spun around, greeted by Sapphire's grinning face. She waved at him.

"Oh bloody hell, not her!" he cried. He slumped down

in a booth, head in hands, for long enough that Sapphire was growing impatient in her tiny dress and uncomfortable heels. Eventually, gathering himself, he gave Sapphire a second glance and sighed. "I suppose you are not *completely* terrible to look at."

"Thank you."

"Come back tomorrow. We open at six, don't be late."

"I won't." Sapphire stood with a huge smile.

Giles walked away, then spun around and pointed at her. "What is your name?"

"Melissa Cambridge," Sapphire answered, prepared like a girl scout.

"Oh-for-the-love-of…not your *real* name. Your stage name. You have got one, haven't you?"

"Er, of course. It-it's…" Sapphire stuttered, not so prepared after all.

Giles rolled his eyes then held his hand up, telling her to be quiet. "Buddy! Did Candy die or is she still alive?"

"Alive."

"Bugger."

Sapphire waited, prepared to handle whatever stereotypical stripper name he would assign her. What would it be? *Roxy, Muffin, Sparkle?*

"Well, we haven't had one of those since the last one got offed, and you're so bloody green you're almost blue, so I'm thinking…" he paused. "Sapphire."

You gotta be kidding me.

. . .

When Sapphire looked at the framed Rorschach inkblot paintings on the wall she saw blood spatter. When she looked at the busty receptionist, she saw a potential victim. When she looked at the older man on the other side of the waiting room, she saw a possible killer.

Next to her, John rubbed his legs. He was as nervous as she was. It was weird, considering he was the reason they were there.

Sapphire had been on her way home from the audition,

excited to get started on the preparations for her first day of work, when John called, reminding her of their appointment.

Sapphire glanced at him and realized there was something else off about him. He hadn't proposed sex for an *entire* hour. He always did that.

To which Sapphire always responded: "No sex before marriage."

To which he would respond: "Don't buy the cow if you can't taste the milk first."

To which she would respond: "That's not the saying. In fact, it's a total contradiction of the saying."

To which he didn't respond at all because John—despite being a fifth generation Harvard student—didn't know what "contradiction" meant.

"Sugar Plum," John said. "I didn't see you after the fire the other night. Chrissy and I looked for you and you didn't answer your phone."

"I had a migraine. I decided not to bother anyone and just go home."

"That's funny because Rick was taking Bieber's new Jag for a spin, and he thought he saw you a few blocks from Whole Foods."

"Nope, I was in bed." Sapphire grabbed a magazine. "Must have been someone else."

John sat silently, glancing at the receptionist's giant boobs every so often.

"He lives there," he said with a hint of anger. "That cop you know lives around there, doesn't he?"

Sapphire looked at him, surprised. Was it possible that there was activity behind that blank stare of his? A functioning mind that put two and two together?

"Dr. Rues is ready for you now," the receptionist called. John's attention diverted back to her giant rack.

Mrs. Vanderpilt had convinced John that they should get premarital counseling to work out any bumps prior to walking down the aisle. Her real intentions lay in trying to stir up arguments that would lead John to change his mind about marrying Sapphire.

Please, let it be so.

They entered the elegant Beverly Hills office and sat down on a suspiciously comfortable couch opposite Dr. Rues, who was seated with a polite smile, looking them over.

Sapphire cleared her throat. She tried hard not to look guilty. Psychologists and psychiatrists freaked her out. She'd had a few in her childhood. It was a standard in Beverly Hills. Some people's Chihuahuas even had shrinks. But when she started hunting serial killers she avoided them like the plague, afraid they'd be able to access her mind without her consent.

She cleared her throat again and glanced over at John, who appeared just as comfortable as Dr. Rues. He had that empty look he got when he thought of nothing, which was often.

"Sooo…," Sapphire said, tapping her hands together. She stopped, scared Dr. Rues would take it as a nervous habit and determine that she devoted her life to capturing serial killers.

Instead, he began, "I like to start these sessions with a conversation, then move onto hypnotherapy. Now, have either of you ever had hypnosis before?"

"I only had it once," John tossed out. "I'm not contagious anymore."

Dr. Rues' eyebrows pushed together. "I'll take that as a no."

Hypnosis? Sapphire was positive her heart stopped. Who knows what she could blurt out?

"I have developed a more modern technique where the depth of your relationship is targeted so that I can eliminate flaws."

Sapphire hoped John would object, but based on his look, he still thought hypnosis was an STD.

"I don't think I am comfortable with that," Sapphire said.

"It is, of course, your choice. But keep in mind that you were referred to me because I am the best in the country," Dr. Rues said without sounding pompous. "You can spend ten conversational sessions together leading up to your wedding date or one hypnosis session right now."

Spending hours upon hours with John Vanderpilt on a suspiciously comfortable couch versus one tiny session? How bad could it be?

"We'll do it," Sapphire said. Maybe she could pretend to be under, to fake it somehow.

After one hour of excruciating relationship analysis, Dr. Rues sent John outside so that Sapphire's session could start.

"Is that your family?" Sapphire asked, looking at a photograph taken of Dr. Rues with what she imagined was his wife and son.

"Yes," he smiled. "Please, make yourself comfortable."

"Is that your house?" she pushed, trying to delay. "I think I've driven by it. Very nice neighborhood. Do you like the neighborhood?"

"Mhmm. Would you mind lying down for me?"

"Why Dr. Rues, at least buy me dinner first," Sapphire joked, cringing when Dr. Rues' uncomfortable gaze drew to his lap.

"Ms. Dubois, *please*. Lie down and make yourself as comfortable and relaxed as possible."

Sapphire lay down, tensing her entire body to try to fend off whatever he was going to do next.

"Before we start, I just want you to understand that for this process to work you have to imagine exactly what I'm relaying to you." He took a deep breath then spoke in a serene voice. "Imagine yourself in an elevator as it moves up through the last numbers. 22. 23. 24. 25." Dr. Rues snapped his fingers.

Sapphire didn't see an elevator. She saw nothing.

She let Dr. Rues blabber on about some sort of meadow of peacefulness while boredom took over.

"Do you see a door?"

"Sure," Sapphire lied, playing along.

"Very good, Ms. Dubois. Open it…now," he said, intense about the door that wasn't there.

The best in the country, my ass. Sapphire bit her lip, holding back a laugh. She'd worried for noth…in…

CHAPTER 6

Slam! A tattered door smacked shut. The lock on the doorknob twisted on its own, letting out a longwinded creak.

Sapphire yanked on the locked knob and then turned around to face her surroundings.

She was in a bizarrely red-themed motel room. Everything inside—the bed, the carpet, the wallpaper—was deep crimson.

There were three people: a man, a woman, and a child. They were oblivious to her, as if there was nothing but air in front of the creepy door.

Sapphire's body tensed when she realized who they were.

The woman was her mother. The child playing with a toy in the corner by the door was Sapphire, age three or four.

Sapphire studied the man. Though she'd never seen a picture of him, or gotten a proper description, Sapphire knew he was her father. His dark eyes and hair were the exact color of her own.

Vivienne laughed and twirled in a red dress. They were dancing to the static music from an old radio. Their movements were too fluid as they hovered ghost-like over the carpet.

Sapphire had never had a memory before the age of five—after Vivienne and Sapphire moved into Charles's mansion—but that was exactly what this was: *a memory.*

Sapphire watched her father and mother treat the confined space like a ballroom and realized she should be feeling grateful to finally get to meet her father. She had wanted to know everything about him. Now she'd been given a happy memory from childhood. This exceeded anything Vivienne could have described to her.

But Sapphire was terrified. Her heart hammered and her

body shook. She wanted to run, but a nightmarish fear crept over her. Her muscles were unresponsive.

Vivienne fell onto the bed with a satisfied sigh, exhausted from the dance. Sapphire's father's gaze slid from Vivienne to Sapphire.

His head cocked to the side. "You're not supposed to be here."

The door opened, letting in a blinding white light.

• • •

"Step off the elevator feeling refreshed and ready to be with the man you love."

Sapphire opened her eyes to find herself back on Dr. Rues' couch. She felt as though she just came out of a deep sleep, but without the drowsiness.

"How do you feel?"

"Great," Sapphire lied. She felt like throwing up. Despite her attempt to fend off the hypnosis, it was clear that she had been under. "Did I say…anything?"

Dr. Rues shook his head, looking as if he was about to ask a question, then shrugged. "You were excellent."

Sapphire walked out of his office feeling overwhelmed. She wasn't sure why such a happy memory frightened her, but she wanted to bury it. Put it back wherever it came from.

"Hey," John said as they left the building. "How about we go to dinner then go back to my house and get in the hot tub?"

There it was: the quest for sex. He seemed desperate now, a tinge of anxiety in his voice.

"No sex before marriage." She was sick of the line. A part of her felt badly for him.

John had always been a horn dog, but since he proposed he'd stopped cheating on her. He no longer smelled like perfume when he embraced her, and she no longer received guilty looks from the girls at the country club.

She wished he would cheat again and that everyone would find out. A big scandal would be the mother of all excuses.

Nobody would call her insane. Stupid, perhaps, for letting all that money go, but not insane. Why did John suddenly have to insist on monogamy?

John stood ill at ease, squeezing her hand in his. "Dr. Rues explained something to me before my session." He paused. "You know why I'm marrying you?"

"No?" She honestly didn't know. She was trailer trash to the Vanderpilts. He claimed he loved her, but this wasn't the feeling she got from him. His unyielding commitment to Sapphire made no sense to her or anybody else.

He looked down. "I broke up with you when my father told me your inheritance was too small. Dr. Rues said that I realized something then. My entire life, I had always done exactly what my parents wanted me to do and that's why I decided to marry you. It's like, even if I wanted to be with someone else, I couldn't because that's what they would want."

"So we're getting married because you're rebelling?" Sapphire said dryly.

"Yes!" He was relieved she understood him.

A fiery hope lit inside Sapphire, and she squeezed his hand back.

"John…" she said slowly. "Don't you think love should be involved?"

"But Sapphire, I *do* love you. You're like my Porsche."

"Ah, of course."

"I think of you as mine. I'm the only one who's allowed to drive you. And once we're married…" he peered down, paying extra attention to her boobs, "I'll upgrade the parts."

Sapphire looked down at her chest. Most girls got their first saline-based implants at eighteen but she had refused her mother's wishes.

John hugged her tight. "Consider yourself the luckiest girl in the world, Snuggle Bunny. I'm not going anywhere."

"Yay," Sapphire said, face inside his rigid embrace.

Kill me.

She had to remind herself she still had plenty of time to come up with a plan.

John pulled back and kissed her. He let his long, pointy tongue slide over her lips, mouth, and teeth before he pulled away.

"So how about that hot tub? Don't buy the cow if you can't taste the milk first."

*   *   *

"If you really want to kill someone," Aston said, "there are three letters you've got to remember. H-L-H. Heart, liver, head. Shoot someone in the chest or back, he might live to avenge your shot. I once made that mistake with a homicidal pimp. However, shoot someone in the eyeball, the liver, or the heart, he doesn't have a prayer." He paused to bring a spoonful of sugary cake to his mouth. "Now, the trick is to stand close enough to get an accurate aim, but far enough away so that his nasty brains don't spray all over your face." Aston glanced down at his audience and took a swig of beer to wash down the cake.

"What's brains?" asked Dylan, the chief's six-year-old son. The other kids on the lawn nodded, a sea of bobbing red cowboy hats.

"And what's a pimp?" another boy asked.

Aston suffocated a burp. "Well, to know what a pimp is, you really need to know what a hooker is first…"

"Okay!" Chief Anderson interrupted. He motioned the kids to run along. "I think Uncle Aston needs a break."

Aston didn't even shudder at the title anymore. The more time he spent with the chief's family, the more he grew accustomed to being referred to as "Uncle." He didn't like it, but it didn't make him want to jam a fork into his eye anymore.

To keep Aston from leaving the BHPD, the chief offered him free range to go after whatever case he wanted, meaning the Serial Catcher. The deal implied that Aston would come to every BBQ, birthday party, and official holiday event he was invited to.

Deep down, there was a miniscule part of Aston that liked it—the same part that felt like the Andersons were more of a family to him than his own father had ever been.

The kids scattered out in the backyard's maze of clowns,

balloons, and bouncing castles.

"Hooker!" Dylan yelled in the distance as he shot one of the defenseless Indians in the eyeball with his toy gun.

The chief blasted Aston a stern look, twisting his beer cap as he settled down in the lawn chair next to Aston's.

"So, where are you on the Serial Catcher? Getting hotter?"

"More like colder than a witch's titty—" A child ran by. "—caca."

"Nice save."

Aston agreed and clinked his bottle to the chief's. There was a no R-rated language rule in the Anderson home. It was set up by the chief's wife, Mona, especially when Aston was around. "The fact that it's a woman hasn't made it easier."

The chief nodded over to Capelli, who was chatting up Mona by the bouncing castle. "I had a conversation with your unofficial partner over there, and it sounds like he's more interested in the fame that comes after, rather than catching your perp. We've had a few cops like that in Beverly Hills, and trust me when I say they're not the right kind of cop. You'd be better off with someone like Barry. He looks up to you, and he's as loyal as they come."

Aston chuckled. He looked over at the pimply Officer Barry Harry, who had been taken hostage by the kids in the bouncing castle.

"Look," Aston said, "I know Capelli, and despite his distractions, he wants the Serial Catcher just as bad as I do… for the right reason." Aston took another swig of his beer and nodded over to Mona and Capelli. "You might want to clear him away from your wife, though; he is a bit of a dog."

The chief's face dropped as he watched Capelli check out Mona's ass while she bent down to fix the bouncing castle's air plug.

"I knew there was a reason I didn't like him," the chief muttered and moved to save his wife. He turned to face Aston, walking backwards toward the castle. "If the Serial Catcher is a woman, maybe you shouldn't focus so much on how to catch her and focus more on how she's catching them!"

Aston froze, his beer halfway to his mouth. The chief's words triggered a launch button in his mind.

That's how she did it: she lured them in. Playing the victim, then unexpectedly swapping roles and taking charge. It was her advantage over the police.

"Capelli!" Aston called, defusing an old-fashioned boxing match between his Italian partner and his chief of police. The chief had already rolled up his sleeves, ready to rumble.

Aston stood with a smile. He knew exactly where to start.

• • •

"Everybody," Giles called out to his staff. "This is the new girl, Sapphire."

All activity ceased and the girls turned to look.

Sapphire stood in the doorway next to Giles. She had never seen so much nudity in one sweep of the eye. There were girls everywhere: topless, semi-naked, buck naked. Bras and panties of various colors and designs lay scattered across the floor or hung from the large mirrors framed by bright light bulbs. Below the mirrors lay mountains of makeup, razors, and wax products. Sapphire hadn't expected a nunnery or anything, but it was a lot to take in.

"Hi," Sapphire said. "I'm Melissa."

A redhead looked over at Giles. "What is she, retarded or something?"

Giles looked at Sapphire, annoyed. "Always use your stage name. It helps you live the character."

"Sorry, not used to the name. I'm Sapphire," Sapphire said.

"Sapphire?!" The angry redhead's eyes wandered between Giles and Sapphire. "The *real* Sapphire just died a few weeks ago. You don't even wait until the pole is cold, do you, Giles?"

Sapphire, aka Susan Barker, was the second girl taken by the Stripper Slayer.

"If you don't go back to icing your nipples I'll replace you too, Ginger." Giles pointed Sapphire to a mirror in the corner.

"Oh, please," Ginger retorted. "With my training I could've

been a showgirl in Vegas. I'm doing you a favor by staying at this rat hole."

Ginger stood up, intentionally bumping into Sapphire. "Could you be more in the way...Sapphire *Two*?"

Oh, ouch. Was that supposed to annoy her? Sapphire sat down and looked at the costume hanging on the chair. Black leather booty shorts, a bra, and gloves missing the tops of the fingers.

"Ladies, tonight is Free Shrimp Friday. Do not even *think* about going near the buffet. Misty, I'm looking at you," Giles warned. "Sapphire, you're doing go-go in the back cage tonight. Let's hope people will look more at your body than they will your bloody left feet. One can only pray."

The girls snickered, except for Ginger, who belly laughed.

Perfect. Sapphire didn't need to be seen tonight. What she needed was to observe everything, every guest, every employee, and every move.

Sapphire looked over at a girl in front of the mirror next to her. Her shoulders were drawn to her neck and her hair pulled over her face. She looked older than the other girls, yet tiny and scared to death.

The girl whispered something to her.

Sapphire leaned in. "I'm sorry?"

"That is Chastity," a topless girl two mirrors down interrupted in a thick Russian accent. "She is new also."

Chastity whispered again. It sounded like: "Nice to meet you." Or, possibly: "I hate you all."

"I am Misty." The Russian girl reached out her hand for Sapphire to take. "Don't worry about Ginger, she is sunulvabeach."

"A what?"

"Sunulvabeach. You know the word, yes?" Misty said. *"Sun-ulva-beach!"*

"Oooh! Son of a bitch."

"Yes, do you not hear good?" Misty put two ice cubes on her nipples. She clasped on her thin bra, and then winked at herself in the mirror. "Okay, let's go, Sapphire Two."

Okay, now it was annoying.

Out in the club, the bass of the DJ's music was beating like a drum, making the whole floor vibrate. Thick cigar smoke lingered throughout and its overpowering sweet smell was nauseating.

Sapphire got in her cage and closed the door behind her. Thankfully, the go-go duty allowed her to keep her "clothes" on. Unthankfully, the girls at the audition had been right; the leather lingerie *did* make your ass sweat.

Sapphire danced and scanned the room. Going into this, she'd expected cops. Amber's death made it three, which officially meant they were prey to a serial killer. All she'd seen so far was a squad car pass the place. She wasn't complaining or anything; it certainly made it less risky for her, but it just seemed…wrong. The LAPD obviously didn't feel that strippers were worth their time.

Her eyes swept over the crowd. Giles was already out of the picture; he was more concerned about his club than the dead girls, which just made him a prick, not a murderer. She eliminated the obvious bachelor parties, guys' night outs, and the pervy guy with his hand in his pants, who a security guy was about to remove. No serial killer would draw that much attention to himself. There was a man in a cowboy hat. His eyes looked like they were going to shoot out of their sockets when the DJ introduced Ginger as the main act. He looked horny but harmless.

Sapphire's eyes landed on a young, well-groomed man. In fact, she doubted he was even 21. He sat close to her in the back and watched the stage as Ginger did some sort of dirty nurse routine using a stethoscope in a way few doctors would approve of.

There was something cold in the young man's eyes.

A cowboy hat blocked Sapphire's view as another man passed by her on his way to the restroom.

"Ma'am," he said, tipping his hat and sending her a curious glance.

Sapphire turned back to the young man just as he rose. He

tossed a hundred on the table.

She noticed his suit and stopped moving as her mind recorded the detail.

Is it? Can it be?

Yes, it was an Alexander Amosu suit. A suit that cost exactly $100,000.

John bought them all the time and would throw the price out there just in case someone in his vicinity had missed the fact that he was filthy rich.

What the hell was a guy with a $100,000 suit doing at a shithole like the Golden Mirage? He should be at upper-class gentlemen's clubs. He could've been twelve years old for all they cared, as long as he had status.

He was also alone. People like him had chauffeurs or security by their side, especially when visiting this area. Sapphire tripped over a homeless guy before she walked into the club. Though that particular homeless guy turned out to be a nice man named Herbert, there was a good chance this rich guy would get robbed the second he stepped out those doors.

There was only one reason someone like him would choose the Golden Mirage over a prestigious club where they'd let you do whatever sick, twisted thing you wanted, to whomever you wanted, under contracted discretion.

And it wasn't Free Shrimp Friday.

. . .

He watched the girls of the Golden Mirage, waiting for someone special to piqué his interest.

His gem, Amber, was long gone and finding his next was crucial to his mental health. They were all beautiful, but like a talent scout, he searched for someone who had the personality with that *it* factor.

He glanced at his phone to make sure he still had enough time. Ice spread like wildfire through his veins.

Three missed calls. How had he failed to notice? One missed call would have been fine, but *three* was unacceptable.

He knew he had to leave, but the thought of walking another day with that void in his chest was unbearable.

The phone buzzed again and the big nasty letters spread out on the screen, identifying the caller. He had no choice. He moved to the doors and took one last glance around the room.

Within a second he was filled with a lifetime of wonderful and complex emotions. There she was. He had seen her before, but he saw her true colors now. He didn't know when the mood would strike him, but once it did, she would die.

He'd be in trouble for not paying attention to his phone, but he felt good. The world was right again.

He had his *next*.

CHAPTER 7

Sapphire yawned as she passed one of the brown triangular Beverly Hills signs.

Good. She was almost home.

Flashes of red and blue lights appeared on the road ahead, coming from the four-way stop, and Sapphire slowed down.

Two ambulances and a patrol car were blocking both lanes of traffic.

Her shift had ended at 11 p.m., but she had stayed behind to make sure he didn't come back. She snooped around the wait staff quarters to find that none of the waitresses knew his name and that Giles had told them not to card anyone who looked like they could spare the money.

The young man never spoke to them and always paid in cash, leaving no credit card name or trail behind.

It confirmed Sapphire was on the right track, so she left the club positive he was her man…boy.

Her guy without a name: *John Doe, Jr.*

Sapphire stopped in front of the ambulance. Had the accident happened before the famous sign resting on the borders of Beverly Hills had come into view, Sapphire wouldn't have sighed.

She had seen it a million times. It was always the same story. Some celeb or young heir who'd had a few too many drinks or lines of coke. If they got pulled over, what would it matter? They had the best lawyers in the country.

Sapphire leaned forward to take in the accident.

A car that looked familiar had plowed into a black Maserati. The windshield of to the car was gone and lay shattered on the ground.

Matt LeBlanc stood unharmed by the Maserati. He gestured wildly to the patrol officer, rehashing the events of the accident the way only an actor could.

The person who had been flung through the windshield still lay in a hot mess on the ground as the paramedics unloaded the stretcher.

Though she felt compassion for the person, Sapphire was appalled by any rich, stupid drunk who endangered not only the poor Matt LeBlanc but non-*Friends* cast members as well.

Then everything began to register and Sapphire drew a breath.

Her eyes bounced around the accident: the totaled car, the smashed windshield, and finally, the rich, stupid drunk on the ground.

Sapphire ripped the seatbelt off and pushed the door open.

•   •   •

Aston was just about to pull into his parking spot when he got the call. It was Barry Harry, the greenest officer at the BHPD.

Another drunk driver hit another celebrity.

"What the hell makes you think I care about some drunk driver?" Aston snapped into the mouth piece.

Officer Harry made a bad habit out of stalking Aston, calling Aston, and worse, joining Aston for lunch. This, despite the fact that Aston told him to fuck off on a regular basis.

"I just thought...you might want *this* call."

The way Barry said it made Aston turn and head to the scene of the accident.

"Did we get any new lead on the Serial Catcher?" Barry asked.

There was no *we*; the boy was delusional if he thought he was rolling with Aston and Capelli.

"Barry..."

"I thought of something this morning, Detective. The Serial Catcher is probably the person we least expect. So that's where we should look, where it's least expected."

That was a great idea…if you were Nancy Drew.

"Barry…"

"How was Thousand Oaks?"

"Barry!"

"Fuck off?"

"Yes."

They disconnected, and Aston rolled down the window to light a cigarette though he knew the chief would bitch about his "display of unprofessionalism when smoking/drinking/flipping off pedestrians while inside an official vehicle." There were more slashes in there, but Aston dozed off after the first three.

Thousand Oaks had gone *very* well.

He and Capelli reenacted the Serial Catcher luring in George Rath.

They took everything the public knew about the shoe fetish serial killer before George Rath was caught. At least that's what the cops thought he was. As it turned out, the shoes that were taken from the victims' feet weren't stolen by Rath but by passing women. The brand, Chi Chi, which all the victims wore, was a sought-after designer label.

Rath had been adamant about this fact. He did not want the public to know him as the creepy shoe-fetish serial killer. As opposed to the creepy hair-collecting killer he really was.

The Serial Catcher caught on to this and found there were few stores that carried Chi Chi in Thousand Oaks. And there was only one in the perimeter of the murders, — the one George Rath worked in.

Aston and Capelli scanned the shoe store for evidence and questioned the employees.

Aston was listening to the pudgy, middle-aged saleswoman, whose never ending blabber made him want to shoot himself in the face.

"And then," she yammered on, "I had my lunch, which was Lean Cuisine…or subway? No, it was definitely Lean Cuisine because I remember thinking, how many calories are in this low calorie pizza? Four hundred? Five hundred? Six—"

"Tell me you save your security data?" He stared up at

the cameras.

"Yes. Anyway, as it turned out it had five hundred, when I should be on three hundred calories a meal diet…"

"Can you show it to me? Preferably before I chop my ears off."

After a few offended snorts, the saleswoman showed him to the computers and Aston downloaded the two weeks prior to Rath's capture onto his flash drive.

He found his partner across the room, who was generously helping a woman put on a pair of sandals while massaging her feet.

"You have exquisite feet," Capelli said.

"Oh…what the heck. It's only money," she replied. "I'll take them. Do you take MasterCard or do I need to run across to the ATM?"

"Oh, I don't work here," Capelli grinned and stood up, noticing Aston. "What's up?"

The woman's face dropped as she stared after Capelli, then down at her naked, molested feet.

"If she got his attention through his job…" Aston held up the flash drive triumphantly, "then we got her face."

They decided to get some sleep and then meet up early the next morning to dig into the hours upon hours of security footage.

•   •   •

The flashing lights of the ambulance blinded Aston when he pulled over.

A woman was being loaded onto a stretcher and it wasn't until he stepped out that he saw who it was.

Mrs. Dubois.

He searched for Sapphire until their eyes met.

She looked childlike. Her usual head-held-high pose had sunken down into her shoulders.

Though he wouldn't admit it, in a sick, twisted way, Aston was almost pleased that Mrs. Dubois had gotten in a wreck. It meant he got to see Sapphire.

"There's room in here," the paramedic shouted, interrupting their gaze. He waved at Sapphire to enter the ambulance.

"No!" Aston shouted too fast. "I'll take her."

.   .   .

"Coffee?" Aston held out a paper cup.

Sapphire didn't feel like vending machine coffee but took it with a nod, as Aston sat down next to her.

Except for the two of them, the emergency waiting room was empty. The only sound—excluding a doctor's occasional sneaker squeak against the rubbery floor—was the TV, ironically on Comedy Central.

Aston sat next to her for hours, staring at the different comedy acts, pretending he wasn't dead tired. He didn't try to speak to her or laugh at the comedians' jokes. He just stayed by her side, refusing to leave. It was exactly what Sapphire needed.

The lack of conversation helped her not look at him. Every time she did, an unpleasant image of Aston and Angelica Moore in bed shot through her mind.

Her mother had been in for an eternity, and the staff hadn't updated them despite several death threats from Aston.

"So I noticed your Volkswagen is gone," Aston said as if they'd been chatting it up the whole time.

"Got rid of it," Sapphire lied and smiled. She had actually moved it to an Aston-safe location. He thought she used the car to go hook up with men below her class. It was a disturbing theory but better than Aston finding out what the car was really used for. "Why, been checking up on me?"

"Please. I have more important things to do with my time than aimlessly chase you around."

Sapphire put the coffee to her mouth to hide her amusement. *Yeah, like aimlessly chase the Serial Catcher around.*

"I just happened to be out there." Aston studied her, contemplating something. "Actually, I'm not sure what you used that clunker for, but I know it wasn't to go slumming."

He paused and his face softened. "Someone let it slip that I was your first."

Damn you, Chrissy. Aston thought he was being sneaky, but her best friend was the only one who knew that Aston was Sapphire's one and only sexual encounter.

"Well, Chrissy was wrong." Sapphire looked nonchalantly at her nails. "Because that's me alright, a big ol' tramp."

She cringed inside. Yes, *that's* what you wanted to tell the guy you were crushing on.

Aston opened his mouth, so Sapphire hurried to change the subject. "How's your girlfriend, by the way?" She smiled. "Well and pants-less as always?"

"Definitely pants-less…*a lot*," Aston said. Sapphire put the cup to her mouth again, this time in case she vomited.

Aston glanced at her, squeezing something in his hand.

It looked like a flash drive, but he was treating it like a gold nugget. He hadn't once put it down or loosened his grip on it. The way he'd looked at it all night told Sapphire something juicy was on it, and that he wanted nothing more than to go look at its content. Yet, he insisted on staying, even after the sun came up.

She watched as Aston yawned and lost the battle to keep his eyes open.

"Ms. Dubois." The doctor stepped up to them.

Aston's eyes sprung wide open as he and Sapphire jumped to their feet.

"Your mother is doing well…considering. Just a few cuts and bruises. It seems it was the amount of alcohol that knocked her out and not the crash. We pumped her stomach and attended to the cuts—she should be fine."

Sapphire exhaled. "Thank God."

"However," the doctor continued, "unrelated to the accident, I'm afraid we can't do much about the state of her liver."

"Well, you're not a miracle worker," Sapphire said.

"She's awake, so feel free to go sit with her." He eyed Aston. "And, as I'm sure the Detective here would suggest, being as far over the legal limit as she was at the time of the accident, I would call the family lawyer if I were you."

The doctor left and Aston ran his fingers through his hair, looking nervous, clenching the gadget tighter than before. "So…"

His phone rang and he dug in his pocket.

"Capelli," Aston said, taking a few steps back. "We have to push it to 2 p.m. I need a few hours of sleep before going through the shoe store's footage." His face twisted with annoyance. "Don't get your panties in a bunch. We've waited almost three years to find the Serial Catcher; a couple more hours won't make a difference."

Sapphire spun around and sped off before Aston could see the fear rising in her face.

"Hey!" Aston called after her, confused, but she didn't stop.

"Sleep tight," Sapphire pushed out. "Tell your girlfriend I said 'hi.'"

"Oh, I will!" Aston yelled back. "And be sure to tell your future husband he can suck my—"

Sapphire slammed the door shut and leaned against it, trying to calm herself. *I'm on that tape*, was all she could think. She'd been caught on camera.

That fat bastard! She cursed the name of George Rath as her knees gave out from under her and she slid down the door.

She knew what she had to do.

She had to rid the shoe store of its footage and then, more importantly, steal it.

She had to steal Aston's flash drive.

CHAPTER 8

Sapphire slid her makeup mirror under Aston's door. She could see him in his bed. Luckily, there was no sight of his girlfriend. *Barf.*

Sapphire exhaled as she placed her torsion wrench into the key hole. She didn't want to do what she was about to do—not to Aston—but she had no choice.

Earlier that morning, Sapphire placed a call to New York where the Dubois' family lawyer, Mr. Goldstein, had his firm. Mr. Goldstein was one of Charles's closest friends, and she knew he'd take care of everything the minute they hung up. Thanks to him, Sapphire was able to leave her mother in the hospital and proceed with the plan.

She bought the exact flash drive she'd seen in Aston's hand and brought it to an Internet café next to Hollywood High School.

She walked in wearing the shortest, yet most innocent-looking sun dress she owned. Eight hormone-riddled 15-year-olds with minor and major acne problems craned their necks to follow her.

After flirting with the same intensity she offered serial killers, Sapphire had the poor, sweet nerds eating out of the palm of her hand.

"So you're saying this thingy can be used for that?" she asked.

"Hurh hurh hurh," the nerds laughed, amused by her measly mortal knowledge of technology.

"Can *you* do it for me?" she asked, challenging them.

"I can, but it's kind of illegal," one replied.

One was Phil. Another Bill. She had a hard time telling

them apart because both their main facial features were pimples.

"I see," Sapphire said, pouting for effect. "It's just, my BFF posted a naked picture of me, and I want to give her a taste of her own medicine and wipe out her tablet."

The nerds stopped breathing at the mention of the nude picture.

"I'll do it!" They both shouted then fought for the flash drive.

The one with more pimples won and clicked around on the computer, in areas Sapphire didn't even know existed. She tried to absorb as much knowledge as possible, in case she'd ever have to do this again, but most of it was lost on her.

"Alright." He handed her the flash drive and cracked his fingers. "You're all good."

"Thank you," Sapphire gushed. She rewarded each of them with a peck on the cheek.

With the strong taste of Clearasil on her lips, she left the boys, who seemed happy to get rid of her so they could start searching the Internet for a naked picture that didn't exist. She sped down the freeway, leaving L.A. County behind and got to Thousand Oaks in Ventura before the store opened.

She managed to get in through the small window in the back alley, which she had once used to escape the staff, and was on their computer system with a half hour to spare before the sales people came in.

A minute after she inserted the flash drive into the hard drive, the screen's images broke up into an endless number of colorful pixels. The system made a high-pitched beep and a little malicious-looking man popped up on the screen with his tongue out just before it all went black.

Mission one complete. The nerd assured her there would be no traces of any previous data or RAM.

She headed for Aston's knowing her next undertaking wouldn't be as easy.

There were three things she knew for sure about Aston.

One: He was a light sleeper. Two: His handgun was never less than two feet away from him. Three: He slept naked, which was neither here nor there, but not a bad thing for someone who spent hours thinking about the man.

She twisted the pick until it *clicked*. She opened the door to find Aston's small studio apartment dark and silent. He lay on his stomach breathing slowly; his butt was sticking out from the white sheet.

Sapphire glanced at it once—maybe twice—then reached in her bag.

She took out the tranquilizer gun she'd stolen from the vet clinic last year and aimed it at Aston's neck…then changed her mind and went for his butt instead when she realized she didn't want to accidentally shoot him in the eyeball. She was way too fond of Aston's eyeballs.

Sapphire inhaled, closing her eyes. She didn't want to do it, not to him, but she couldn't rummage through his apartment without waking him up.

She squeezed the trigger and the dart launched right into Aston's ass. A second passed, then Aston's dazed eyes shot open.

"SON OF A—" he shouted before quickly trailing off, closing his eyes again as his body relaxed. He was out.

After going through the kitchen, its cupboards, and various boxes of high fiber cereal, Sapphire finally found the flash drive in a small filing cabinet. She snatched it, replaced it with her own, and was just about to close the drawer when a file caught her eye.

It contained everything Aston had on the Serial Catcher. Sapphire sunk to the floor as she started flipping through unsolved police reports, false statements from all the serial killers she'd captured, and lastly, Aston's own sheets of theories.

There was more doodling than there was speculation. Without the evidence of the shoe store's surveillance footage, all Aston seemed to have figured out with the help of George Rath—the tattletale—was that she was a woman. Otherwise, he was nowhere near…for now.

Sapphire got up and lay down on her stomach next to him. It was asinine. Not because it could wake him from the tranquilizer's powerful slumber, but why did she have to keep torturing herself?

Aston was Sapphire's enemy. That would never change, unless she got caught. Aston was as devoted to finding the Serial Catcher as Sapphire was to finding her killers. She hunted them, he hunted her. It was a vicious cycle of cat and mouse; like Tom and Jerry…if Tom had been a handsome cop, and Jerry sickly attracted to him.

She looked at him and couldn't help but smile. He looked charming even when sedated: tousled hair, drool, and all.

Had there been an off button where every thought, emotion, and image of Aston Ridder would vanish from her memory, Sapphire would have pushed it. But there was no such thing, and no matter how much she strived to expel him, Aston was always there, a permanent resident of her consciousness.

Sapphire got up and put the files back. She placed Aston's flash drive in the pocket of her spring jacket and left.

She couldn't fight how she felt about him anymore, but even if Aston had no girlfriend and Sapphire chose to be with him, there would be no winners. It was like having to pick between plague and cancer—either way, Sapphire was screwed.

. . .

Crash!

Sapphire ducked just as she turned into the dressing room of the Golden Mirage. A small bottle lay shattered on the floor and liquor dripped down from the wall where it hit.

"You bitch!"

Ginger was staring at her, nostrils flared and fists clenched.

"What?!"

"Oh please, don't act like you don't know," Ginger sneered. "I've been here forever, I've paid my dues and you think you can just waltz in here and take my regulars?"

"What are you talking about? I haven't even had a customer yet, let alone a regular. I just started yesterday!"

"You should just leave; nobody wants you here. Isn't that right, Chastity?"

Chastity looked up from behind her hair. She whispered an inaudible response then returned to staring at her palms.

"Speak up!" Ginger shouted.

"Leave her alone," Sapphire said, realizing she shouldn't have.

Ginger grabbed the pink razor from her vanity. "I'll cut you!" She flew toward Sapphire.

Before Sapphire had even begun to plan how to knock Ginger out and make it look accidental, Misty stepped in between.

"No! You hev problem, so vat? Talk to Giles, not her fault. You go now."

Ginger's furious eyes darted between Sapphire and Misty. She snorted, bull-like, then took a step back.

"Don't think I won't cut you too!" Ginger pointed at Misty then walked out, ignoring other girls' stares.

Sapphire felt touched by her newfound Russian friend's action and gave Misty a warm smile. "Thank you. I'm sorry if I've caused you problems."

Misty shrugged. "So vat? She always say I vill cut this, I vill cut that. She's a lying sunulvabeach. She forget, you see."

"What was she mad about?"

"Giles did not tell you?" Misty asked. "There is a man who is regular. Before he vants dance from Ginger, now he vants dance from you. Big tipper. Come."

Sapphire's heart skipped. She crossed her fingers for John Doe, Jr. as Misty led her up to the stage entrance and pulled the thick curtain aside.

Sapphire's mood sank as Misty pointed to the man with the cowboy hat.

"Giles says he see you in the cage last night and he vants private."

Sapphire let out a sigh. She'd looked forward to spending another night in the perv-safe cage where she could observe John Doe Jr. to try and figure out what he was into.

If she even could. Had she figured out what type of girl he liked, Sapphire would have morphed herself into whatever his twisted heart desired, but there wasn't. She'd spent hours in her attic, matching the victims to one another. Excluding the M.O. of killing only strippers from the Golden Mirage, John Doe, Jr. didn't have a physical type, favorite weapon, or any victim whose death was similar to the others. He seemed random and sporadic, and it was hard to anticipate his moves. She needed to observe him and now she'd have to waste time dancing for some sleaze ball.

Misty tilted her head confused. "Why you are sad? This is promotion, yes?"

"Oh no," Sapphire tried, "this is how I look when I'm happy."

Misty gave her three encouraging pats on the back that felt more like the slaps one gets when choking. "Lucky girl, you are terrible dancer."

"Thanks."

Misty left to go wax a body part Sapphire didn't know was waxable, and she stood there for awhile, disappointed, staring out as a few customers entered the establishment.

The doors opened and he stepped inside.

John Doe, Jr.

• • •

"Fuck me." Aston shook his head.

"Man, you can say that again," Capelli agreed.

"Fuck me." Aston shook his head.

He stared down at the broken keyboard that he used to smash up the hard drive which had collapsed when they inserted the flash drive.

Capelli sat next to him staring at the black computer screen, arms crossed.

Aston was so excited to get the identity of the Serial Catcher that he ignored the fact that he had slept through his alarm, had strange dreams of people in his studio, and had the ass-ache of the century. He skipped breakfast, a shower, and a few red lights on his way to the Beverly Hills Police Station.

At first he thought there was an error with the computer, but when he saw the vicious little man flashing his tongue at them, he knew it was a virus. After a quick call, they found out the shoe store had the same problem. The tech department told them the virus was immediate and final.

It was gone. All of it. There was no way to retrieve the information. The Serial Catcher, who was hooked and ready to be reeled in, had bitten off the line and escaped back into muddy waters.

"How does breakfast sound?" Aston asked, grabbing the flash drive. "Coffee, bagel, bullet-to-the-head, eggs?"

They walked down to the station's cafeteria. Aston stared at the flash drive in his hand. *Something smells fishy.*

And it wasn't Capelli today, who instead reeked of bad cologne.

"Coffee. Black," Capelli ordered at the counter.

"You should try the caramel macchiato," Aston suggested. "It's delightful." When he got no reply, he turned to see Capelli gawking at him. "What?"

"You should try the caramel macchiato, it's delightful?" Capelli repeated. "This from a guy who used to reheat instant Folgers in the microwave and laugh at people with their foo-foo coffee drinks?"

Aston was just about to defend his caramel macchiato, because it really was delightful, when it hit him. He grabbed Capelli's arm so violently that the black coffee splattered all over the counter.

"Fine, I'll try your damn macchiato. Relax."

"The computer yahoos said the virus was instant, right? And the shoe store's system was clean last night. I had the clean flash drive in my hand from the time I got it to when I went to bed. I put it in my filing cabinet, went to sleep, slept through my alarm for the first time in my life, then took the flash drive straight here and inserted it." Aston and Capelli looked at each other, their brains connecting.

"So either someone infected your flash drive too, then put it back," Capelli said. "Or..."

"This isn't my flash drive," Aston said. One thing became clear to Aston as he and Capelli stared down at the black, two-inch article in his hand.

"She knows who I am."

CHAPTER 9

"No touching, no snogging, no nipples, definitely no BJ. And don't get any ideas, no CBJ either."

"Okay."

"No number, no talking, no flashing, no Italian. No shagging on the side, period."

"Okay." She didn't have a clue what Giles was talking about.

"Good." He looked less concerned. "Also, for anyone else, I'd tell you that security's right outside if you need them, but if you call them in on this guy, I will kill you with my own bloody hands, Sapphire Two. If he gets out of line, you handle him. Ginger always did."

"Okay."

He took her right hand and held it up as if she was pledging an oath, then closed his eyes. "Repeat after me: I will not fock this up."

"I will not fock this up."

"Very funny," Giles sneered, letting go of her. "Let's have a piss at Giles who is down to one decent customer and has his willy strung up in one of those medieval devices because the world has been in a bloody recession and half his staff has either left because they are scared of dying or off being dead themselves." He paused. "I *need* this bloke. So please, do the dance we practiced, don't fock up, and I promise I will not kill or sack you…or both."

"So basically, no pressure."

"Go on then." He smacked her on the ass, sending her in the right direction.

Sapphire collected her nerves as she stood in front of the curtain to the private room where the cowboy was waiting for her.

Whatever you do, Sapphire told herself, *do not punch this man in the face*. She slid the curtain to the side and smiled.

"Why, howdy," he said, licking his upper lip. Sapphire's fist automatically clenched.

"Howdy," she answered, attempting a coy voice.

He sat in a plush chair—taking up the majority of the space in the small room—drinking whiskey, and undressing her with his eyes. Not that he had to work hard at it.

Giles had tried to make it easy for her. All she had to do was take off a small see-through shirt, her gloves, and a tiny skirt held by Velcro, leaving her in black booty shorts and a bra that was stuffed with nude cutlets to give her "something resembling cleavage" as Giles put it.

When the cowboy's favorite country song started playing, Sapphire took his hat and put it on her head, like she and Giles rehearsed. Though she found it hard to dance to the DJ's hardcore techno, she found it harder to be sexy to a country song titled: *Momma get the hammer, there's a fly on daddy's head*.

Despite two missteps and the twenty-second struggle to get her shirt off, it was going well. The cowboy seemed into it.

It was when Sapphire turned around to do a dip that it all went south…literally.

The cowboy stood up and grabbed her ass. Then came the unmistakable sound of cowboy jeans being unzipped.

As Giles's voice echoed in her mind, warning her not to fock up, Sapphire turned to him. She pushed him back and wagged her finger in a no-no motion.

"Oh come on," he said with groggy eyes, "we both know how important I am to this joint." He approached her again, this time aggressively. "Just do what I want and no one will be upset."

His cattle-trading fingers reached for her throat and Sapphire snapped into defense mode. He could have been reaching for a body part less hostile, like her boob, but in Sapphire's mind—more accustomed to murderous men—he was going for the kill. Her body responded before her commonsense had time to stop her.

She grabbed his hand, twisting it. He winced in pain and his pants slid down to his ankles. His other hand searched toward her face and Sapphire kicked him back into the chair.

There was a moment of stillness while Sapphire's foot was still on his face—pushing his lips and his cheek to the side—his eye flicking between her and her boot.

Not sure what to do, Sapphire slowly removed her foot from the cowboy's face—frozen in some indescribable emotion—then removed the hat and neatly set it to the side. She stayed for an awkward moment then bolted.

Shit. Sapphire's heart raced as she dashed down the hallway. She'd get fired. Giles would never let her come back once the cowboy opened his mouth.

She ran to the dressing room to change her clothes and noticed that someone—Ginger most likely—had written *die bitch die* in red lipstick on her mirror.

It wasn't until she got into her Volkswagen and her panic settled that she was able to start thinking.

Sapphire sat in her car across the street from the Golden Mirage.

She couldn't give up now. John Doe, Jr. was still in there and he was brutal, a psycho. She couldn't let him get another girl. If Sapphire didn't catch him, who would? Strippers getting killed and disfigured right and left obviously wasn't a priority for the LAPD. Without Sapphire, these girls didn't have a chance in hell. She *had* to stay.

She would wait for the cowboy to exit then use whatever tactic she could to convince him to tell Giles he needed to keep her. If the cowboy spoke, Giles listened. That part was clear.

The door of the Golden Mirage opened and a familiar face appeared.

Except it wasn't the cowboy.

It was John Doe, Jr.

There were a few standard rules to stalking a serial killer, and since the bookstore didn't carry a copy of *Stalking Serial Killers for Dummies*, they were rules Sapphire had created herself.

Rule Number One: If you don't have a plan while stalking

your predator, keep your distance.

Which is exactly what she did.

The streets lay dark while Sapphire crept after the man-boy as he passed both humans and other creatures lurking in the shadows.

The nightlife in downtown L.A. consisted of hobos, prostitutes, and the occasional lowlife criminal waiting for a chance to rob a hobo, prostitute, or a much more lucrative lowlife. It wasn't often that you saw a young man wearing a $100,000 suit strolling carelessly through a part of L.A. the city didn't even bother to keep properly lit.

A few blocks down he stopped by a gas station and tried to hail a cab that was already taken. It confirmed Sapphire's theory.

Why wouldn't he just get a cab outside the Golden Mirage? He didn't want to be seen and recorded by one of the cab cameras at the place he picked his victims.

There was a whisper in Sapphire's ear. Fortunately she wasn't getting carjacked. It was her own voice telling her to violate the regulations that had kept her alive so far.

Rule Number One was about to be broken.

Sapphire pulled up to the gas station. She took a breath before she rolled down the window.

"You need a ride?"

. . .

"Hey…" *Sluuurp*. "Did you hear about that downtown case?" Barry asked.

Aston cringed as he gazed at his own apartment building across the street. They were watching his building, hoping to spot the Serial Catcher staking him out.

"It's strange," Barry continued. "The LAPD doesn't seem to be doing anything about it." *Sluuurp*.

"Trust me," Aston said. He took another bite of his whole grain bagel, trying to stay calm. "They're doing something, just not in the public eye." He had no idea what case Barry was talking about but felt obligated to defend his old station.

Sluuurp.

Aston counted to ten, annoyance for Officer Barry Harry making his skin crawl.

After a lot of awkward begging, Aston had let the boy come along. Partly because he felt sorry for him and his lack of experience, but mostly because he needed Barry's ugly buggy to stay incognito.

Barry was the greenest cop Aston had ever come across. Having spent his first year as a cop in Beverly Hills, Barry's ass was used to cushy assignments that ended with all parties smiling and shaking hands. In contrast, Aston got stabbed on his first day at the LAPD. His left ball was never the same.

Sluuurp.

"Give me that!" Aston snatched Barry's juice box and threw it out the window. "What are you, five?"

"Sorry, Detective," Barry said wide-eyed, reaching for his potato chips instead.

Crunch. Crunch. Crunch.

Aston had just started putting Barry in a headlock when a car blew past them going at least 55 mph. It took Aston a second to recognize the car and two more to react.

"What are you doing?"

"What does it look like? We've got a five-ten." Aston searched for his siren in the backseat before remembering this wasn't his car.

"Um, three things, Detective," Barry said, grabbing onto the side handle as Aston floored it. "How are you going to pull someone over without the siren? How are people going to know you're coming without a siren? And why are you worried about a five-ten when we're on an important stake out?"

"Don't know yet. Don't care. And stopped listening after the first two."

"OH MY GOD!" Barry squeezed his eyes shut as Aston pulled between two cars in a nonexistent lane. The boy was overreacting. Aston had tons of margin—at least one inch on both sides.

The other car took a sharp left at the next intersection

and drove down Rodeo Drive. Aston turned, cutting off a yellow vehicle.

Barry looked over his shoulder. "That was a school bus, you know. With *kids* in it."

"Then they're lucky. I had to walk to school."

Aston maneuvered into oncoming traffic, driving alongside the perp with only the palm tree decorated median separating them. He accelerated to the intersection, then grabbed a hold of the emergency break as he pulled a sharp right.

The buggy squealed to a stop in front of oncoming traffic in the intersection.

Barry's girly scream rang out as the perpetrator's car plunged toward them, skidding forward. The Porsche emblem nicked Barry's passenger side door.

"Got any ticket books?" Aston asked.

White as a sheet, Barry shook his head then his cheeks puffed up with either air or vomit. Nope. Definitely vomit.

Barry hurled into Aston's bagel bag.

"You owe me $6.98," Aston said. He grabbed his sunglasses and something to write on. He stepped outside, patting down a few out of place hairs.

Aston approached the car calmly just as the man in the driver's seat recognized him.

"Sir, are you aware of the speed limit on residential streets?"

John Vanderpilt stared back at him in disbelief. *"What?"*

"It's generally 30 to 35 miles per hour. I suggest you don't ever go over 45, unless you're on a highway or freeway. I'm gonna go ahead and issue you a citation." He handed it to Vanderpilt.

"Are you kidding me? This is not even a ticket. It's the back of a tacky takeout menu!"

"Sir, please don't take that tone with me. Taco Pete's is a fine establishment."

John crumpled up the menu and tossed it at Aston's chest. It bounced to the ground.

"Why don't you add littering to that?" Vanderpilt said and eyed him up and down. "Unlike some people, I can afford it."

"Listen to me, you little prick," Aston spat. "If I catch you driving 55 in a 35 zone again, I'll make you regret the day daddy bought you this Porsche."

"For your information, my *mom* bought it for me," John said, "And don't think I don't know what this is about."

"Oh yeah, what?" Aston said dryly.

"You want something I have," Vanderpilt smirked.

"A receding hairline?"

"No," he said, as his hand flew to his hair. "Do you really think Sapphire wants some little meter maid that makes as much in a year as she spends on her electric bill? Then you're day-lusional." He arched a brow. "Where do you live anyway? An *apartment?* Ha!"

Aston was happy he'd put on the sunglasses; they hid his reaction. Maybe it was true. Maybe he was day-lusional. What could he ever offer Sapphire Dubois? A yearly salary of 45 grand wasn't enough to cover her lifestyle. The notion hit him hard, harder than Aston was used to being hit.

"I have *everything* she'll ever want." John twisted the knife. "Just look around. I *own* that store." He pointed. "And that restaurant and that bank. And that's just on this block."

Aston looked at the bank, his jaw clenching. His eyes drew to a tiny camera on the outdoor ATM and his something in his mind sparked.

The lady whose feet Capelli molested had said there was an ATM across from the shoe store. No ATM came without a camera. If it was even in the vicinity of the shoe store there was a chance something—anything—was caught.

"Barry!" Aston shouted, ecstatic. "Call Capelli and tell him to meet me at the shoe store, asap."

"Yes, Detective," Barry said, puke still on his shirt.

"You're right, by the way." Aston turned back to Vanderpilt. "She would never want me for my money."

"Of course I'm right," Vanderpilt said into the rearview mirror, counting hair strands.

"Must have been the legendary size of my dick that made her come home with me that one time."

Vanderpilt's hand froze and his face dropped.

"Now you make sure you pay that ticket, *son*." Aston tapped the top of the Porsche, maybe a little too hard.

Aston peeled off and enjoyed the silent ride to his destination. It wasn't until twenty minutes later that he realized he had stolen the Buggy and left Barry back on Rodeo Drive.

All and all, not a bad day.

. . .

Sapphire's palms were so sweaty they stuck to the wheel. Inside her car, two feet away from her, sat a serial killer. He reeked of both blood-lust and guilt.

She shouldn't have broken her own rule, but the circumstances called for it.

If she couldn't get back on Giles's good side—which was likely since she'd planted a foot on his best customer's face—she might never get the opportunity to be near John Doe, Jr. again.

She knew she didn't really exist to him yet. She needed to establish a relationship by reaching out and introducing herself as his next victim. *Fingers crossed.*

Sapphire had asked several questions, trying to pump him for information, but he didn't tell her anything of value.

"I'm sorry," Sapphire said, "I never caught your name."

"Um, David."

Sapphire sniffed, smelling smoke. It seemed a fire had originated somewhere in the general area of um-David's pants. He was small and scrawny, but a big fat liar.

"So, David," she said ready for one final push, "I'm not gonna beat around the bush. I've heard from some of the waitresses that you're pretty generous. The reason I picked you up was because I thought you might like a private dance."

He glanced at her.

"I could give you one," Sapphire continued. "Outside of work."

Take the bait. Take it. Taaaake it.

He glanced over at her again then his eyes shot in the opposite direction.

"Mmm…no thanks," he said, as if she had asked him if he wanted the rest of her ice cream.

Sapphire smiled to hide her frustration. This man-boy did not want to kill her *at all*.

He didn't have a type or any other physical preferences. Meaning it could be any girl at any given moment as long as she was a Golden Mirage stripper. So why not Sapphire? Not that she was vain or anything, and she tried hard not to take it personally, but seriously, what was it? Her hair? Make up? Breath? Something about her made him think she wasn't killable. She never had any complaints before.

"That's me over there," he said and she pulled over. She found it hard to believe that the man with the world's most expensive suit lived in such an average apartment building.

"If you change your mind…" Sapphire started, about to give him an e-mail address she would set up later.

"I won't. Thanks for the ride." He slammed the door shut.

Sapphire gasped as he walked off. First, he refuses to kill her, and then he slams her already loose door? This killer was psychotic AND bad-mannered.

He walked up to the entrance of the building and fiddled with his keys.

Sapphire drove off then pulled into an alley and parked.

John Doe, Jr. looked around then walked away from the building. Sapphire let him get way ahead then crept after him, lights off.

He walked until he reached a part of the city where there were streetlights and no hobos or prostitutes in sight. He stopped at Skyline, downtown's most retro building, where some of the richest people in finance and a few celebs lived.

Sapphire watched him exchange a few words with a passing woman and shook her head.

The misconception of serial killers often being middle-class was a bad one. It tricked people into believing they were safe around the wealthy. Wrong. Rich people were worse. They were bored. Sapphire should know.

She waited the few minutes it took for him to get up the

elevator. Then a light from the apartment farthest to the left on the thirty-second floor came on.

"Gotcha."

CHAPTER 10

Sapphire's eyes snapped open. Her whole body was soaked in sweat, and her heart beat something fierce. She was awake, but she couldn't get the images out of her head.

She'd come home from stalking John Doe, Jr. and hit the sack right away. The second she fell asleep, she was back in the crimson-colored motel room with her mother and father.

Sapphire looked at her alarm clock. It was only 3 a.m. but it felt like she'd been trapped in the dream for hours, trying to get out. The scenario kept repeating, ending with her father saying, "You're not supposed to be here."

She got out of bed and stood by the window looking out into the darkness. Something wasn't right, she could feel it. Dr. Rues made Sapphire go somewhere she wasn't supposed to and now her mind was stuck there, on repeat.

She noticed a white Audi outside of the mansion. Its lights were off, but fumes came out of the rear. Sapphire would not have reacted to it except the car didn't belong. It wasn't that it was ugly and cheap like Sapphire's Volkswagen. It was too average. People in Beverly Hills spent millions on their homes and vehicles to make sure they could never be called average. The word was detested.

Sapphire clapped. When the light didn't come on, she remembered her mother recently upgraded the house lighting system. God forbid anyone actually walk over and flip a switch.

"Lights on." The room burst into a bright yellow.

The Audi sped off, leaving a cloud of exhaust behind.

Of course, it could have been a pizza delivery driver, a maid, anyone.

Of course, this was not what Sapphire Dubois believed.

. . .

"You said we were going to Napa!" Vivienne cried.

Sapphire rolled up the window as she watched her mother and the rehab facility get smaller in the rearview mirror.

Mr. Goldstein had managed to work his magic, getting Vivienne out of both jail time and excessive fines. Had the judge not been a Matt LeBlanc fan, Mr. Goldstein would have gotten her out of the week-long rehab requirement as well. But the judge was and had asked Matt, more than once, to say, "How you *doin?"*

Sapphire's mother, who was still in denial about the whole thing, had to attend rehab.

It hadn't taken much to get Vivienne into the car, despite the fact that she preferred not to spend time with Sapphire. A promise of a mother-daughter week at a vineyard in Napa Valley—"vineyard" being the key word—and she was good to go.

Sapphire yawned, trying to keep her tired eyes steady on the dirt road. She hadn't been able to sleep after the nightmare. She stayed up and watched the road in case the white car returned. It never did.

She pulled out from the gates meant to keep people in more than out, and actually felt bad for her mother, who looked helpless in the mirror as she stared after the Range Rover. All that was missing was a teddy bear in her arms.

Sapphire glanced at the clock on her dashboard: 6:05 p.m.

She would have been at the Golden Mirage now if she hadn't beaten the crap out of their best customer. Big mistake. Now she would have to figure out a way to get into John Doe, Jr.'s apartment, which was nearly impossible.

The Skyline was a state-of-the-art new apartment building with all the best amenities and topnotch security. They had cameras everywhere and security guards patrolled every floor.

Sapphire had been there once, at the grand opening. Chrissy dragged her there. Now she was glad her best friend had. She knew the obstacles and could prevent her face from getting plastered on a screen…again.

She put her phone in the port as she realized that the person who got her in before, could probably get her in again.

"Call Chrissy," Sapphire ordered.

"Right away Ms. Dubois," the robotic female voice replied. "Calling: California Pizza Kitchen."

Sapphire scowled at her new phone. They didn't get along well, the two of them, not like her and her old phone. She would still have the old one if Chrissy hadn't traded it in, insisting Sapphire's was three months out of date and therefore an embarrassment.

"No," Sapphire scolded. "Call *Chrissy.*"

"Calling: Father O'Riley."

"No. Call…well, okay."

They hadn't talked since she found her new killer, and he had a knack for shedding light on most situations.

"Father O'Riley is out of the coverage area, Ms. Dubois."

Sapphire sighed at the rectangle machine. "No, he's thirty miles away. Last week I went to West Hollywood and you told me I was in *Guam.*"

"Searching…Guam."

"No! Call Father O'Riley," Sapphire insisted.

"Calling: Chrissy."

Sapphire banged her head to the steering wheel, accidently honking at an elderly couple crossing the street.

"Um, hey, Saph," Chrissy's voice filled the car. "I, eh, can't talk. Shopping."

"Wait. Remember when we went to the Skyline's grand opening?"

"Barely, it was boring. I ended up sleeping with the Prince of Finland because I was so bored."

"Finland isn't a monarchy."

"Then who did I sleep with?"

Sapphire sighed. This was a question that came up a lot. Over the years it became a weekly game titled: Who did Chrissy sleep with at (insert event)? Most cases remained unsolved.

"Anyways," Sapphire said, not having time to play, "do you

know anyone there who might have a party or gathering in the near future?"

"I'll see what I can do," Chrissy sneered.

"What's up with you? Is something wrong?"

"I didn't—I mean *nothing*. Quit questioning me. What are you, my mother? I said I can't talk!"

Click.

Sapphire looked at the screen. Yep, something was definitely wrong.

. . .

"Sir, I already told you, you can't smoke in here."

"I'm not."

"Then what's in your hand?"

"Oh, whoops. I'll just finish this one then."

The bank director gave Aston a cold stare then opened the window, coughing and waving her hand.

Becoming a cop was the best decision Aston ever made. People tended to argue less over things that clearly weren't okay. They assumed he knew what he was doing because he was a cop. Joke was on them, Aston rarely knew what he was doing.

After coughing some more, the director left the room and Aston and Capelli went back to staring at the small screen, featuring the security footage.

Aston's phone rang and he looked at the screen. It was Moore.

Reject.

He liked to believe he was passing on no-strings-attached sex because he just didn't have time, but he knew the real reason; it was the look on Sapphire's face when she saw Moore at his place. It had been on replay in his mind ever since.

His actions had hurt her and he hated that, even though she was engaged to someone else. The whole thing was fucking confusing.

"Nice ass," Capelli said.

"Thanks, I've been working out."

"The bank director's."

"Oh, I didn't notice."

"Really?" Capelli leaned back, putting his hands crisscross in his armpits. "Aston Ridder, the infamous downtown womanizer 'didn't notice.' I used to think alien abductions were a crock, but now I'm not so sure."

"If anybody has changed, it's you," Aston sneered.

"I hate to tell yah, but I'm the same as I've always been. That Moore chick has done a number on you. You won't go to boobie-bars, and you don't even glance when a smokin' ten walks our way. Frankly, your behavior is alarming, Ridder."

Aston was taken aback. Was he the one who had changed? He laughed despite the headache he had from staring at the poor-quality footage. "Trust me, Moore isn't the reason."

Capelli scoffed, not believing him. "Okay, so if not Moore, then who?"

"Her, right there." Aston pointed at a slender blonde on the screen. "Watch."

"We've already watched her, she goes in, ten minutes later she comes out. Nada."

"Exactly, read the list."

Capelli sighed and looked down at the notebook. "Femmy guy, purchased shoes. Brunette, nothing. Lady with dog in her purse, a new purse for her dog. Redhead, nothing. Weird woman with limp, purchased surprise, surprise, shoes. Blonde, nada."

"Different women, go to a shop, and none of them bought anything?"

"Dear God," Capelli exclaimed, sarcasm dripping from his tongue. "Book 'em Dano."

Aston snatched the remote from Capelli and rewound the tape, pausing with every woman.

"Brunette, redhead, blonde. Rath collected hair from his victims. She lured him out by switching her appearance to figure out what hair color he wanted."

Capelli squinted at the screen. "Christ. We've got the back of the Serial Catcher's head."

They both tilted their heads and Aston pushed pause.

"Do you see what I see?"

"Yup."

· · ·

Sapphire walked into the kitchen to see the Dubois' family physician, Dr. Wells, and Charles with their weekly checkup underway. Behind them, Berta was mopping and farting, making Dr. Wells uneasy.

"Hello Sapphire, haven't seen you in awhile," he said.

"Jacket," Berta ordered and Sapphire handed it to her.

Berta scowled and shook the jacket vigorously to make a point of its dirtiness.

"I'm glad you came, Sapphire." Dr. Wells put down his stethoscope and his forehead creased with concern.

A knot materialized in Sapphire's stomach and she looked at Charles.

"I heard your mother is in re…er…away, and legally Charles's secondary guardianship falls on your Uncle Gary, but his office said he is in India on business and not due back until next week. This means all decisions fall on you."

"What kind of decisions?" She couldn't lose Charles. Growing up she never had that father-daughter relationship with him. Whenever Charles wasn't away on business, he seemed oblivious of her, like she was air to him. But in the years after his stroke, they had grown closer. The idea of a life without Charles and his lopsided smile was inconceivable.

"Um," Doctor Wells said. "The medication your mother has kept Charles on doesn't do much but maintain the state he's in. Over the last few years I've been trying to convince your mother to put Charles on a program that could improve his health quite a lot."

Sapphire knew the answer, but she had to ask. "And why did she refuse?"

"Well-um," he said, "the treatment is rather expensive, and she said it was a financial issue."

Eeer! Wrong answer. Charles was a multimillionaire.

Vivienne did it to keep Charles immobile until the day he finally croaked. Even Dr. Wells knew it.

Sapphire cringed thinking about what her stepfather had been through over the years. She always thought Charles had the best help, but her mother had let him suffer on purpose.

"Yes, you have my permission," she said, her voice hard.

"Great. It may work quickly, or in few cases, not at all. It varies from patient to patient." Dr. Wells gave her forms to sign, handed Berta a prescription for extra strength Gas-X, and was out the door.

Sapphire looked over at Charles. Since she knew her mother felt no guilt at all, Sapphire felt it was her responsibility to feel guilty enough for the both of them.

"Charles…"

He looked over at her with his sweet gray eyes. Sapphire marched over and hugged him. He was surprised by the forceful embrace, then tried to hug her back, but just leaned into her.

"I say we order the messiest food we can find then picnic in front of the TV on mom's darling $65,000 ivory carpet."

"Hoa He!" he said. It generally translated to: *Hell yeah.* Or, during baseball season: *Those damn Yankees.*

Sapphire's phone rang. She assumed it was either her mother calling to beg Sapphire to take her back, or, more likely, the staff calling to beg Sapphire to take her mother back.

She didn't recognize the number but answered anyway.

"Where in the hell are you?" an Englishman spat.

"Giles?" she asked, stepping away from Charles and into the hallway.

"Yes, Giles! Who did you think it was, Hugh-bloody-Grant?"

"Not really." Hugh usually called Vivienne's cell, not Sapphire's.

"You better have a valid reason for running out in the middle of a shift and not showing up at all tonight."

"I'm not fired? I mean, the cowboy…?"

"He said, and I quote, 'her sass was refreshing.' It's too late to get your routine right tonight, so come in early tomorrow and we'll see if we can get you on stage and straighten out your problem areas, so *all* your areas."

Sapphire smiled. She wasn't fired and she'd be on stage. Perhaps John Doe, Jr. would accept her as a victim. It was possible he was only drawn to the dancers featured on stage.

"So?" Giles asked.

"Sooo…I'll see you tomorrow?"

"So what is your excuse for not showing up? Make it a good one please. I've heard everything from 'my grandmother died again' to vaginal reconstruction surgery."

"Well…" Sapphire headed for the closet to get Aston's flash drive, which was still in her pocket. "I had to take my alcoholic mother to court-ordered rehab because she smashed into Matt LeBlanc's car. Then I had to spend time with my vegetative, paraplegic stepfather, who has been kept like that by my alcoholic mother so she can have sex with other men and still inherit his money."

The other end of the line was silent as Sapphire grabbed her jacket.

"Good one," Giles finally said. "Though I'd lay off the soap operas if I were you."

Sapphire hung up. She was back on track.

She dug into her pocket. The flash drive needed to be destroyed. Demolished. Hell, blasted by high-powered artillery, to make sure all evidence of Sapphire as the Serial Catcher died a fiery death.

There was only one problem.

It was gone.

CHAPTER 11

"Get off the stage!" Somebody hurled a shoe at Sapphire and she ducked.

Some Golden Mirage customers booed while others played with their phones. One guy was snoring. Not the greatest moment in Sapphire's short career as a stripper.

She arrived at the Golden Mirage at 3 p.m. Giles spent the next few hours pouring his British heart into molding Sapphire into an acceptable stripper. Based on the booing and shoe throwing, he'd failed.

The DJ killed Sapphire's techno music, and she left the stage embarrassed.

She went to the dressing room to plant her head on the desk in front of her mirror. She was so tired from not sleeping for days that her mind and body were on autopilot. Last night, she closed her eyes and was back in the motel room. After waking up screaming twice, Sapphire had given up on sleep and searched the whole mansion for Aston's flash drive without result.

Berta would probably just set it aside if she found it, but having that kind of evidence on the loose was nerve wracking.

Sapphire banged her head against the desk a couple times.

"It's okay, Sapphire Two," Misty said, "when I was little girl in Russia, I dream of coming to America and see my name in big lights. Perhaps this is not good dream for you. Perhaps, butcher or prostitute." She gave Sapphire one of those painful Russian encouragement pats.

Ginger skipped past them and over to her mirror.

"What, no gloating?" Sapphire looked at her. "No comments about shoes being thrown?"

"No need," Ginger said, then held her hand up, counting

down with her fingers. Three. Two. One.

"Sapphire!" Giles stormed into the room. "You are done for tonight. You were such rubbish up there, you make Chastity look like bleeding Michael Flatley in comparison."

All eyes turned to Chastity. She blinked at them from behind her hair, then shrunk down into her seat.

"But it's only nine," Sapphire tried. "I'll take the back cage."

"I am actually in pain right now because the law prevents me from strangling you," Giles said. "So please get out of my sight, come back tomorrow, and try, please God try, to…suck less. Can you do that for me? Suck less?"

"Yes."

After getting heckled by Ginger and encouraged once more toward prostitution by Misty, Sapphire walked out of the Golden Mirage feeling tense.

She could feel John Doe, Jr. craving his next kill. She didn't see him at the Golden Mirage tonight. She was afraid she'd missed him and that he'd already snatched someone. She even tried to do a head count on the strippers.

Sapphire headed for the garage and made sure not to trip on the homeless man this time.

"You hungry, Herbert?" she asked, digging in her purse for money.

"No, just had a big expensive steak dinner." Herbert smiled up at her from under his foil hat and long gnarly hair.

Aw, delusion. Sapphire was just about to force the money on him anyway when her phone rang. Her mind went to the only person in the world that could make her feel better.

Of course, it wasn't him. Aston was probably at home and in bed with his cop girlfriend…using cuffs. The thought made her feel like someone was stabbing her in the chest with a butter knife. It wouldn't kill her instantly, and she'd suffer longer.

"What's up, Chrissy?"

"Who's the best BFF ever?" Chrissy's tone was an attempt at normal. "My friend Hayley Hasselhoff knows a guy who is cousins with Jennifer Aniston, who was in a movie with Paul Rudd, who is friends with Judd Apatow, whose wife knows

Rachel McAdams."

"And do any of these people know Kevin Bacon?"

"No."

"Then I think you've misunderstood the game."

"No, Rachel McAdams lives at Skyline. She's having a party tonight, and I'm totally invited. I got you down as a plus."

Sapphire smiled. "Chrissy, I could kiss you right now."

"Don't. That's what Lohan said right before I turned her gay."

"It's a saying."

"Not the way I do it."

Sapphire hung up feeling downright satisfied. Whether he was at the party or not, this was Sapphire's ticket into the building and into Doe's lair.

* * *

The Skyline was one of the most ridiculous things ever built by man, Aston thought, looking up at the towering monster. Twisting and turning, the structure looked more like an art piece than a place where people live.

"Does this tux make my muscles look too big?" Capelli asked.

"No."

Capelli looked down at his body, disappointed. "You sure?"

Diana, Capelli's date, smiled and patted his shoulder. "You look great; let's go inside. Come on, Ashton."

Aston shuttered. "It's As-ton, actually." He tossed his cigarette and held back a few curse words for Capelli.

Aston should be at the station now that they were so close.

While reviewing the bank's recording, Aston and Capelli both saw it. The Serial Catcher turned her head upward, just enough for the shoe store's shiny logo to catch her reflection. They took all the original footage to the Beverly Hills station where the Serial Catcher could never get to it.

The image caught was so unclear that the computer nerds at the station said it could take days or even weeks for it to process into something recognizable. Still, Aston wanted to sit there until the picture got processed. Unfortunately, Capelli's date was a makeup artist for something or another Adams. She was going to a ridiculous Hollywood party and got three pluses.

Capelli nagged Aston into coming along and leaving Barry on the job instead.

"Hello!"

Aston didn't have to look to know who it was. Officer Moore's high heels clacked on the road as she hurried up to them.

"What's she doing here?" Aston whispered.

"I invited her for you," Capelli said and slapped Aston's chest. "You're welcome, man."

"*Thanks.*" Capelli was too busy staring at his date's ass to notice Aston's sarcasm.

They went inside, past a doorman, security guards, and forty-seven security cameras.

"Jesus," Aston mumbled, as they passed by a fourth security guard when exiting the elevator. "That much security for a building shaped like a deformed penis?"

Capelli chuckled, then changed his mind and shushed Aston when he saw his date's disapproving head shake. It was obvious he hadn't gotten into the makeup artist's pants yet.

Whipped, Aston thought and laughed out loud.

They entered the lavish party, and his heart stopped when he saw her. Christina Kraft. Which meant one thing: Sapphire Dubois was near.

Whipped, Aston thought again. This time he didn't laugh.

*　　•　•　•*

Okay, maybe it wasn't the brightest idea she'd ever had.

Sapphire was perched on the skyscraper's platform, five-hundred feet above racing traffic below.

After scoping security a second time, it was clear she'd be on camera, and maybe even get arrested by one of the security guards if they caught her where she didn't belong.

Climbing out Rachel McAdams' bathroom window and

scaling the twisted building's platform was, oddly, the best plan Sapphire could come up with.

She was starting to regret it now that the wind picked up and dizziness kicked in.

Luckily, she had one platform below her feet and one right above her head to hold onto. The hard part was passing by the windows unseen. She crouched down while passing the window of a naked guy playing the harp, a woman crying hysterically to *The Bachelor*, and a labradoodle cleaning his privates. It was an awkward moment for both of them.

She reached John Doe, Jr.'s bathroom window and grabbed her tools. She'd managed to hide them from security by slipping them into her cherry lip gloss and mascara. The latch gave in, and Sapphire ripped open the window and tossed herself inside.

Based on her visit to Rachel McAdams' condo, she was pretty sure there were no security cameras inside. Rich and famous people liked their private lives classified. She banked on the serial killer being of the same mind.

Inside, Sapphire looked down at her watch and timed herself. She couldn't stay too long. She wasn't worried about Chrissy noticing, more the other complication who had arrived.

They'd strolled into the crowded party, Sapphire searching for John Doe, Jr., Chrissy for the hostess, grabbing a few salmon tartares as the tray passed by. When they found the actress, Chrissy handed her an $800 bottle of Belvedere Vodka and wished her a happy birthday then leaned into Sapphire's ear. "She's just an actress; they think this cheap crap is expensive."

Rachel McAdams frowned, which meant she either heard like a bat or Chrissy wasn't as good at whispering as she thought she was. Sapphire went all-in on the latter.

Her eyes swept through the crowd and stopped on the man-boy. John Doe, Jr. was standing in the middle of the dance floor, bored to death by two reality stars.

Next to her, Chrissy yanked the open bottle back from the actress and chugged about half before returning the gift.

Sapphire turned to see the other John, her fiancé, enter the party while doing the *Daniel Craig*. He tossed his jacket to a random guest to go hang and was followed by his posse of Beverly Hills boys.

He saw them, made a face reminiscent of a lobotomy victim, then waved. It was Sapphire's cue.

"I have to go to the bathroom, I think the tartares were bad," she whispered to Chrissy.

Rachel McAdams frowned again. She *did* hear like a bat.

Up in Doe's apartment Sapphire spent an hour going through closets, cabinets, and drawers. Then she looked behind rows of mundane photographs and abstract art pieces. She found nothing.

She sighed, impatient. She'd already been gone too long. She knew John was looking for her and Doe may decide to leave at any minute; he looked like he was falling asleep down there.

She was just about to head back when she stopped at a row of wannabe-artsy photographs. The man-boy wasn't only into buying art but liked to snap pictures himself.

She ran back to the living room and went through the bookshelf of photo albums until she found one with a small lock on it. She picked the lock and opened it to find a scrapbook of familiar faces.

Page after page featured the girls from the Golden Mirage. Across the photographs words were written with a red marker.

Ginger: *Too scary*. Misty: *Maybe*. Chastity: *Small, easy kill*.

Sapphire stared at the words, disgusted but relieved. She got to him before he got to Chastity. She seemed to be next in line.

"What the hell are you doing in my home?!"

John Doe, Jr. stood over her, staring down at his precious scrapbook with fear.

"Oh," Sapphire said, mystified. "Is this...not okay?"

Doe held his hands out at her preposterous question. *"No!"*

"Duly noted," Sapphire said and kicked him in the groin.

He grabbed his crotch and fell forward, a scream stuck in his throat. She moved out of the way and let him hit the ground. She climbed on top of his back and let her legs encircle each of his arms before she leaned backward, pulling him with her.

Panicked by his imprisoned arms, John Doe, Jr. kicked as

she positioned her arm around his throat in a 90-degree angle and forced his head forward, squeezing his Adam's apple.

"Sleep tight," she whispered, as he closed his eyes.

Sapphire felt proud; this was her first choke-out, and it had been successful. It was her old martial arts instructor who taught her that move. Had the bastard not turned out to be a serial killer himself, she may have sent him a thank you note.

Sapphire released the pressure and glanced down at John Doe Jr. taking his nap.

Finally, she had her killer.

• • •

Paul Butler watched the girls fight from his corner.

It reminded him of a dream he once had, except there was less of them slicing at each other with knives and more pulling of the hair.

Ginger, the fiery redhead, had a problem with Misty, the Russian, who had stuck up for the new girl, Sapphire, the one who couldn't dance. It wasn't very entertaining so it helped that he imagined them covered in each other's blood. Like a mud wrestling match but more amusing.

Misty caught Ginger about to cut up one of Sapphire's uniforms and had taken the scissors away from her.

"I'll cut you, bitch!" Ginger screamed.

The moment the the words left her lips a switch flipped in his mind. He'd only had a candle-wick-sized flame of interest before. Now he was consumed.

Oh no, bitch. I'll be the one cutting you. The mood had hit him.

He would cut her open and gut her like a pig. He would take his time until she gave up her dominance and allowed him all the power. He would make her admit that he was stronger and that she was a nobody. If there was one thing Paul loved, it was to break a controlling and confident woman. There was no sweeter kill than a lioness turned kitten.

Yes, *now* Ginger would die.

A strong vibration came from the phone in his pocket and

he didn't have to look to know who it was.

Perhaps he could ignore it. Just once. Perhaps, this one time, his victim could come first.

Who was he kidding?

Paul sighed, disappointed.

"Yes, Mother?"

CHAPTER 12

"I told you, I've never killed anyone!"

Sapphire stared down at Joseph Young, the 19-year-old co-founder of a trending software program; the next Mark Zuckerberg, he had called himself. It was the first thing he'd told her after he woke up all frazzled, as if his status would save him.

She didn't believe him, not for one second. It didn't add up. Even if she took away the scrapbook, there was the odd behavior, and she'd seen it in his eyes. He was a killer. She knew it as much as she knew her name was Sapphire Dubois. Er Green.

Joseph squirmed, uncomfortable—might've been the yard of duct tape she'd wrapped around him or the art deco chair, meant to be looked at and not sat in. Surely, he was regretting that purchase right now.

He whined again and looked at Sapphire, searching for compassion. She felt none. He shouldn't be such a baby; it could be worse. She hung George Rath over a meat grinder for Pete's sake.

"Okay." She held her finger over the state-of-the-art answering machine. "This is the last time, and then I swear to you, I will lose my patience." She pushed the button, and the machine was ready to receive his message.

Because of security, she wasn't able to bring a tape recorder, which she had planned on incase anything like this should happen. Although the photographs were probably evidence enough, she didn't want to leave the police with anything that wasn't rock solid. The answering machine was the next best thing.

"I did not kill anyone! I keep telling you!"

"Oh yeah?" Sapphire tapped the album. "Then what's this? Personally I call, 'small, easy kill' evidence, but maybe that's just me."

"So sue me. I like to take photographs of hot girls and write funny things. Why are you even stalking me? I told you I didn't want a private dance!"

"So I suppose it's just a coincidence that you have pictures of all the dead girls from the Golden Mirage?"

"I don't."

Sapphire opened her mouth to toss out a snappy reply— her favorite kind—then flipped through the album.

Crap! He was right. The girls who were dead weren't in there.

"Well, obviously you took them out, once you *took them out,*" Sapphire tried, hopeful.

"Listen to me: I am very, very powerful, and I can have my lawyers put you in jail for this."

He wasn't as powerful as he thought he was. He was what the people at the country club liked to call New Money, and New Money wasn't Old Money.

Sapphire sat down on the couch opposite Joseph and pinched her lips together, thinking.

"I guess there's only one thing I can do," she said, trying to sound concerned. It wasn't hard; she *was* concerned at this point.

"Let me go?"

"Close. Kill you."

"How is that *close?*" Joseph shrieked.

"Do you prefer stainless steel to the throat, or are you more of a plummet-out-the-window type of guy?" She got up and grabbed a knife from his kitchen drawer. She waved it around, pretending to be on the crazy side.

"No," Joseph pleaded. "I'll do whatever you want. You can dance for me! I'd love it, see?" He tried to smile and nod to prove his point, but fell short.

"Too late Joseph, you should have wanted to kill me when you had the chance." She brought the knife closer to his throat, watching his eyes grow wider with her every move.

"What was it?" she asked. "Was I too tall? Too short? Too skinny? Too fat? Too…brunette?"

"Please don't! I didn't kill anyone!"

"Don't tell lies, Joseph."

The blade touched his throat and Sapphire held it for as long as she could before she had to start digging in. She sawed lightly, allowing the knife to break skin.

"You were fine!" Joseph shouted. "I already had too many choices!"

"What?" Sapphire pulled back but kept the knife pointed at him.

"I hadn't picked anyone yet. I was trying to, but I hadn't. You just started there and I didn't need more options."

"You didn't kill any of the dancers?"

"I've had the fantasy for years, and then this guy started to kill off the strippers at the Golden Mirage, and I thought, great, I'll just do it once, and it will get pegged as one of his. They'd never suspect a second killer."

Sapphire lowered the knife, put out. "So you're like a lamer version of a copycat?"

"I don't know…" Joseph was on the verge of tears. "I just thought I'd do it once and get it out of my system. You don't understand what it's like to have these…thoughts and fantasies! They never go away. No matter how hard you try." It seemed like he was relieved to get it all off his chest.

Sapphire sat back down on the couch, deflated. Three things went through her mind. One: She had a serial killer on her hands who hadn't killed—hard to nail someone for victims who weren't dead yet. Two: She was glad she caught him before he did kill someone. Three: The Stripper Slayer was still out there, and Sapphire was back to square one.

Joseph Young sobbed. His tears ran down his chin, streaking his Cavalli shirt.

"I got rich when I was sixteen," he bawled, choking on his tears. "You don't understand what it's like to have everything. You want more. Something to make your heart pump and your adrenaline shoot through the roof. You just don't understa-ha-haaand."

Well…

Sapphire discreetly pushed the answering machine

behind her.

"I understand that it's wrong," Joseph continued. "But it feels like it should be right! I want to kill. Girls especially. I just want them dead. Does that make me such a bad person?"

Sapphire pushed the button behind her. "Well, yes, Joseph. Yes, it does."

The machine beeped and played back Joseph Young's new greeting. His eyes became engorged with shock.

"Here's what's gonna happen," Sapphire said. In a way, she felt sorry for the deranged little rich fellow. "You will see a shrink and pop pills for the rest of your life so that you'll stay away from murdering innocent women. I will always…*always* be watching you."

One lonely tear trickled down Joseph's cheek, and he looked about eleven years old.

"And if you so much as look at the Golden Mirage or hunt for a kill, I will send your confession to the police along with your name, and that will be it. You'll be nailed for murders you may or may not have committed."

Joseph nodded.

"So cliff notes: Get help. Don't kill. Me watching you. M'kay?"

He nodded again.

"And also," Sapphire said as she unhooked the contraption. "Buy a new answering machine because I'm taking this one." Sapphire walked toward the bathroom, cramming the answering machine into her tiny purse.

"Are…aren't you gonna untie me?" Joseph shouted after her.

"Do you have a weekly maid?"

"Yes."

"Then no."

.   .   .

It was about five drinks in and several bad celebrity impressions later that Aston realized Sapphire wasn't there. Chrissy said she was, but Chrissy wasn't the type of person who paid attention to anyone but herself.

The five drinks were a good idea. They helped release the Serial Catcher energy he'd stored up for the past few months. The celebrity impressions he did, not so much.

Danny DeVito punched him in the gut—the only place he could reach—after Aston shouted the Batman line, "I'm not a human being. I am an animal!" maybe one too many times.

One actor launched a kumquat at him after he caught the Titanic star doing a line of cocaine in the kitchen and asked: "Is that *really* something the king of the world would do?"

Aston stumbled into one of the four bathrooms and took extra care in locking the door. A tall woman with an Adam's apple had been chasing him around all night.

He unzipped his fly and sighed as he relieved three of his five drinks.

A squeak followed by a loud thud came from outside.

Aston double shook, zipped back up, and pulled the bath curtain aside to find the window open. He stuck his head out. The person he'd been looking for all night hung onto the edge of the building, her feet dangling 500-feet above ground.

"Hi?" Sapphire said, more confused to see him than fearful of falling.

Aston looked down at her, holding on for dear life. "What the hell are you doing?"

"Thought I'd admire the view." She looked over her shoulder. "And…done. You gonna just stand there or help me up?"

"I don't know. I already pulled you in from a skyscraper once. It's time you learn these things on your own."

"God, you're hilarious, but can you…" A strong gust of wind grabbed a hold of Sapphire's body. She squeezed her eyes shut and her knuckles whitened from the tightened grip.

Aston took a deep breath, focused on Sapphire, and reached for her. Heights weren't his thing.

She put her arms around his neck and he pulled her in.

When he put her down on the floor, neither of them let go

of each other. Their lips were only inches apart and they were both very aware of it. Aston's eyes slid from her lips down her neck, over her chest, along her arm and stopped at—

"Why do you have an answering machine in your purse?"

Sapphire scoffed. "Obviously…I didn't want to miss any calls."

She frowned at her own words then pulled away and ripped the door open. Capelli was standing on the other side, blocking her.

"Where have you been, man?" Capelli asked. "How do you expect me to work this place without my wingman?"

"Didn't you come with a date?"

"What are yah, a feminist now too?" Capelli said, then noticed Sapphire. "Oh, were you guys in there…together?"

"No!" Aston and Sapphire sneered at the same time, equally appalled.

"Well in that case…" Capelli grabbed Sapphire's hand, kissing it. *Kissing* it! "Aren't you going to introduce me, Ridder?"

"No."

"Excuse me, I was just leaving," Sapphire said. She pulled her hand out of Capelli's rigid grip and pushed past him.

"You wanna go watch the two girls make out in the hot tub upstairs?" Capelli asked.

Aston shook his head, watching Vanderpilt grab Sapphire on the dance floor where people were moving to a slow song from a Green Day cover band. Or maybe it was actually Green Day.

"Suit yourself," Capelli said and walked away.

Aston cringed as the rich snake slithered his arm around Sapphire's waist, letting his hand rest on her ass.

Moore came up to Aston and leaned in. "Hey, I'm leaving. Can you thank Capelli for me?"

She looked from Aston to Sapphire then rubbed her eye, seeming tired.

Across the floor, Sapphire's eyes drew back to Aston and landed on Moore. Aston couldn't lie; he enjoyed the jealousy that he could see erupting in her.

"Moore, you wanna dance?"

"Angelica," she corrected.

He pulled Moore to the dance floor, right in front of Sapphire and Vanderpilt. Sapphire saw them and pulled Vanderpilt to her and started moving to the music.

A game began as they kept their eyes locked on each other across the dance floor. If Sapphire pulled the snake closer, Aston pulled Moore closer, which made Sapphire pull the snake even closer. Aston retaliated by gabbing Moore's ass cheek.

Sapphire's eyes narrowed, so Aston grabbed the other ass cheek too.

Sapphire took Vanderpilt's face in her hands and pulled him in for a hard kiss.

A typhoon raged in Aston and he took out his anger by clenching his fists. Regrettably, Moore's ass got caught in the crossfire.

"Aooouu!" She pushed him away and rubbed her butt.

Sapphire broke the kiss, pushing John's wandering hands off her and saying something to him. Aston wasn't a master at reading lips, but he swore Vanderpilt's response involved the word "cow."

After casting one final scowl Aston's way, Sapphire took off toward the door.

As Officer Moore went to mend her ass, Aston watched Sapphire leave, feeling more bummed than he was when he was eight and his drunken father set his Lincoln Logs on fire.

This was getting ridiculous. They had one night months ago and had Aston had his way back then, their relationship would have ended when he closed the door behind her.

Capelli popped up next to him looking paranoid. "We should leave. I just got caught peeping at the girls in the tub, and the mayor's pissed at me."

"Why would the mayor care?" Aston asked, eyes still on the door.

"He was there too."

As they walked up to the elevator, Aston made three decisions. He would never go to another party with Capelli. He would spend all his energy on the Serial Catcher. He would forget about Sapphire Dubois. This time he *really* meant it. For sure.

"That brunette, what was her name?" Capelli asked as they stood in the elevator shoulder to shoulder, waiting for the doors to close.

"Sapphire Dubois." Aston said it as if he was uttering the name of a cruel dictator.

"What's the story, are you trying to hit that or what?"

"No."

"Mind if I give it a go, then?"

Aston shrugged. It was fine by him. He was over it. Over *her*.

"She's gay," he said and the doors closed.

*   *   *

When Sapphire entered the mansion her phone rang again.

"Reject," Sapphire ordered once more.

John had been calling her like a maniac since she left the party. She didn't have the energy to talk to him. All she wanted to do was sleep, but she knew her nightmare wouldn't allow it.

"Accepting," the phone said.

"No, I said RE-JECT! Abort-abort!"

"Sapphire?" John's voice catapulted through the speaker. "I need to ask you something, and don't worry, I already know it's a lie…"

"What?"

"Did you ever sleep with the cop while we were together?"

Sapphire's mouth opened as she stared down at the phone. She wanted to shout *"YES!"* but cheating on a Vanderpilt, Kraft, or Rockefeller was the worst thing you could do if you weren't part of the elite yourself. It would be like Kate cheating on William, the consequences would be gi-normous. A letter from the country club stating Sapphire's presence was no longer desired would arrive within days.

"Sapphire?"

It was hard to muster up a lie and fight for something she didn't want.

"Obviously you didn't," John said. "You're quiet because

you're shocked I would even ask." John was in denial and it had nothing to do with love. He didn't want to believe someone else had driven his Porsche. "Uh, right."

He laughed. "Like *you* would ever cheat on *me*."

Sapphire wanted to cry, scream, maybe even tear out some hair. His, not hers.

"Had you..." he turned serious. "I'm pretty sure I could take him."

"John..." Sapphire sighed. She had to come up with a plan.

"Love you too," he said and hung up.

Sapphire stared at her phone, her nemesis. "I really do hate you."

She found Charles in the living room, still up. Normally he would have been put to bed at 10 p.m. by her mother, whether he was tired or not.

"How you doing, Charles?" Sapphire leaned down to kiss his forehead but froze, surprised. He was sitting up straight, instead of his usual slouch, holding onto a photograph.

The new program was working. Just a couple of days ago, Charles couldn't lift his left hand, let alone manage to hold onto something as small as a photo.

He smiled at her, and she noticed something else that was different about him.

For the first time since the stroke, Charles's eyes were clear—not muddled by drugs and drowsiness. His previously pasty cheeks were rosy, full of life. He looked a good ten years younger.

"Can I see?" Sapphire sat down and looked down at the black and white photograph of Charles as a boy standing next to a man in his forties. The photograph's edges were burnt.

"Is this you and your dad?"

Charles sighed and gave her a peculiar look.

"You guys looked so much alike," she said, tracing her finger around a burnt corner. Charles's parents had died long before Sapphire and Vivienne came into his life, and this was one of a few photographs she'd seen of either of them.

She handed Charles the photograph, but he pushed it back

to her. *Keep it.*

"What? No." Sapphire placed it on his lap. "You keep it. It must be special to you."

Charles gave an intense look and tapped the picture. He formed his mouth, pushing the sounds out. "Berr Crrfu."

"Whatever you say, Charles," Sapphire smiled and patted his arm. He sighed again, leaning back.

They sat in silence as Sapphire's eyelids grew heavier and heavier. Her body was crying out for sleep. She knew that once she closed her eyes she'd be right back in *that* room, but she was so tired.

"Goodnight, Charles." Sapphire kissed his forehead and headed upstairs. She stumbled to her bed and let her body fall onto her overstuffed down comforter.

Finally, sleep, Sapphire thought, letting the pleasant slumber pull her in.

. . .

Sapphire sat up covered in sweat, shaking from the fresh images of the motel room.

She looked at the time. She'd only been asleep for fifteen stinking minutes. The fear settled and was replaced by anger.

Sapphire had a killer to catch, and in order to catch that killer, she needed to be smart. In order to be smart she needed sleep. In order to get sleep she needed to go back to the person responsible for her nightmare.

Sapphire ripped her covers off and grabbed her keys.

CHAPTER 13

Bam! Bam! Bam!

Aston stood in the middle of his pitch black studio, buck naked, trying not to breathe too heavily. He had to admit, it wasn't the first time he had done this.

More like the seventh...or eighth if you counted this incident.

"I know you're in there Aston," she shouted, pummeling the door once more. "I saw your lights under the door before you turned them off!"

Aston sighed and checked his microwave for the time. If there was one thing you could say about Officer Moore it was that she was persistent. After five minutes, she still hadn't given up. He craved a cigarette but couldn't light up knowing she'd smell it.

"It will take two seconds!"

Nope. Don't believe that.

"I have something for you!"

Or that.

If there was one thing about the seven other times that Aston had stood naked, in the pitch black, hoping that whatever woman was outside would leave so that he could go back to watching his reruns of Magnum P.I., it was that he never *considered* opening the door. Now, strangely, he was tempted.

The dance might've sent Moore the wrong message, that they were good to go. It probably negated the effect of the rejected phone calls. It was his fault, not hers. He felt guilty.

Maybe Capelli was right. Maybe Aston was the one who had changed. Or maybe he just really wanted that cigarette, because the next thing Aston did was turn the lights on and open the door.

Officer Moore stopped with her fist midair, stunned. "Oh, hi."

"Listen, Moore…"

"Angelica."

"I'm…sorry if I sent you the wrong message; I didn't mean for that to happen. We both said this was nothing serious, and it's time for it to end."

"I know. I got that when you didn't pick up the phone for the third time." She pulled a shirt out of her bag. "I was meeting Laura for a drink two blocks down, so I figured I might as well return your shirt while I'm at it."

Son of a bitch. She had stolen his favorite shirt.

"Sorry about the tear," Moore said. "It got caught in the car door."

Son of a bitch. She had torn his favorite shirt.

Aston grabbed his old Dodgers shirt, deciding never to let go again. "So you're okay then?"

"Yes, why wouldn't I be?" Officer Moore smiled. Her eyes searched the apartment behind him. "Alone tonight?"

"Who else would be here?"

Moore shrugged then let her eyes search down to his crotch.

"Me?" She inched closer.

"Okay," he said, annoyed. There was not one part of him that wanted to sleep with her. Not even his penis part. "I mean it. It was great, but I think we better just be coworkers, who don't have sex…at all…ever."

Moore's eye twitched and she groaned, rubbing it.

"Are you crying?" Aston knew he sounded apprehensive. He hated when women cried. It made him feel awkward and bad at the same time.

"No, I'm not crying, I have something in my eye." She chuckled. "Don't flatter yourself, Aston. You're good in bed, but you're not *that* good."

Ouch. It was okay though, neither was she.

"Relax, it was just a thought," Moore continued. "Are you in love?"

"Ahem…"

"Not with *me*, bonehead!" Moore rolled her eyes. "Her, what's her name…Stephanie?"

Aston laughed. Did he have a weird infatuation with the Dubois girl? Yes, absolutely. Was it love?

"No." He shook his head amused. "I don't do that. I've always been positive that I'm missing that gene. Either way, whatever that was, I'm done with it."

Moore tilted her head, giving him a patronizing look. "Hon," she smiled. "If you were done, don't you think we'd both be naked right now?"

Aston laughed again, but stopped when he realized her statement confused him.

"Just be careful with her, Aston," Moore said and walked off. "I don't want to see you get hurt."

He stood in the doorway until he saw his favorite nightshift security guard. "How's it hanging, Burt?"

Burt's eyes widened, then he dove into the elevator, refusing communication.

Aston looked down and realized he was still naked.

"Fuck me." He closed the door. He was caught off guard. Not because he'd just asked another dude 'how's it hanging?' while his penis was out. It was Moore's words.

As a cop, he learned to look at the evidence and let it speak for itself, no matter previous assumptions.

The Evidence:

1. *Aston passed on no-strings-attached sex.*
2. *He'd had a weird feeling in his gut since the day he met Sapphire Dubois.*
2. *Aston passed on no-strings-attached sex.*
3. *He never stopped thinking about Sapphire.*
5. *Aston passed on no-strings-attached sex!*

Conclusion: Aston Ridder wasn't as genetically different as he always thought.

He was in love.

• • •

Sapphire broke into Dr. Rues' house and sat in his living room, spinning around on a leather chair, trying to figure out how to wake the good doctor without rousing his entire family and having the cops called on her.

She didn't have to ponder long, because the light came on in the hallway and Dr. Rues passed by in his tighty whities.

Sapphire cringed. Tighty whities should be banned for anyone over the age of eight.

He clanged around in the kitchen before he entered the hallway with whipped cream, chocolate syrup, and honey in his arms.

"Never pegged you as a late night snacker, Dr. Rues."

Dr. Rues let out a yell as the food crashed to the ground. Then he recognized her.

"Ms. Dubois! What on earth do you think you're doing in my home?"

She'd been getting that question a lot lately.

"Oh, I'm sorry…" Sapphire wanted to get the jump on him before he jumped on the phone. "Am I interrupting your sleep? Because I wouldn't know about interrupted sleep since you actually have to be asleep for that to happen, which I haven't been able to do since you hypnotized me."

Dr. Rues blinked at her. "If you have concerns may I suggest you make an appointment at my office instead of *breaking into my house!*"

"Shhh," Sapphire urged, "you're gonna wake up your family. I need sleep, doc. You broke me and now you have to fix me."

"You're crazy! I'm calling the cops." He reached for the phone on the wall.

"Honey?" a woman's voice called from upstairs.

"I told you to be quiet," Sapphire hissed, "and now you've woken your wife."

"Who's here?" the woman said.

"Just a deranged patient of ours," Dr. Rues said, dialing the phone.

Dr. Rues' wife peeked into the living room.

Odd. Sapphire stared at the giant pair of boobs entering the room a freakishly long time before the rest of the body followed. She'd seen the picture of Dr. Rues' wife at his office and the woman hadn't seemed as busty in the photograph.

A smile spread on Sapphire's face.

"Why Dr. Rues, *that's* not your wife," she chirped as if he didn't know. "Here I was accusing you of being a late night snacker. The whipped cream was clearly only meant for recreational purposes between you and your receptionist."

Dr. Rues' top-heavy receptionist threw a confused glance at Sapphire and then at her lover.

"As kindhearted as it is of you to lend your wife's side of the bed to your receptionist while your family is away," Sapphire said, "I don't know if your wife would see it that way. What do *you* think?"

Dr. Rues swallowed, putting the phone down.

"Darling," he sighed, turning to the receptionist, "why don't you go on up while I do a quick session with Ms. Dubois?"

The receptionist shrugged and left, then came back to snag the whipped cream.

"Please, make yourself comfortable on the couch," Dr Rues said. Sapphire moved to let him take the chair.

"So, you said you couldn't sleep." He put his finger to his chin, resuming a position of authority. "Can I assume nightmares, night terrors?"

"Nightmares that, um…I'm sorry," Sapphire said, staring at his junk pushing against his underwear. "It's really hard to take you seriously right now."

Dr. Rues muttered and covered up his tighty whities with a blanket from the chair. "Proceed."

She told him what she felt he needed to know.

"So can you fix it?" She settled into the couch. It was just as suspiciously comfortable as the one in his office. "And where the hell do you get these couches, IKEA?" She turned, searching for a tag.

After a moment, Dr. Rues spoke. "It's possible you tapped

into a repressed memory when you went under hypnosis." He watched her for a second. "Speaking of which, there was something I meant to ask you during our last session. I decided not to because you seemed to be doing well, but while you were under you were clenching your fists."

"And?"

"Based on my studies, most patients who clench their fists during hypnosis are experiencing reluctance from the subconscious mind. Many times this can be linked to severe childhood trauma." He studied her again, probably until he felt he'd made her uncomfortable enough. "Have you, Ms. Dubois?"

Sapphire chuckled. "If you'd ever walked in on your mother having sex with your second grade teacher, you'd probably be traumatized too."

Dr. Rues wasn't amused. "What about recurring nightmares prior to the hypnosis?"

"No." *Yes.* From time to time, over the years, Sapphire had woken up screaming, never able to remember the dreams.

"Any unhealthy obsessions or urges? Things you are compelled to do, perhaps without understanding why?"

"No!" *Yes.* The bastard was reading her mind, emptying it of everything tagged *serial killer.* "I grew up in Beverly Hills, Dr. Rues, how traumatic can it get?"

That seemed to do it. Dr. Rues let go of the intense stare. "Either way, your mind won't be satisfied until you've seen what you are supposed to see and have accepted it."

"I saw it, accepted it, and now I want it to go away."

"I can target your sleep cycle and try to remove the images from there," Dr. Rues sighed. "But I can't guarantee they won't appear while you're in other states of mind. Sometimes when we consciously try to suppress something the memories grow instead of weaken."

"Will I sleep?"

"Most likely."

"Then do it." Sapphire lay down and closed her eyes.

• • •

Sapphire was in a meadow, surrounded by bright blue skies, feeling tranquil. She knew everything she experienced was fake, conjured by Dr. Rues, but she felt wonderful.

"This place of harmony," Dr. Rues said, his voice echoing in the sky, "is where you'll find yourself every time you go to sleep."

Sapphire noticed her mother. She was standing in the middle of the meadow holding a shoebox. She looked around, paranoid.

"Sapphire…" Vivienne clenched the box. "Don't tell your father we found it."

· · ·

Dr. Rues snapped Sapphire out. "How do you feel?"

"Good," Sapphire said. This time, she did feel good. She was ready to do some serious sleeping and prodding.

"Great." He clapped his hands. "Then please get out of my house and feel free to find a different doctor."

Rude.

Dr. Rues slammed the door behind her, and Sapphire dialed her phone, going for the prodding first.

"Vivienne Dubois, please."

"Ma'am, it's five in the morning. Our residents aren't woken until seven."

"It's an emergency. This is her daughter."

The receptionist put her on hold as Sapphire paced the sidewalk outside of Dr. Rues' home.

"Is it Charles?" Vivienne panted into the phone. "Has he died?" She didn't even bother hiding the hope in her voice.

"What was in the shoebox, Mom?" The box could have been nothing, a fake image like the meadow Dr. Rues had created for her, but it felt real.

"I don't know what you're talking about."

"What was in the box?" Sapphire's tone grew more urgent as she stepped into the road, heading for her car.

"I don't…how do you…you were so young…"

"What was in the goddamned shoebox?!"

"Killers!" Vivienne blurted out. "Newspaper clippings about murders, victims. Sick, horrible, things that nobody should save, that nobody should collect!"

Sapphire stopped in the middle of the road.

"I found the shoebox in the back of the closet. He never thought I knew anything. I'd see him glued to TV reports about killers and murders with this worried look on his face. I got the feeling he thought he could help and be some sort of, I don't know…"

"Vigilante," Sapphire filled in. Everything started spinning. The expensive houses with their greener-than-green grass, the street, the cars, even a Corgi whirled around Sapphire as if she was in the eye of a tornado.

"Yes," Vivienne said in a disconnected tone. "Any more painful memories you'd like to rummage through or will that be all?"

Sapphire exhaled and the tornado settled.

"Just one more thing. Screw you for sleeping with Mr. Welsh; he was my favorite teacher." Sapphire hung up and moved toward her Range Rover.

Like father, like daughter, she chanted in her mind. She supposed she should feel happy about sharing a connection with her father, but something didn't feel right. *She* didn't feel right about it.

It would explain his sudden disappearance. He was either killed by one of his adversaries, or chose to leave because he couldn't lead a double life anymore. It hit home…more than Sapphire wanted to admit.

Perhaps her father was still out there somewhere, doing what she did. *Two* Serial Catchers. Aston's brain would explode.

Sapphire was just about to unlock her Range Rover when she saw the white Audi parked a few yards down. The same Audi that had been outside the mansion. It reversed and peeled off in the other direction.

Sapphire stared after it.

Once was nothing. Twice was trouble.

CHAPTER 14

Tick. Tick. Tick. Fifty-three minutes.

Sapphire stared at herself in the wedding dress in the 360 degree mirror and felt the sweat accumulate above her lip. It was suffocating her body and its tight, off-the-shoulder straps squeezed her arms into submission.

She'd gotten home from Dr. Rues' that morning ready to see if the hypnosis worked. She didn't even bother stripping out of her clothes before collapsing on her bed. She'd just closed her eyes when the door bell rang. Berta was out with Charles so Sapphire zombie-shuffled down to the door and opened it to find Eloise, the wedding planner from Hell.

"Oh great, you're ready," Eloise said.

"Um, ready fooor…"

Eloise's eyes exploded with rage. "Ready for your *fitting!* I've sent the itinerary more than once!"

Sapphire was forced by limo to the bridal shop on Rodeo Drive and jammed into the Vera Wang.

Since the dress was designed for Sapphire by Vera herself, it wasn't the fitting that took time; it was the accessories. Tiara, no tiara? Veil, no veil? Gloves, no gloves?

The company only made it worse. Chrissy sulked into her glass of red wine, which she insisted she *had* to have the moment the staff announced there could be no colored liquids near the dresses. Mrs. Vanderpilt, however, was cheerful, but only because Eloise gave her a Xanax. And Petunia and her mother, Heather, were having a blast attacking Sapphire.

Tick. Tick. Tick. Fifty minutes until she had to be at the Golden Mirage.

"Have you gained weight?" Petunia eyed Sapphire. "I get it,

with your mother in *rehab*, it's probably stress eating. She is the only family member you are *actually* related to, and she's not even here. Carefuuul, don't want to look fat on your honeymoooon."

Sapphire opened her mouth but found no words.

Heather and Petunia had always taken stabs at Sapphire not being a real Dubois. Usually their comments barely grazed her, but today Petunia's remark actually hurt. She'd never liked the name Dubois, but Sapphire Green felt too foreign.

"It must be so hard for you, Petunia," Chrissy cut in, taking a sip of her wine. "Sapphire marrying a *Vanderpilt* has to remind you of how super single you are. I'm curious, how do you cope? By shopping discount designer wear from last season?" She nodded to Petunia's fur vest.

Sapphire sent an appreciative smile, but Chrissy was already back to sulking.

"I have a boyfriend," Petunia mumbled. "He could propose *any day*." This was all she dared to say. The Krafts weren't social enemies you wanted to make.

Petunia's sudden need for marriage had nothing to do with social pressure...or love. She was in a lifelong competition with Sapphire. Anything she had, Petunia wanted two of.

Sapphire remembered the moment she realized her cousin couldn't be the child of her kind Uncle Gary—that she was, in fact, the spawn of Satan.

It was the event of the season at the country club. Petunia and Sapphire had been 8 years old, sitting next to each other in their puffy dresses—no doubt made from unicorn pelts. Petunia had loved it, but Sapphire had felt trapped. She had stared at the exit, praying for the night to end.

Run. Sapphire had thought, before making her first mistake.

She had turned to Petunia and whispered, "Hey, let's see if we can trick the chauffer into driving us somewhere." Sapphire had felt a thrill run through her. "Anywhere but Beverly Hills."

Petunia's eyes had narrowed. "Why would we want to leave Beverly Hills?" She turned back to the stage. "You're so weird."

Sapphire had sunk back in her seat. "Yeah, no, I was kidding." She had sat still for five more minutes but she couldn't stand it anymore.

"Pardon me," Sapphire had nodded to Petunia, Uncle Gary, Charles, and the nymphomaniac staring at the waiter's crotch: her mother. "I'm going to the ladies' room."

She had hurried to the bathroom and climbed up on the sink to open the small ceiling window, before leaping from the sink, grabbing onto the window, and pulling herself out. She had been halfway through when the dress's puffy skirt got stuck. She couldn't move.

"Sapphire!"

Sapphire had turned to see Petunia in the doorway.

"Petunia," Sapphire had exhaled in relief. "Help pull me in. My mom will be so pissed if she finds out I tried to run away again." A few seconds passed. "Petunia, hurry!"

Sapphire had squinted back into the bathroom. A smile crept onto Petunia's lips. It was an evil, satisfied, version of glee.

"Oooh, Auntie Vivienne!" Petunia had called, turning on her heel.

Sapphire had been grounded for trying to escape and for embarrassing Vivienne. It had taken three servers to get her out.

From that day on, Sapphire disliked Petunia. Her cousin, however, felt more than just a mutual dislike. Petunia *hated* Sapphire, she knew it.

Tick. Tick. Tick. 45 minutes to get to the Golden Mirage.

"Chrissy." Sapphire turned to the only other person who didn't want to be there…who was she kidding? Nobody—except for Eloise—wanted to be there. "You were going to show me that thing in the dressing room?"

"What thing?"

"The *thing*." Sapphire gave her a look.

"Riiight, the *thing*." Chrissy used her whole face to wink, making it obvious to the whole room.

Sapphire closed the curtain behind them. "Chrissy, can you help me get out of here? No questions asked."

"Why?" Chrissy asked, taking a sip of her red wine.

"Do you not know the meaning of *no questions asked*?"

"Whatever. You sure?"

"Yes."

Chrissy shrugged and tossed her glass.

Sapphire exited the dressing room with the stained Vera Wang, and the women's cries of despair were heard by the whole county.

•   •   •

Long, dark hair. A sharp but rounded nose. The eyes were the important part, taunting and full of darkness.

Richard Martin stared at his drawing on the napkin and took another bite of the dry breadstick. *Yes.* It was her.

He was back in L.A., and he'd searched all over the county. Marina Del Ray. Burbank. Santa Monica.

He was in West Hollywood now. It was 7 p.m. and the sun had set, reminding him of another day gone. Another failure.

Every day she faded more in his mind, and he hoped the sketch would help him remember her face. He used to love drawing when he was a kid on Park Avenue in New York. Once his nanny quit, and there was nobody around to praise his work, he grew sick of it.

Now, it seemed, he'd grown sick of killing as well.

He'd tried killing that college girl at the restroom in Utah, but as he stood there ready to slice her throat, he couldn't do it. He let the girl run away in tears when he realized she wasn't *her*. None of them would ever be the Serial Catcher.

That's how powerful she was. She didn't even have to be present to keep taking things from him. Her actions in the forest months ago had caused an everlasting ripple effect of negativity on his life. She had made him impotent.

If the victim wasn't the Serial Catcher, he didn't want to kill. If he didn't have killing, Richard Martin had *nothing*.

He licked the pencil tip and blackened her irises.

Who are you? He wondered. *How will I find you?*

"Another." Richard emptied his beer and slid the glass to the bartender.

"Pretty." The bartender nodded to the sketch.

"She'll be prettier when she's dead," Richard mumbled.

"Excuse me?"

"I said, can I have some more bread?"

The bartender grabbed the bread basket, and Richard turned to a group of celebrating women that had just walked in. Their scant party dresses should have made his carnal being roar, but there wasn't even a whisper.

He hated the Serial Catcher for it. Richard had killed a lot of women in his days; he never hated any of them. On the contrary, he loved them all, a little.

He heard her laugh again, taunting him from the past. He grizzled his teeth and pushed the pencil to her eye so hard it pierced the napkin. Putting a hole in her felt good and made him chortle. His laugh grew hysterical and people turned their heads. He knew his hate for her had poisoned his mind and was making him crazy, but he didn't care. He kept laughing until his stomach ached and his eyes watered. He sighed and wiped his cheek.

The chattering group of women sat down in the stools next to him.

"I can't believe he *proposed*!" one of them yelled. "How'd he do it?"

The engaged woman showed them a strange blue ring and told them the story of the spontaneous proposal. "I'm sure he'll be working on replacing it with a real one soon…" Her eyes landed on the counter then drew up to Richard and never strayed.

Maybe she liked the looks of him and was in need of a last hoorah before she got married. Or maybe…she recognized him from the news coverage of his trial.

Richard pulled his ball cap over his brows and shot out of his seat. He could not get caught before he found the Serial Catcher.

After he'd killed her he wasn't sure he cared what happened to him. What would there be for him after she was gone?

He hurried out of the bar and tried to look natural as he shoved his hands in his pockets, matching the other pedestrians' pace.

"Excuse me!" The hand with the odd blue ring touched his shoulder.

Tense, he turned to face the newly engaged woman. This would be the first time he would kill a woman out of necessity and not want.

How peculiar. Like killing a man.

"You forgot this." She held out the napkin with the sketch.

"Oh, thank you." Richard exhaled and relaxed. When he tried to take it from her, she held on, eyes locked on him.

Back to plan A?

"I have to give it to you." She nodded to his sketch. "You've got some skills…"

"Mmhm." Richard scanned the crowd. Would anyone notice if he dragged her into the alley?

"I recognized her right away."

Richard's heart jumped. He looked at the woman, then down at the drawing of his nemesis. "You know who she is?"

She smiled.

• • •

"No!" Ginger shouted. "I want the black one or I'm not going on!"

"The bloody number is called Randy Red Riding Hood," Giles said, the patience in his voice running thin. "You don't suppose wearing red would be more appropriate?"

Sapphire, Candy, and some of the other girls sat in silence observing the power struggle like they were watching a tennis match. Ginger wanted to wear a black, bathing-suit-style, one piece. Giles wanted her to wear a two-piece, red-laced bikini.

Sapphire hadn't slept in forever. She was moody and as impatient as Giles. They were sucking away prime killer-finding time.

Ginger glared at her boss and tightened the strap on her robe in protest.

Giles threw his hands to the sky, mouthing, *"Why me?"* before turning to leave.

"I could have been someone!" Ginger shouted after him. "I could have been a Vegas showgirl, but I'm here for *you*!"

"Jesus Christ, just put it on!" Sapphire erupted, immediately regretting it. She tried to cover it up by looking behind her to see who may have said it.

Ginger didn't fall for it. Sapphire swore the redhead's hair turned into actual flames. Her muscles tensed, and in a second Ginger had grabbed Sapphire's hair.

It would have been so easy to take Ginger's free hand and twist her body into submission, but Sapphire was there to find the Stripper Slayer, and catty strippers didn't even break the top-ten list of justified ass-whoopings. Although, there was a small... medium...mammoth-sized part of Sapphire that wanted to toss Ginger to the ground and shut her up, once and for all.

"Listen to me, Sapphire *Two*," Ginger ordered an inch from Sapphire's face. "Do you know why I don't like you? You and your shitty dancing drags down the credibility of this place, which makes me lose money, which makes me angry. If you ever open your mouth again, I'll cut your face and then we'll see how long the cowboy wants you!" Ginger pinched the corners of Sapphire's mouth together, pushing her lips out.

Sapphire was two seconds from head-butting her when Misty walked in and Ginger let go.

"Watch your back," Ginger hissed, then strolled out the alley door. Her robe flew up in the wind, revealing her bare ass.

"Sapphire Two, are you okay?" Misty asked , sitting down by Sapphire's mirror.

"Peachy." Sapphire forced a smile.

"She is sunulvabeach. You want me talk to her? Maybe punch?"

"No, that's okay," Sapphire laughed.

"I am heppy today. Giles hev big news when I come in." Misty turned to the mirror to fill in her lip liner. "I am number two. Not like you, bad number two, but good number two. After Ginger it is me."

"That's great." There was something innocent and lovable about Misty. She was too good for the underworld of Los

Angeles, and Sapphire felt the urge to help her get out of there. "Hey, Misty, isn't there anything else you'd rather do? I know this sounds strange, but maybe I could help you. I mean, help you get away from here and have a different life. A *good* life."

In the middle of applying her lipstick, Misty looked perplexed. "This *is* good life. In Russia I hev bad money. Bad name. Here I dance. I am *Misty* and I will finally hev my photo on the wall."

"Aha," Sapphire said, feeling foolish. Since she walked into the place, she assumed all the girls were there because it was their only option. Misty obviously loved her job. "Wait, what wall?"

"You hev not seen wall? Come."

They walked to a corridor in the back where the wall featured rows of headshots.

"Number one girls and number two girls, the stars of the show."

Sapphire scanned the wall. Ginger was the most recently added, then it went backwards chronologically. Next to her was Amber, the girl who got killed in the parking garage. And next to her…

"Giles says I will hev my picture taken on…"

"Misty," Sapphire interrupted. "All the newest additions on the wall are dead."

"I know. Giles tell police this. I tell police this. The police is sunulvabeach."

This meant Sapphire would have to work her ass off to become part of the wall and…something much more important.

"Not Ginger," Misty shrugged.

"No, not Ginger." Sapphire started jogging back toward the dressing room. She ripped the back door open and smacked right into a dark figure.

"Jeez, I'm sorry." The DJ stepped into the light.

"Have you seen Ginger?"

"Just saw her walk across the street."

She sprinted to the other side of the road. The quiet night was interrupted by a scream.

"Please stop!"

The words bounced between the walls of the adobe buildings and up to Sapphire. It was definitely Ginger.

Sapphire turned the alley's corner to see a car pulled over by a dumpster. Next to the car a dark figure was slamming Ginger's head into the side of the container.

Ginger cried out every time she took another hit. The man dropped her to the ground then kicked her in the abdomen. She coughed, gasping for air.

"I'm gonna cut your face, bitch! And then what will you do?" He snarled and bent down to spit on her.

Sapphire bolted toward them, using a couple of wooden crates as stepping-stones. She jumped up onto the closed dumpster and leapt off, crashing down on him, her her elbow smashing his head. A sharp pain exploded in her arm and she landed on the ground, hoping it hurt him more than it hurt her.

"What the fuck?!" he yelled, disoriented. He touched his bleeding forehead.

Sapphire sent a punch straight to his throat, and he grabbed it, wheezing.

"Run, Ginger!" Sapphire screamed as he attacked.

Ginger just stood there, staring at them in shock.

"I said GO!" Sapphire yelled, trying to fight the man off. But he was stronger than her. He pulled her to the ground and sat on top of her.

Sapphire clawed at his hand as his thumbs pushed in on her esophagus. She fought for air, feeling the panic. Her lungs ached and darkness closed in on her.

She forced her hands away from his grip, and her thumbs dug into his eyeballs.

When he yelled out and let go, Sapphire slammed her head into his nose. His eyes rolled around for a bit before he fell backward, his head hitting the pavement with a crack.

Sapphire clamored to her hands and knees. Her eyes watered and her lungs burned as they filled with air. She grabbed the dumpster and stood, feeling her head throb.

"First of all, OUCH!" She pointed to her forehead. "Second of all..." she glared at Ginger, who still hadn't moved a muscle, "since you insisted on staying, couldn't you have at least clonked him over the head with something?!"

"How…how…did you do that?" Ginger's voice was a mix of confusion and admiration.

Sapphire shrugged to avoid the question. She looked down at her killer, ready to take in the glory of another successful capture. Her eyes fell on the scattered hundred dollar bills that lay on the ground. Her glory was replaced by doubt.

"Ginger, please tell me he wasn't robbing you?"

"No…," Ginger pushed out. "He…he's…"

Sapphire looked from Ginger, to the unconscious man on the ground, and back to Ginger. "What?!"

Ginger gazed down at her feet in silence.

The robe she refused to take off had opened during her struggle and Sapphire noticed the old green and purple bruises lining her ribs. The marks would have gone unnoticed in the black one-piece. The man on the ground was *not* the Stripper Slayer.

"He's your boyfriend," Sapphire said, finishing Ginger's sentence.

Ginger's aggression made sense now. She was like an abused child-turned-bully.

"It's not like that. It's not what you think."

"Okay."

"I don't stay with him because I love him. I stay with him because if I leave, he'll kill me."

"As opposed to now when he was a big teddy bear?"

Ginger closed her robe. "He takes my tips. If I do well nothing happens. If I do badly, like this week, he thinks I've been stealing the rest of the money. I tried to tell him that I lost my best regular, but he didn't believe me."

The cowboy. A pang of guilt hit Sapphire.

They stood in silence, their breath the only thing filling the empty alley.

"If you can do that…" Ginger nodded down to her boyfriend, "why didn't you do that to me?"

Sapphire cleared her throat. "I specialize more in psychotic men."

"Oh." Ginger still looked confused.

"You should leave."

"I told you, I can't," Ginger said. "He knows everyone in L.A. He'll find me."

"No, I mean leave the state. Go be a showgirl. Take the money and drive straight to Vegas."

Hope flashed in Ginger's eyes and then faded. "That's his car, he won't let me get one, and he'll report it stolen if I take it."

Sapphire closed her eyes as she dug into her pocket, saddened to the depths of her soul by what she was about to do.

"Here." Sapphire hung her head and raised the car keys to Ginger's face. "Take mine."

"What?" Ginger looked at the keys in disbelief.

"It's the old Volkswagen on the third floor. It's held together by duct tape and smells kind of like Cheetos, but it'll take where you need to go. The door's broken so you have to give it three kicks and a knee to open it. There's a couple of grand taped under the passenger seat. Use that, too."

"But…" Ginger tried.

"I'd say you have a few hours before he wakes up, so go home, grab only the essentials, and get on the road."

A slight smile reached Ginger's lips. Tears of relief sprang from her eyes.

"Thank you, Sapphire Tw-…Sapphire." Then she was gone, leaving Sapphire with the unconscious douchebag on the ground. So she did what any good citizen would do. She stripped him of all his clothes and locked him in the trunk of his own car, then tossed his keys in the gutter.

That ought to slow him down.

Sapphire could hear *Amazing Grace* as she held a mental funeral for her beloved Volkswagen. She thought of all the good times they'd had together—all the serial killers they'd caught.

When she walked back into the Golden Mirage she smiled, knowing two things for sure: Unbeknownst to Ginger, she had just saved her life, and there was a new spot open on the Golden Mirage's wall.

It belonged to Sapphire.

CHAPTER 15

Barry and Aston stared at the computer screen. Barry: half dead, eyelids closing. Aston: eyes wide open, junked up on gallons of coffee.

Capelli had left the office hours earlier to go run some errands and had never returned. It was fine by Aston. He and Capelli had spent so much time together lately that he'd forgotten why he liked the dude in the first place.

Aston put the cup to his mouth and emptied the last of it before knocking Barry on the arm. He kept his eyes glued to the screen.

"Barry. Out. More." They'd stopped speaking in full sentences seven hours ago.

Barry yawned, grabbed the cup, and went to refill it. "Need break."

"Take five."

"Longer. Need sleep."

"Sleep when dead."

Barry sat back down, disappointed. He handed the fresh cup back to Aston, who took it without letting the screen out of his sight. He didn't want to miss a second. He could be one pixel away from deciphering her face.

Barry closed his eyes again and his head soon fell on Aston's shoulder. Aston pulled it away and Barry's face smacked into the desk.

The newbie swore, confused, as Aston's phone rang.

"Ridder," Aston said, eyes still on the screen.

"I have a problem," Capelli said.

"For the last time, if it lasts more than four hours, go see a doctor."

"No. I accidently got a bit hammered while running errands. I can't drive back."

"Take a cab."

"Spent all my cash on the errands and the ATM fee here is like five bucks. Freakin' robbery if you ask me."

"So when you say errands, you mean strip club."

"What did you think I meant, picking up my pink skirt at the dry cleaner? Come on, man."

Aston sighed, letting his gaze stray from the computer. He blinked, letting his eyes regain moisture. "Where are you?"

"Downtown. Place called Golden Mirage."

Aston hung up and turned to Barry. "Going to a strip club to pick up Capelli."

Barry's face lit up and he stood, suddenly awake. "We're going to a strip club?"

"*I'm* going to a strip club. Call me with updates."

Barry sunk back down in disappointment, and Aston moved through the station.

"Hey, Ridder, congrats, I just heard!" Officer Fatso smacked Aston's back as he passed by. "Laura just told me. Nice."

His name wasn't actually Fatso, but Aston could never remember it. If Laura the receptionist knew, the Serial Catcher case was no longer on the DL. This was just a taste of the congratulations that would come after the Serial Catcher was behind bars.

Aston smiled as he stepped into the elevator. He and Capelli would become legends at every station in So-Cal, and Aston would pack up his shit and head for the FBI's training facilities. Everything he wanted would be waiting for him there...

His smile fell.

Minus one heiress.

*   *   *

Sapphire threw back the shot and sent the empty glass back to Buddy. Ten minutes and forty-seven seconds left until Sapphire had to go back on that God-awful stage and try to rock the pants off the horn dogs in the audience to make the wall.

"Another?" Buddy asked and Sapphire nodded.

She'd never had a job before, but she'd assumed that drinking on the clock was frowned upon until Giles turned to her in the dressing room. "Sapphire, go have Buddy give you a bloody cocktail if it means you will stop dancing like my blimey Aunt Mildred!"

He was upset about losing his star, and Sapphire didn't want to argue.

She leaned against the bar and scanned the crowd. Joseph Young was nowhere to be found.

Good boy, she smiled. If she ever ran into him again, in a non-serial-killing setting, she'd pat his head and give him a treat.

"Buddy…" Sapphire turned to him as he put the shot glass in front of her. "Am I really that bad?"

Buddy sighed as he wiped the counter the way only a wise bartender could. "When I see you up there it doesn't look like you're having a lot of fun. It looks like you're uncomfortable, which makes the audience uncomfortable, which leads to people throwing their shoes at you."

"So I'm supposed to have a big grin on my face? How do I look like I'm having fun?"

"Come here and I'll share the secret."

Sapphire leaned in closer.

"You have…" he tossed a few looks over his shoulders. "*Fun.*"

Mind blowing, really. Sapphire gave him a stare but couldn't help but laugh.

"Look at Misty." He pointed at the stage where Misty was rallying the crowd with the sensual Red Riding Hood number. "She's enjoying herself up there."

"I have fun, okay? Maybe not up there, but I have plenty of fun."

"Okay, so when?"

"Tsssk," Sapphire sneered, then thought back. She couldn't say *"Capturing killers."* And she couldn't think of anything else. This probably wasn't normal.

"I've gotten pretty good at judging character and you, my dear," Buddy said, handing her a bottle from the tall beer fridge, "are uptight."

"Trust me, I'm not."

"I see you up there and I can tell you care way too much about what everybody else thinks of you." He tossed the rag over his shoulder. "So let me ask you something? When you're on your deathbed looking back at your life, what do you want to look back on? A life you lived for someone else? Or a life you lived for you?"

Sapphire froze in the middle of sipping her beer. Buddy struck a chord. Maybe several, like G, B, and F.

"Things aren't always that simple, Buddy."

"That's the sad part," he smiled. His crow's feet spread like cobwebs around his eyes. "Things are *exactly* that simple. Not everything is life and death, you know."

Weeeell...

"You're up," he said, nodding to the stage.

Sapphire disrobed and hurried to the red curtains, reminding herself to breathe. Giles came over and handed her a small masquerade mask that went with her black lace costume.

"Sometimes, the mask helps," he said with an encouraging smile, hiding worry. He walked to the other side and grabbed the curtain rope as she put the mask on. It covered her eyes and part of her nose.

"Just have fun," she whispered to herself. "You've captured eight serial killers. Having fun can't be that hard."

Misty smiled as she came off the stage and dabbed perspiration with a towel.

"Good luck."

"Misty!"

Misty turned, still smiling.

"Promise me you'll have someone walk you to your car when you leave and make sure nobody follows you."

Misty's smile faded for a second, then she waved Sapphire's words off. "Don't vorry, I hev strong Russian arm." She flexed, demonstrating.

"Alright, gentlemen and...lady," the DJ announced, "Please welcome S-s-s-apphirrre!"

Her techno song started and Giles pulled the curtain.

Despite the mask, the spotlights blinded Sapphire. The crowd clapped, and some whistled, but only because she hadn't started dancing yet. Once she did, they'd shut up for sure.

The techno blared as Sapphire began her first sequence of moves. Whoever he was, he was out there and she could feel it. He was watching her, judging whether or not she'd be a good kill. Her eyes swept over the room, looking at expressions and facial features.

She tried to keep up with the tempo of the music but ended up doing the wrong moves with the wrong motions at the wrong time.

Her eye caught the cowboy sitting in his throne-like chair, bored. A waitress came by and tried to give him another drink, but he declined it and got up.

A single *"Boo"* echoed through the crowd just as Sapphire stumbled on a cord Giles had told her a thousand times *not* to stumble on. She felt like she fell in slow-motion before her ass hit the floor.

The room was still for a moment as she sat on the ground before the laughter broke out.

Giles motioned the DJ to cut the lights. The stage went black and the venue was filled by complaints and moans.

"Jesus Christ," Giles hissed from the side of the curtain. "Get off the stage, now. You are so bloody sacked."

Sapphire stayed there, glued to the floor, knowing the minute she got up it was over.

"I'm sorry, gentlemen...and lady," the DJ said, eyeing Sapphire. "We're experiencing some technical difficulties. We'll have it solved in just a moment."

The crowd grew impatient, some of them heading for the door.

Sapphire knew she had to do something new. Something different. She needed to forget about the killer for a second and focus on her job.

This was a last ditch effort. She had nothing to lose.

"Did you not hear me?" Giles sharply whispered. "You're sacked. Fired. Get off!"

Sapphire stood up, ignored Giles, and hurried over to the DJ. She placed both her hands on his arm, pleading. "Do you have anything else? Anything older with actual lyrics?"

He frowned. "Older like oh-nine?"

"Older."

"Oh-seven?"

Sapphire shook her head.

"Wait," he said with an excited glimmer in his eyes. "I have a remix of the perfect song."

"Put it on."

Sapphire took her position in the dark and waited for the spotlight.

* * *

Aston walked past half-naked women, various horny men, and up to Capelli who was sitting in a puffy chair with three girls on and around his lap.

The stage lay dark halfway across the room and the DJ had just apologized for some sort of technical difficulty.

"Yo!" Capelli shouted and motioned to the empty chair next to him. "Have a seat. Have a girl."

One of Capelli's girls put her arms around Aston's neck and started dancing.

"I'm here to pick your drunk ass up, not waste time. Let's go."

"Right, that," Capelli said, eyes on the dancing girl. "I may have exaggerated how wasted I was."

"Say what now?" Aston asked, struggling to peel the girl off his body.

"Come on, Ridder. You look goddamn miserable these days." He stood and grabbed one of the girls by the hand. "I'm just trying to get you back to your old self."

When Aston was about to storm off to slash Capelli's tires,

the center spotlight on the stage turned on. In its light, stood a girl in a black mask.

A sultry voice sang out through the speaker and Aston watched as the girl started moving sensually to a remixed *Hey Big Spender*.

"I'm going to the private room with Candy here." Capelli tapped him on the shoulder, but Aston barely noticed it. "That's more like it, Ridder."

Capelli vanished as the remaining spotlights turned on and the dancer picked up pace with the music. The crowd, who'd been frozen, snapped to life. They started hollering and threw singles at her feet.

Aston was attracted to the girl. This was the first time he'd felt drawn to someone since she-who-would-no-longer-be named.

He was wrong. Moore was wrong. Mrs. Dubois, who said the very same thing months ago, was wrong. How could Aston be in love with Sapphire Dubois if he felt so drawn to the girl on the stage?

The girl's hips popped every time the music did, and she let out just a little smile every now and then to let the audience know she was with them.

Halfway through the number, someone tossed her a fedora and put a chair out. The girl put the hat on and climbed on the chair without hesitation. She peeled her gloves slowly, enticing the crowd.

Aston moved across the floor, inching closer to the stage. He looked at her tight stomach, hinting a six-pack. Even in his early days, stripteases had zero effect on Aston, but this was different. It was classy, sensual, and he felt like he could watch this girl forever.

He edged closer. He stood behind a man in a cowboy hat tossing Jacksons on the stage, screaming, "Take it off, baby!"

The beat of the song picked up again and then climaxed. The girl did a spin around the pole then walked to the music up to the front of her stage. The cowboy looked back at Aston and raised his eyebrows in excitement.

At the song's last beat, the girl tossed off the hat and smiled. Aston knew something wasn't right. He knew that smile.

"Alright!" the DJ shouted. "Give it up for Miss S-s-sapphire!"

Just before the DJ uttered her name, Sapphire took off her mask and flung it across the room.

Aston's face fell as his insides turned. The blood boiled so violently in him that it could—no doubt—poach a fucking egg.

Son of a bitch!

The men cheered and Sapphire smiled at them. Her eyes searched the crowd and landed on Aston. Sapphire's jaw dropped and her eyes went big in disbelief, then bigger in realization.

"How 'bout a private tonight, Darlin'?" the cowboy urged. He reached his grubby hand toward her body.

Aston's egg-poaching anger boiled over, spewing water and steam.

Obviously, it wasn't this cowboy's fault that Sapphire stripped. He only did what men in strip clubs do, so *clearly* Aston didn't punch the man.

Okay, he did.

The cowboy went out like a light and plunged to the floor. It didn't help; Aston was still livid. Anyone looking at her deserved to die.

The crowd roared at the sight of the brawl, and Sapphire stared at him. Aston did exactly what he no longer had the jurisdiction to do; he grabbed Sapphire by the wrist and pulled her off stage, flashing his badge around the room.

"BHPD! This is a raid!"

The DJ killed the music and stared down at Aston. The other strippers gasped, horrified. Some of the perverts ran out the door in fear. Only a few men remained in their seats, curiosity written all over their faces.

"I'm the owner here!" A British man rushed up to Aston in anger. "Please take your hands of my twelfth-best dancer."

"Yes, Aston, please take your hands off his twelfth-best dancer," Sapphire said through her teeth, pissed off.

Not more pissed off than him though. Aston turned her

around and slapped the cuffs on her wrists.

"ASTON!" Sapphire shouted. "What the hell do you think you're—"

"Sapphire!"

"What?!"

"You have the right to remain silent, anything you say can and will be used against you…"

CHAPTER 16

Aston slammed the rear door closed and went around to the driver side, getting into the car without a word.

Sapphire squirmed in the back; the cuffs made her shoulder blades pinch together uncomfortably.

Aston pulled out, staring straight ahead, refusing to meet her gaze in the rearview mirror.

"Aston," Sapphire said, trying not to sound as angry as she felt. This could've been the night she'd figure out who the killer was. "That was fun and all, but let's be real here, you're not really arresting me."

Aston kept his gaze fixed ahead, his face unyielding.

"You can't arrest me. There's nothing to arrest me for. Stripping isn't against the law, is it?"

His eyes finally drew to the rearview mirror. Sapphire thought she was angry, but it was nothing compared to what she saw in Aston's eyes.

"What were you doing there?" he asked in a cold voice as he lit a cigarette.

The second her eyes landed on Aston inside the Golden Mirage, Sapphire started working on the answer to this question.

"I was researching." It was a partial truth.

Aston's brows drew together. "You were *researching.* Researching what?"

"A screenplay. I'm writing a screenplay."

Aston laughed in mistrust. "So, you're writing movies now? What's it called then?"

Curve ball.

"The stripper and the…naked guy!"

"That's a stupid ti—" Aston slammed his brakes. The car

screeched to a halt an inch from the crotch of a terrified naked guy in the middle of the street.

Damn it! Ginger's boyfriend had found the trunk's release catch sooner than she had expected. Most people didn't know all cars made after '02 had them.

After the initial shock, Aston rolled down his window. "Get your dick off my car and get off the street, moron!"

Ginger's boyfriend cupped his hands over his crotch and scampered to the sidewalk, trying to cover both his naked front and back as he ran past the other non-naked pedestrians.

Sapphire looked at the time on the dashboard and smiled. Ginger was already halfway to Vegas.

"Can't believe I used to miss this place," Aston muttered.

"Aston," Sapphire said again, "I'm really tired, and I'd like to go home now. Just drop me off here and I'll walk back to my…" She realized she didn't have her Volkswagen anymore. "House."

"How does your precious fiancé feel about you doing this?"

"I suppose he feels the same as your girlfriend feels about you going to strip clubs."

"She's not my girlfriend." He sounded honest, and Sapphire's insides gave a standing ovation, wolf whistles and everything. She wished she could tell him the same thing about her and John.

Aston's phone rang and his shoulders tensed as he scrambled to grab it.

"Ridder," he answered. "Wilson?"

His shoulders dropped, and Sapphire caught concern in his profile. "Thanks, Wilson. I owe you one."

He hung up and glanced back at Sapphire. "I'm sorry I arrested you, okay?"

Sapphire's neck pulled back in surprise. She'd never heard Aston apologize, didn't think the word *sorry* was in his vocabulary—excluding the sarcastic kind.

"I'll drop you off at home, but we have to make a pit stop."

"Fine, but can you take off the cuffs first?"

"I don't know," he said with a teasing smile. "I kind of prefer you locked down. Makes my life less stressful." He accelerated and took another long drag of his cigarette.

Sapphire leaned back. "You really should quit smoking. Those things will kill you, you know?"

"I'm pretty sure if something will be the death of me, it's gonna be you." Aston held her gaze in the rearview mirror a long time before he pulled over and got out.

Sapphire leaned forward and watched Aston walk up to an old homeless guy, who was drunker than her mother on a Tuesday morning. It was pretty impressive; not very many people pulled off being that drunk and alive at the same time.

The old man tried to fight him off. Sapphire could hear a lot of swearing.

After a long match, Aston managed to wrestle the guy into the backseat next to Sapphire.

Aston slammed the door shut and went around to the driver's side.

The old man stunk of dirt and sweat, and Sapphire had to breathe through her mouth so she wouldn't throw up.

After a few seconds the drunk turned to her. "So, what are you in for?"

"Stripping. You?"

"Don't know." He nodded to Aston. "Ask my son."

*   *   *

Paul Butler had watched as the cop dragged the new girl out kicking and screaming with her hands cuffed behind her back. It was kind of sexy. The energy between the cop and the girl was contagious and *really* put him in the mood.

He had to get his hands on Ginger. Not tomorrow or the day after, he wanted her *now*. And Paul always got what he wanted. Except when it came to his mother.

It looked like the place was closing early tonight because of the crazy cop's raid. It suited him; he had to be home by 11:30 p.m. Now he wouldn't have to rush, he could take his time and enjoy himself.

When Paul first saw the badge, he stood there petrified and

covered in sweat until he realized the cop wasn't there for him; he was there for the new girl.

Too bad. She'd improved tonight. She had blossomed before his very eyes. Of course, her attitude would need to change for anything to happen. She was much too nice of a person right now to piqué his interest.

He left the building by the alley exit hoping to run into Ginger before her boyfriend picked her up like he did every night. He would take her right there, pull her into his car, and slice her open. Or if he changed his mind, which could happen, he might drown her in the lake. He'd never drowned anyone before. It would be new and exciting.

He waited, watching Giles, Candy, and a few of the other girls leave the building. Where was she?

Come to think of it, he hadn't seen her since the beginning of the night.

Misty, the Russian girl, came out the back door wearing sweats and a t-shirt. Her face was stripped of makeup, and she didn't look nearly as appealing as she did on stage.

At first, she froze, coming across someone in the dark alley. Then she recognized him and smiled in relief.

"Oh, sunulvabeach, you scare me," she said, patting her hand over her heart. "Walk with me to the garage, there is a killer out, yes?"

"I'll walk with you," he said, grateful that it gave him a chance to pump her for information on Ginger. Maybe she'd even give him an address.

Misty smiled and they began their promenade.

"Did you see Sapphire Two tonight? She vas good, yes?"

"Yes, she was good."

"I am heppy for her. She is good person, yes?"

He didn't like how the Russian always ended her sentences with a question whether it belonged there or not. It reminded him too much of his mother. She insisted on playing twenty questions before he left the house.

"Where are you going? When will you be home? Are you really wearing that? Would you like a sandwich? Hot pocket then? Why aren't

you answering me? Do you have to slam the door?"

Hearing her voice tumbling in his head made him angry. His need for Ginger grew stronger. When the moment came, he'd knock that bitch's cocky smirk off her face and pretend it was his mother's.

Misty smiled and held the elevator door for him. Lucky Misty, she was too nice for him to kill. It wouldn't be any fun, would it? He couldn't extinguish a flame that wasn't already burning, could he?

"I barely saw Ginger all night," he said as they stepped into the elevator.

"Oooh, she qvit."

"She qvit?!"

"Yes."

"Why?"

"She call Giles and say: I qvit, never coming back."

He stared at the elevator's floor numbers as they grew higher. "Maybe you should go see her, make sure she's okay. Do you know where she lives?"

Misty shook her head and dug for her car keys.

"What about her phone number?" he urged. "Do you have her phone number?"

"Yes, but Giles says phone is now off…" Misty's eyes narrowed, and she studied him. "Vhy?"

The elevator stopped and the doors opened sluggishly.

"Oh, no, there was just something I wanted to do with her."

"Okay…" Misty's voice was drenched in uncertainty. "This is my floor." She waved and stepped off.

"But I guess you'll have to do," Paul said and reached for her hair.

•   •   •

Aston, Sapphire, and the old man, who wasn't a homeless drunk at all, but Aston's father, shuffled toward the small single story house.

Sapphire glanced at Aston. This was a new side to him. He

guided the old man up the steps, a hint of embarrassment on his face with every little bump along the way.

"You're just like the cold-hearted whore," the old man spat. Aston sat him down on a chair inside the confined kitchen and took off his dirty jacket. "Ah, fuck me, enough with the fussing!"

It was pretty clear Aston had inherited his vocabulary.

"Pops," Aston pleaded, "can you promise me you'll stay here while I drive her home?"

"I won't promise shit," the old man muttered. "Pulling me off the street, you goddamned brat."

"Pops!" Aston snapped. "Watch your fucking language, there's a lady here."

A giggle escaped Sapphire and Aston's dad looked up at her as if he just realized she was there. "I didn't know you got married, Ashton."

Sapphire raised her eyebrows and watched Aston do everything to avoid eye contact.

"Ashton?" she asked.

"We're not married," Aston corrected, ignoring Sapphire as he sat a glass of water in front of his father. "Listen, you're not gonna move a muscle until I come back, you hear me?"

"Fuck you."

"Ashton?" Sapphire prompted again.

"Drop it," Aston said, turning back to his father. "Get up, pops. You're coming with us."

"I'll stay," Sapphire said.

"I'll be here all night. I have to bathe him and make sure he doesn't run back out."

"I'll stay."

"Thanks."

Thanks AND sorry in one day? Maybe Aston was running a fever. Sapphire sat down on the chair opposite his father.

"You gonna introduce me to your wife or not?"

Aston sighed, pouring Sapphire a glass of water.

"Pops, Sapphire. Sapphire, Pops."

"The name's Joe," Aston's father held out a soiled hand . "You're lovely, nothing like the cold-hearted whore who gave birth to this guy."

Aston grabbed Joe by the collar and lifted him up. "I'm gonna give him a bath." He nodded to Sapphire. "There's nothing in the fridge, and I doubt he paid his cable bill, but help yourself."

After a screaming match between Aston and Joe, which involved a lot of blaming the cold-hearted whore, Aston joined Sapphire on the porch. His shirt was wet from bathwater and had pasted itself to his stomach. Sapphire tried not to look at his muscles through the shirt. She forced her eyes to her cup instead. Aston frowned, sitting down in the other chair.

"You found coffee?"

"Bouillon cube," Sapphire said, taking a drink.

"Oh, I bought that bouillon," Aston said and his mouth twitched into a smile, "in 1998."

About to swallow, Sapphire spat the bouillon back into the cup and pushed it away.

"Does your dad always drink like that?"

"Oh, he wasn't drunk. He's way worse as a drunk." Aston lit a cigarette. "He drank until I was twenty-five, then had to quit because of his liver. His brain was already fried though. Psychosis. He's got about two marbles left, but sometimes he loses them and wanders the streets until he comes to his senses or someone finds him. Wilson, my ex-partner at the LAPD, happened to be in the area, recognized him, and called me."

"Sooo, the whole *Ashton* thing is because he's confused?"

"Ah, yup."

Liar. They sat in silence for awhile, letting their eyes rest on the rotten picket fence and the long weeds taking over the yard.

"There's someone by the door, Ashton," Joe yelled from inside.

"There's no one at the door, Pops. It's three in the fucking morning!"

"Maybe it's the milkman!"

"It's not 1952!"

"Maybe there is someone there," Sapphire whispered, paranoid.

"Trust me, there never is." Aston stubbed out his cigarette and got up. "And hey, don't think you're off the hook on the whole stripper thing. We're going to talk about it later."

"Now there's someone in my bed!" Joe yelled.

"Maybe it's the goddamned milkman!" Aston shouted and slammed the door behind him.

Sapphire looked after him—*her hunter*—as he disappeared inside. Should she have stayed? No. But to not be allowed to see Aston was like being on a strict diet and walking around with a constant hunger. Now, somebody had handed her a plate of her favorite food.

She wouldn't eat it. She just wanted to hold the plate and take in its aromas. At least that's what she wanted to believe.

Sapphire sighed, then grabbed the bouillon and took a sip.

"Damn it," she said and spit it back out.

• • •

Aston punched the crap out of his pillow, trying to get comfortable. The couch was older than him and he doubted he'd get any sleep.

He gave Sapphire his childhood room once his father was in bed for the night.

Aston groaned when he heard the shower that connected to his room turn on. It meant Sapphire Dubois was less than fifteen feet away, naked. Very, very, naked. With water and soap, all sudsy. He sighed at the image. Now he definitely wouldn't sleep.

After another ten minutes of tormenting himself, Aston threw the blanket off.

He knocked twice and listened as Sapphire got up to open the door. Her hair was still wet from the shower, and she was wearing his old high school t-shirt. It was too big for her and ran halfway down her thighs. Aston intended a quick peek, but when Sapphire cleared her throat, he realized he was staring.

"I just…" Aston searched for words, "heard you showering and wanted to make sure you found a towel."

"Found one."

He nodded and braced his elbow against the frame of the door, leaning in. Sapphire's body followed his lead. They stood close, bodies almost touching, Aston a head taller than her looking down.

"Need anything else?" he asked, his voice coming from down deep.

"No."

"Sheets?"

"No."

"Pillow?"

"No."

"Water?"

"No."

"Ovaltine?"

Sapphire laughed and shook her head.

"Okay." He finalized it with a nod. "Goodnight."

"Goodnight." She closed the door.

Aston left and swore at himself. Then he went back, and left again. He repeated the procedure three times. Back at the door, he raised his fist to knock.

Sapphire reopened before he could.

Aston pushed through, grabbed her by the waist, and kissed her. He lifted her off the ground and pushed her back against the door, slamming it shut. Their bodies pressed together as if a force from either side had launched them toward each other. Their kiss, deep and arousing, caused Aston as much pain as bliss. He savored her but knew she wasn't his to keep.

His hand slid up along her warm thigh, pushing the shirt up, and their kiss went primitive.

He pulled her to his bed and slid her panties off, then pushed inside her.

• • •

Sapphire started to wake up, feeling rested. She'd slept soundly—no motel room nightmares. Whether it was because of Dr. Rues or Aston's calming effect, she couldn't say. She felt great, happy.

It was a different happiness from the kind she felt when she hunted; it was more tangible. Sapphire and Aston waking up in bed together felt natural.

She opened her eyes to look at him.

Except, there was no Sapphire and Aston in bed. Just Sapphire and Disappointment. And Disappointment wasn't nearly as attractive as Aston.

Sapphire's eyes narrowed. Had he abandoned her at his father's house? The last time she spent the night with Aston, he couldn't get her out of his studio fast enough.

How could she be this stupid...*twice*?

Sapphire ripped off the covers and searched for something to wear. Aston had dragged her out in her itty-bitty costume. In the morning light she saw the walls of Aston's room caked in posters of Magnum P.I, James Bond, and Miami Vice: male role models, no doubt. Made sense. She found a pair of shorts next to a pile of charred Lincoln Logs.

Self-conscious, Sapphire tiptoed to the kitchen where she found Joe drinking coffee and smoking a cigarette, watching the news on a small TV with the volume low.

"Good morning." He motioned to the coffeemaker. "I borrowed some coffee from the neighbor."

"Nice."

"No, she's a hag."

"The coffee, I mean."

"Oh, right. Would you like a cup?" His mind was clearer today. It was hard to believe this was the same man who'd been shouting about invisible people the night before. "Ashton walked to the store to get some breakfast for you."

"Oooh." Sapphire cringed at how relieved and girly she sounded. "So *Ashton*...what's up with that?"

Joe handed her a cup and sat back down. "That's his name. I might have been a little tipsy when I went to fill out the paper work and forgot the H. Once the kids learned to read in school, they started teasing him about the name being spelled wrong, along with some...other things. He used to come home with bruises, broken arms, black eyes, you name it. It made him a hell of a fighter though."

"I see." It explained why she'd seen him cringe at his name being mispronounced.

"I only remember bits and pieces from yesterday, so I'm sorry if I said anything insulting. Not really the first fucking impression you want to make when you meet your daughter in-law." Joe peered into his coffee.

"You know Joe, Aston and I aren't really marr-hi…" The TV caught her eye.

A picture of a girl framed the corner of the screen.

"It was right here," the reporter stated, standing in front of a lake by Arrowhead, "this morning, that the drowned body of a young woman was found." The picture of the girl in the corner blew up covering the whole screen.

Sapphire went deaf and the room around her dissolved. All she could see was the image of the girl.

She shot up and her chair crashed to the floor. Joe looked at her in surprise.

"I have to leave," she managed to get out. She had to go to the lake *now*. She had to find him.

She ran out of the house. It wasn't supposed to go like this. Sapphire was supposed to be next.

It wasn't supposed to be Misty.

CHAPTER 17

Aston walked in the door feeling like a million bucks. It was a good day. Hell, it was a good life.

He was close to finding the Serial Catcher, something he'd dreamed of for years. Above all, he'd spent the night with Sapphire. He felt...what was it, giddy? Aston had never felt giddy before. He had such a rush of energy his bad leg didn't even hurt when he jogged to the grocery store.

Aston found his father staring out the kitchen window with a cup of coffee to his lips and burning cigarette filter between his fingers. For once, the house smelled of coffee instead of mold.

Aston put down the grocery bag filled with everything he thought a vegetarian might want in an omelet.

"She still sleeping?" he asked, pouring himself a cup.

"Um, well...not really."

Aston stared at his old man as he swallowed the first sip. "What do you mean not real..." The giddy-million-bucks-the-house-smells-of-coffee-not-mold mood left him. "She left, didn't she?"

"Yup."

"And she stole my car, didn't she?"

"Yup."

"Son of a bitch!" A sharp pain stabbed his chest.

It was clear. Last night meant nothing.

"She saw something on the news and just took off," his father said, shaking his head. "Women."

"Ooh-hoo," Aston chuckled on the brink of madness. "See, that's what she wants you to think to suck you in, but trust me, she's not a woman. She's a freaking *siren*." He tossed the cup into the sink. It hit the edge and shattered, which was too bad.

His dad only owned three coffee cups to begin with.

He reached for his cell and waited impatiently.

"Yes?" Barry's voice was thick with sleep.

"Get your ass out of bed."

"I just got my ass *in* bed."

"I need you to drive me to the Dubois mansion."

"Is this one of those times where you ask me to drive you, but then you end up stealing my car and leaving me stranded on Rodeo?"

"Probably not, but we'll see."

. . .

Sapphire stood on the hill above the lake watching the Sheriff's department and reporters leave the scene.

It was hard to believe that such a peaceful place surrounded by mountains, forestry, and fresh water was the place Misty took her last breath only hours ago. Sapphire cringed, imagining the appalling scenario that had played out below. None of the girls deserved to die. But did it have to be *Misty*?

Sapphire slid down the hill until she reached the water. She'd watched the Sheriff's department comb the area and knew she wouldn't find anything, but she paced at the water's edge anyway.

Why this specific lake? There were several lakes closer to the Golden Mirage and downtown L.A. The longer he drove with a woman in the trunk the riskier it was, so why go out of his way? Perhaps this lake had sentimental value to him, or...

Her gaze landed on the few cabins scattered in the surrounding forest, smoke ascending from their chimneys.

Or he lived there.

It wasn't out of his way at all. It was on his way home. Sapphire ran back to her car and jumped inside. The mountain town had no more than a couple hundred people. With a bit of luck, she might find him today.

She'd stolen Aston's car that morning and rushed home. She had run up to the attic to change and pack her bag, flown downstairs, snatched a banana from the fruit bowl, and headed for the door just as Charles and Berta got back from their morning stroll.

Charles's wheelchair had blocked her exit and he eyed her, mystified. Not strange considering she was wearing black jeans, black boots, and a tight black t-shirt—none of which were Prada.

When she squeezed by him, Charles had grabbed her arm with such force that it startled her.

"Charles, I really have to go," she had said, gently pulling on her hand.

Charles had opened his mouth, taking a breath before pouring all his energy into forming his lips. "Be...careful."

Sapphire had blinked at him, processing his words and the clear voice she hadn't heard in almost a decade.

"I-I'll see you later," she had stammered.

Still taken aback by Charles's words, Sapphire had gone to the driveway knowing what she had to do. There was a reason she stole the Volkswagen years ago. Her Range Rover with its sparkling rhinestone-covered grill and rims screamed, *look at me, look at me*, in Chrissy-like fashion. Not to mention that it was in her name.

She couldn't have a cab haul her around to hunt a serial killer, and Aston's car was sure to have a tracker on it, most cops' did. The Range Rover had to do.

Sapphire got to her 100th dirt road in the mountains when it hit her.

"Shit!"

She never closed the attic door. How messed up was her mind if she'd forgotten to protect the *one* thing in the mansion that connected to her Serial Catcher life?

She panicked, debating whether to turn around. Then she calmed down. Her mother was in rehab, Charles was wheelchair bound, and Berta had already cleaned her room the day before. She should be safe.

She continued down another dirt road and searched for residential houses hidden among the trees. For the past hour the view hadn't changed. She felt like she was having constant déjà vu.

Tree. Tree. Elk Warning sign. Tree. Tree. Bush. Elk Warning sign. Tree. Bush. Elk Warning sign. Tree. Tree. Elk...

ELK!

Sapphire slammed the brakes and veered away from the animal in the road, heading straight for a tree. The hood bent, hissing steam, and her airbags exploded.

She stumbled out and looked at her totaled car, then at the Elk responsible. He still hadn't moved.

"I'm okay, thanks for asking!" Sapphire looked around the deserted road and grabbed her phone. "Call nearest tow truck."

"You have no service, Ms. Dubois."

"Then how are you talking to me?" Sapphire sneered.

"My verbal communication feature is not connected to the network. Please review your owner's manual."

Sapphire climbed up on the car's roof. She waved her phone around, searching for reception. It wasn't working.

"Look," she said sweetly to the screen. "We've had some rough times, you and I, where we both said things we didn't mean. I just need one bar, that's all...please."

Unyielding silence, then:

"You have...absolutely no service."

Sapphire let out a frustrated yell as the Elk ogled her.

"Bet you think this is funny."

He pooped.

"Sweetheart, are you in trouble?"

Sapphire turned to an old, sweet-looking lady standing in the middle of the road and looking up at her.

"Oh, those things almost never work out here," the lady chuckled at the cell phone. "You need to use my telephone? I live right up the hill."

Sapphire sighed. "Yes, thank you."

"Come on then," the old lady said, smiling from ear to ear. "I've got tea on the stove and key lime pie in the fridge."

Sapphire dropped her phone into her boot and followed the old woman. They hiked until they hit a small dirt road. It led to a cute house that bordered a steep hill.

"I'm sorry," Sapphire said. "I'm…Jill. I didn't catch your name."

"Oh, how silly of me, I'm Maggie." She closed the door behind them. "Maggie Butler."

•   •   •

Barry stepped out of the buggy in the Dubois driveway and walked up to Aston's car. "Good news. She left the keys in the ignition."

Aston slammed the buggy's door shut. "How very noble. I'll be sure to thank the thief." He didn't give a shit about his car. He gave a shit about her reason for taking it.

He rang the golden doorbell sixteen times before a big-boned housekeeper ripped the door open, angry as a bee. Or in her case: moose.

"Nein!" She slapped Aston's hand off the buzzer. "Nein. Nein. Nein."

Aston was stunned by the woman. He wasn't used to people scaring the crap out of him. He scrambled for his badge. "We're looking for Ms. Dubois."

"Gone. Goodbye."

She slammed the door and Aston looked over at Barry whose eyes were bulging with terror. He rang the doorbell again, only once. The large German ripped open the door again—no shit—breathing fire through her nostrils.

God, Aston missed the old one, Julia. "Where did Ms. Dubois go?"

"Gone. Goodbye." She reached to close the door again, but Aston stuck his foot in the crack. Over the angry German's shoulder he saw Mr. Dubois watching from his wheelchair.

"B…Berta, no." The old man waved to let them in.

"Come," Berta commanded. She escorted them to the kitchen where Barry and Aston sat down on stools. When Berta was about to park Mr. Dubois' wheelchair, he held up a hand and stood up, slowly.

Aston watched him in shock. Last time he was there the

rich old fart couldn't walk, let alone speak.

"I'm sorry," Aston said as the look on Mr. Dubois' face made him realize that he was staring. "I was under the impression you were a full-time cripple."

He must have said something insulting because Mr. Dubois frowned before he settled in the chair, pridefully.

"Wh...what...is this...re...garding?"

"Sapphire," Aston answered, "she stole my car."

A smile danced on Mr. Dubois' lips. "K...kids." He shrugged as if Aston had just told him that Sapphire had taken his ball and wouldn't give it back.

"But she was here first before she left," Aston tried. "Did she say anything? Grab anything?"

"Banana."

"I don't suppose you know which way she went?"

"F...fruit bowl is that way." The old man pointed, barely holding back a smile.

Aston ignored the comment and hopped off the stool. "Well if she comes home, let her know to—"

Somebody farted. All eyes slowly turned to Berta who was mopping by the fridge.

"Um...to call me," Aston continued before smacking Barry on the back of the head. "Let's go."

As they passed Berta, she bent down to grab something. She put the two inch black gadget on the counter and returned her attention to the mop.

Aston glanced at it. He moved through the hallway as a strange and unwelcome feeling grew inside him. He reached for the front doorknob and got stuck. He was immovable by an invisible force field.

It was only a flash drive. Plenty of people owned the same brand. It didn't mean anything. Pure coincidence.

"Are you okay?" Barry asked. "You look kind of pale."

"I'll meet you at the station, Barry," Aston said, holding his voice steady.

"But..."

"Go."

After a moment of disappointment, Barry exited.

Feeling sick, Aston went back to the kitchen, snatched the flash drive, and was out of there before Mr. Dubois and Berta had turned their heads.

Clenching the flash drive in his hand Aston's eyes drew to the staircase. His throat felt dry and thick.

Technically, he needed a warrant to go up to Sapphire's room without permission. Technically, Aston didn't give a shit. Berta and Mr. Dubois didn't even know he was still there.

He had to look at it *now*. He wanted to be proven wrong.

He moved up the stairs, his eyes fixed on the goal. A speeding train of images raced up toward his consciousness. The evidence came in waves. With each heavy step he took, another image crashed into him.

Step 1: *The Serial Catcher was a woman.* Step 2: *It was someone who knew of Aston's case.* Step 3: *Somebody who overheard him speak about the flash drive.* Step 4: *She'd bolted after watching the news this morning.* Step 5: *The beat up Volkswagen to stay undercover. Her trained body. Her odd behavior. The lying. The religious serial killer's true reason for wanting her dead last year.*

Aston stopped in front of Sapphire's door. He let his mind catch up.

Barry's words were the final step: *"The Serial Catcher is probably the person we least expect."*

An heiress.

Aston walked over to her computer; the tiny gadget weighing a thousand pounds in his palm.

He inserted the flash drive, staring down at the screen. His heart raced, pushing his blood pressure to a new high.

The file popped up on the screen. A file that he recognized well because he himself had put it there. Aston's air passage closed and he backed away from the computer.

It *was* his stolen flash drive.

His eyes landed on an opened attic flap above Sapphire's bed.

Aston had been in her room plenty of times. He'd never noticed an attic before.

He wobbled over, feeling as if his legs had been stripped

of their bones.

Aston inhaled, taking a moment. He knew his world was about to change. He pulled himself up the flap and exhaled at the view.

Sapphire Dubois was the Serial Catcher.

CHAPTER 18

Sapphire glanced at the loud grandfather clock again; it had only been twenty-eight minutes since she called the tow truck and he told her it'd be two hours.

Under any other circumstances, twenty-eight minutes would be short. But this was twenty-eight minutes of Maggie's endless stories about her son, *Dancing with the Stars*, and Alex Trebek.

"Are you sure you don't want some tea?" the old lady urged for the 135th time.

They were in the living room, surrounded by trinkets, cat ceramics, and baby pictures of Maggie's son.

"No, thank you…again." Maggie was as sweet as they come, but Sapphire no longer accepted drinks from strangers. Last time she did, her old MMA instructor hung her from a skyscraper.

"Okay," Maggie said. In two minutes, she would probably have asked again…twice.

"That's one fancy car you have out there," Maggie said.

"Mhmm," Sapphire mumbled and got up in search of something to change the subject. She grabbed one of the photographs of Maggie's son, around 8 years old. "Cute."

"Oh yes, back in the day when he still allowed me to take pictures of him. He'll always look that way to me even though he's going on 43 now."

"You must miss him."

"Not at all."

Sapphire turned and Maggie laughed at her surprise.

"He still lives at home."

"Oh." Sapphire glanced at the grandfather clock again. It had been a full minute since last time she checked. "Are you sure that clock isn't broken?"

"Works like a charm. Tea?"

Sapphire closed her eyes and turned back to the shelf, noticing a college diploma made out to Paul Butler. "Paul, that's your son? What did he major in?"

"Yuck, he was away from home for four whole years. He wanted to be a chemist, but I felt it was much too dangerous for him. He works in the city, downtown, just a few nights a week. It's not for the paycheck. His father passed and left us with enough money to live on."

"What place?" Sapphire turned to Maggie, her stomach tightening in anticipation.

"Golden Nugget? No, the Golden Mirage? Yes, that's it. Tea?"

Sapphire turned back to the shelf, knowing her face was one of alarm. This sweet old lady was unaware of what a monster she gave birth to.

Poor Maggie, Sapphire thought, studying the diploma. She realized she should leave, car or no car. She didn't want to risk exposing herself to Paul Butler before she could trap him at work. She just had one more question.

"So," Sapphire said, turning, "what does Paul do at the—"

A sharp pain exploded from the back of her head. Sapphire's eyes blurred and her knees buckled under her. Dazed, she touched her head. When she pulled her hand back, it was covered in blood.

Maggie stepped into her field of vision, which was shrinking with each passing second. In the palm of Maggie's hand was a blood stained candlestick.

"You should've had the tea."

Before the world turned black, Sapphire knew one thing: this sweet old lady wasn't so sweet after all.

•   •   •

Pictures, drawings, red strings connecting one thing to the other and newspaper clippings caked the attic wall. A small bag with wigs and clothes that would drive most men crazy lay in the corner. The answering machine that Sapphire had in her purse contained a voice of an unidentified man confessing to wanting to murder women.

There were the files: Tomas Broker; Richard Martin; Harold Marlow; George Rath. Each of them assigned a number in the order in which they'd been captured. Each one a dangerous serial killer twice Sapphire's size. Except for Rath, who was closer to four times her size.

Last year, when he first met Sapphire at the police charity ball and brought her home to his bed, he thought she was the typical Beverly Hills chick: spoiled, dimwitted, clueless. As it turned out, Aston was the thick one.

He sat in the middle of the dusty wooden floor, surrounded by evidence. Her wall was breathtaking but bordered on mental illness.

Clearly, Sapphire had kept this secret for years and probably began plotting years before that. Which would make her what, fifteen, sixteen? What sane teenager would spend her life doing such a thing? Or which Beverly Hills heiress, for that matter?

Sapphire denied knowledge of the Batman ring attached to Shelly McCormick's dismembered finger. Now Aston knew she had lied.

Who was the millionaire Bruce Wayne, if not a man who chose to leave his rich and comfortable life at night to go catch bad guys? It sounded pretty damn familiar.

Was that it? Had she started all of this inspired by an unrealistic work of fiction?

Aston felt like an idiot when he spotted the content in the middle of the wall: articles on murders connected to the Golden Mirage. Had Aston's mind not been so set on the Serial Catcher and failed to notice news and headlines, he might have connected the dots as soon as he saw her at the strip club.

It was obvious now. Sapphire had gone undercover, working her way from the inside like a cop would. Not that he ever believed her screenwriting lie, but *this* never crossed his mind.

"Jesus," Aston sighed, lighting a cigarette. He felt overwhelmed. It was a big change; he usually moseyed around feeling underwhelmed.

What the hell was he going to do? It was Sapphire. *His* Sapphire. He couldn't just drag her into the station, toss her on the floor, and say, *"Tah-dah!"*

The person who he'd hunted for so long was someone he knew. Someone he had slept with. Someone he wanted nothing more than to protect from harm. Someone he...loved.

This was *fucked up*; a sick joke from the universe. Detective Aston Ridder, the cop, was in love with the Serial Catcher.

He couldn't arrest her, could he? He needed time. He needed to get his shit together. Nobody else could know.

He started to put everything back where he found it. Sapphire was the most important person to keep it from. If she figured out someone had been here, she might take off.

Correction. Sapphire was the *second* most important person to keep it from. Aston fumbled for his phone.

"Barry, where are you?" He hurried, ripping the evidence off the wall, loading it into a bag.

"Just walked into the station."

"Run to my office. And not in that girly way you run, I mean really fucking haul ass. I need you to do something, no questions asked."

"What?" Barry panted from the sudden sprint.

"Delete the photograph. The whole file."

"But...yes, sir."

He was learning.

"Listen to me very carefully, Barry. Capelli cannot know under *any* circumstances, do you understand me?"

Barry's panting stopped and a long silence followed.

"Too late."

• • •

"Where were you? Why didn't you wear the shirt I put out for you? Why is your jacket so dirty? Did you remember to wipe your boots off?"

"Yes, Mother." Paul wasn't even over the threshold yet.

His mother took his jacket and hung it up the only proper way, her way.

"I have a surprise for you," she said.

"Meatloaf?" He moved to the kitchen to get a glass of water.

"No," his mother said. She took his glass away from the faucet and poured milk into it instead. He didn't want milk. "You know how I don't like you having to go out there to do your *thing* when you could be here with me. I've finally found a solution to our problem."

She handed him the glass of milk as Paul stared at her.

It wasn't their problem. It was *her* problem. He loved going out in the world to find his next.

"W-what do you mean?"

"Today, I ran into this lovely girl whose car had run off the road. And I thought, why on God's green earth is Paul having to leave everyday when he can do it all right here. At home."

"At...at..."

"Yes." She put a bendy straw in his milk. "We'll spend tourist season grabbing the college girls that do illegal camping by the lake and bring them to the basement. When you're done doing your *thing*, you can burn them in the woods. You'll never have to leave me now. Isn't that great?"

Paul stared at his mother, repeating her words in his mind.

He'd *never* leave. Going out to find his next was his only freedom, his air. Without it, his mother would suffocate him. He'd end up hanging himself like his father had.

"Paul...Paulie. Paul! Say something."

"It's great..."

"Oh, I knew you'd love it!" She kissed him on the lips, too long, like always. "Do you want some pie with that milk?"

"I'm not hungry."

She took the milk and replaced it with a fork and a slice of key lime pie. He hated key lime pie.

"And now for the rest of your surprise."

"There's more?" He wasn't sure he could take more.

"Of course there's more," his mother beamed and led him toward the basement door.

This was not how he saw his life when he finally told his mother what he did. He'd expected her to kick him out. To his disappointment, she didn't. She'd held on tighter.

"Okay, Paulie. Open the door."

With pie still in his hand, Paul peeked down the basement and shut the door quickly. "There's a girl down there."

"Yes, you can enjoy yourself while I start dinner."

"You picked…a girl…for me?" He couldn't grasp it.

"You'll love her. She's so sweet."

Sweet. Sweet?!

Paul didn't do *sweet*. He was the only one who picked his *next*. He loved killing over-demanding, hyper-controlling women. Killing them gave him his manhood back. The manhood his mother always stole from him. *Sweet* did not do the trick.

"Oh, and here, give her six or seven of these. It'll overdose her." His mother held up her jar of sedatives. "It's better, less messy. She completely ruined Grandma's candlestick before."

Paul stared at the sedatives. The same pills she'd dropped into his tea when he was an unruly child.

It was the last straw. She wanted him to kill people with *sedatives*.

The basement was a plan. Everything about it would be calculated to the smallest detail. A routine. His kills would become like his mother: sensible and boring. Paul Butler didn't *do* plans. He loved the spur of the moment kill. He lived for the adrenaline, the excitement.

He had to say no to his mother. He could not live under these conditions.

"Mother…" Paul pushed.

"What?" She gave him the authoritarian look, knowing he was going to argue.

Paul's lips moved but no words came out. He sighed. "Nothing."

Out in the world, he was assertive, cool, and well-spoken. The minute he walk through these doors he became a child again. He wasn't able to say no to his mother. Not then. Not now. Not ever. That would never change, unless…

"Good," his mother said. "Dinner will be ready in—"

Paul jammed the pie fork into her eye. She fell onto the ground, and he watched her body twitch until it remained still. Her eye with the fork in it stared at his boots.

Freedom rushed through him. Finally, he'd killed the right bitch.

He opened the basement door. The girl was unconscious and cuffed to a pipe. They were the same cuffs Paul's mother used on him when he was a child. They'd kept him inside when all he wanted was to go out and play with the other kids.

He gazed down at her face, swallowed by the basement's darkness. He would let the fire take care of her. He had no want to kill her himself. She wasn't his next. She had been his mother's.

He doused his mother's house in gasoline and stepped outside before he dropped the match. He watched the fire grow, his nostrils filling with the intoxicating smoke.

Paul turned his back on his childhood home with a smile. Soon he would start his new life as an adult. The only voice that controlled him from here on out was his own. But before he left, he would end his old life with a bang and do something grand.

He would kill them all.

. . .

Sapphire's eyes stung and her lungs squealed with every breath. She coughed and opened her eyes to find more darkness.

She should have played more Clue and less Uno with Julia when she was a kid. Had she, perhaps she would have foreseen it: Mrs. Butler, in the lounge, with the candlestick.

Sapphire moaned and reached to touch the back of her head. Her muscles were anemic and she had to fight for every movement.

Her hand snapped back. It was cuffed to a metal pipe behind her. Her eyes adjusted to the dark and she saw it. Thick, gray smoke came through the bottom of the basement door. The smell of fire burned her nostrils.

Sapphire shot up at full attention, her head pounding.

The house was about to go up in flames, and she was cuffed to it. She yanked on the pipe, a sharp pain spreading from the back of her head to her cheek bones.

If only Sapphire would have worn her hair up with pins today, she could have picked the cuff. Instead, she had chosen a ponytail. A stupid, fatal ponytail.

She dug into her boot and fished out her phone.

"Text Father O'Riley with coordinates and *help*."

"You have…no service."

Sapphire roared, feeling the panic devour her. She had to find a way to escape.

She shoved the phone back in her boot and looked around the basement for something useful. She tried to squeeze her hand out of the cuff, knowing it wouldn't work. Her thumb was in the way. Her stupid, fatal thumb.

Sapphire's adrenaline raced when the idea hit her. She peered down at her thumb and swallowed. She needed to do it before she lost her nerve.

Close to tears, Sapphire prepared herself. It was the only way to get out.

She braced herself with quick exhales through the nose, squeezed her eyes shut, then bit down on her thumb, overriding her mouth's reservations.

CHAPTER 19

"I can't believe it, man," Capelli said as he rang the Dubois' doorbell. "An *heiress*." He shook his head. "And she was right under your nose. Have yah heard of something called cop instincts?"

"I dunno, Capelli, it sounds pretty unlikely," Aston said, avoiding eye contact.

"Trust me, I never forget a face. This was the girl in the photo." Capelli scratched his head. "Yo, when you see the photo, don't show anyone else at the station before we've nailed her. We don't want them to get to the media before us."

Aston nodded, pretending to agree.

He'd tried everything to delay bringing Sapphire in for questioning, but there wasn't an excuse in the world that would keep Capelli from the Serial Catcher. He'd left the mansion, met up with Capelli, and pretended he'd been at home, just to go right back to the mansion.

"How did you say you knew her again?" Capelli asked, ringing the bell again.

Berta ripped the door open.

This time she didn't scream in German, and instead looked at Capelli's body, her eyelashes flapping like bats out of hell.

"Hello," she smiled, revealing teeth of varying shades.

"We're here…" Aston started.

"Suush!" Berta quieted Aston, gestured for Capelli to continue. "Yeees?"

"We're here for Sapphire Dubois," Capelli said.

"Again?"

"Not again," Aston jumped in. "Just this *one* time." He turned to Capelli and lowered his voice. "Foreigners."

"Gone," Berta said then winked at Capelli. "Cabbage for you?"

"Er, no thanks. Where can we find her?"

"Country club. Everybody's always at the country club."

"Thank you, ma'am," Capelli said and turned to leave.

"Goodbye," Berta said in a dreamy tone.

"Bye," Aston responded.

Berta glared at him and slammed the door.

• • •

A cry erupted in Sapphire's throat as the pain shot through her thumb and out her hand. The iron taste of blood made her gag and pull her hand back.

Sapphire's thumb was stubbornly attached despite the deep flesh wound her teeth had made. She knew she had to bite down harder this time and it scared her.

Sapphire placed her thumb back in her mouth, took a deep breath, and started to bite down...then stopped. On the cellar floor lay a rusty paperclip.

Sapphire pulled her thumb away, spitting out a mouthful of blood. She launched her hand at the clip and stretched the cuff's chain to its limit.

Above her, the smoke grew thicker and she could hear the crackling of fire.

Sapphire's fingers were almost to the paperclip. She pressed forward feeling as if her shoulder was going pop right out of its socket. The tip of her finger grazed the paperclip and coaxed it closer.

Sapphire snatched the clip, pried it open, and jammed it into the cuff, unlocking it in record time. She sprung to her feet and her head exploded in raw pain, making the room spin. She reached her hand out in front of her to stay straight.

Sapphire coughed and searched for a basement window. There were none. She would have to go through the door, into the fire.

She pulled herself up the railing and yanked on the blazing

door handle. Locked. Of course her kidnappers wouldn't be so kind. Sapphire wasn't even sure what the hell was going on. Maggie Butler had clobbered her on the head just to set her own house on fire?

Sapphire shielded her face and kicked at the lock. It caved and she shoved the door open. The heat rushed at her, burning her face. A spectacle of orange licked away the walls of the Butlers' living room.

Sapphire squinted through the flames as her eyes teared up from the smoke. She couldn't see anything but the wall of fire rising in front of her. It was spreading, pushing her back. She wouldn't make it to the door.

She coughed and tried to shield her face from the penetrating heat, as the flames inched closer, trapping her.

Sapphire squinted and spotted a window behind the wall of fire. She backed up to get a sprint going. She pulled her shirt to her mouth and jumped.

Blazing heat shocked her body before she crashed through the glass.

Sapphire tucked her head, expecting to hit the ground flat, but she never did. Instead, she tumbled down the steep hill next to the house. She tried to grab onto bushes and moss but ended up with most of it in her fists.

Several yards down the decline, she smacked into a tree and stopped.

Sapphire felt a thick drowsiness take over. She tried to get up, but her body wouldn't let her. Her head roared in pain and her arms felt too heavy.

She gazed up at the dark treetops swaying above her and was mesmerized by the stars. They were more prominent over the mountains than above Los Angeles's sea of lights.

How could a day that started so well in Aston's bed end in such despondency? A part of her wished she would have stayed at Joe's house. Had she, maybe the day would have ended the way it begun.

Or?

She suddenly couldn't help but feel like there was somewhere she was supposed to be tonight. Like she'd forgotten something important…maybe on purpose.

Sapphire used the last of her strength to reach in her boot. Her fingers were so weak they barely managed to place the phone on her chest.

"Text Father O'Riley…coordinates with *help*." Sapphire's eyelids dropped against her will.

"You have no…"

The phone beeped, gaining a bar. "Father O'Riley is out of the coverage area."

Sapphire let out a weak, hopeless laugh as she let the warm darkness take her. "You…asshole."

"Texting…"

• • •

"I hate that asshole," Aston mumbled to himself.

"Who?" Capelli asked.

Across the ballroom floor John Vanderpilt swirled his Cognac like it was a sport. He was pretending to be in a conversation with some men but was actually admiring himself in the mirror behind them.

"No one." Aston looked away. He wanted to fight the asshole so badly that his knuckles itched whenever he was near.

How could Sapphire be so stupid to want to…

No, Aston realized, *she couldn't.* Now knowing the true Sapphire Dubois, he understood who Vanderpilt must be to her. A cover, an attempt to retain a persona that fit into the ideal Beverly Hills mold. Obviously the cover had gone too far, and Sapphire was with him against her will, forced by outside pressure to marry the guy.

A relieved smile spread on Aston's face. "Fucking aye."

"Excuse me?!" An old jewel-mongering lady to his left crinkled her nose at him, disgusted.

"I'm sorry," Aston said and leaned in. How rude of him; she was hard of hearing. "FUCKING-AYE!"

The lady walked away, huffing and puffing.

No wonder she's in a bad mood, Aston thought. The crowd had been waiting for hours.

The place was packed with guests of the Dubois and Vanderpilt families, all of them gossiping about why Sapphire Dubois wasn't attending her own wedding rehearsal. Aston had heard everything from Sapphire was getting a last minute boob job—which people agreed was needed—to Sapphire joining her mother in rehab. It was scandalous, and they all loved it.

Who knew where she was? Aston sure as shit didn't. He'd snuck away from Capelli to call the Golden Mirage, anonymously asking for Sapphire. The British guy told him she wasn't there tonight.

The good news: She wasn't getting herself in trouble at the Golden Mirage. The bad news: She was most likely getting herself in trouble elsewhere.

Vanderpilt noticed Aston and his obsessive swirling ceased. He worked his way toward them.

"I don't get it." Capelli nodded to the groom. "I thought you said she was gay."

"She is." Aston kept his eyes on Vanderpilt. "That dude used to be a chick. Sex change. Fake balls and everything."

"Really?" Capelli said amazed.

Vanderpilt came up to Aston. "What do you think you're doing here?"

"I'm afraid I can't disclose that."

"So how do you take a piss with that thing?" Capelli asked Vanderpilt, staring down at his crotch.

"What?"

"Good evening...*again*." A bitter woman held the microphone up on the U-shaped table. "Like I said three hours ago, I'm Eloise Parker...the *wedding planner*." She waited for applause. None came. "Ahem...Since the bride-to-be is still M.I.A., I say we proceed with the dinner. Ms. Kraft, do you mind playing the bride for the speeches?"

Vanderpilt gave Aston a last look of hatred and hurried to the table. He and Chrissy sat down next to each other, bodies stiff.

Aston's phone buzzed and he flipped it open to find a text from Sapphire.

"Capelli," he said, "you think you can hold down the fort?"

"Why?"

"Emergency. They need me at the station." Aston headed for the double doors.

"Ridder! Do you think I'm an idiot?" Capelli grabbed Aston's shoulder. "Don't you think I know what you got on your phone?"

Shitballs.

"A booty text from Moore." Capelli broke into a smile.

"You got me." Aston took the breath he hadn't realized he was holding in.

"Doesn't look like she's showing up tonight, so go get 'em, tiger." Capelli smacked Aston on the ass, athlete-style.

Aston waited until he was outside to start running.

CHAPTER 20

Aston stared at Sapphire sleeping on the other side of the window looking small in the king-size bed. Only in Beverly Hills would the hospital rooms look like something from a five-star hotel.

Aston sighed. He knew what he had to do: the shittiest thing ever. He had no choice— Capelli would never give up. He couldn't avoid it anymore.

He'd found her on the ground in the forest at the text's exact coordinates, unconscious and bloody. He'd picked her up gently and carried her through the dense, dark woods until he got to his car. He'd smelled fire from somewhere but didn't care. All he wanted was to get her to the hospital and have her safe once and for all.

After he got her there, Vanderpilt was notified. Then the whole country club knew, including Capelli, who called Aston to give him the news of the Serial Catcher's whereabouts. They agreed to meet at the hospital the next day, knowing she wasn't going anywhere. Of course Capelli didn't know Aston was already there.

He took one last look at Sapphire then moved to meet Capelli at the entrance, sweating.

Between worrying about Sapphire and second-guessing himself, Aston hadn't slept. It was evident now that he struggled to text Barry with double vision.

He gave the hospital's security guards each a nod and placed himself in front of the sliding glass doors, waiting as Capelli parked and marched up to him.

"Ready for fame, Ridder?" Capelli beamed. "Can you imagine how the girls are going to react when they see our faces all over the news? Their panties will drop before they even know what hit 'em."

Aston cringed. The chief had been right. Capelli didn't give a crap if what the Serial Catcher did was illegal; he just wanted the cameras on him. Not that it mattered.

"I'm ready," Aston said. He wasn't. Even his balls were sweating.

"Detectives!"

They turned to see Barry sprinting across the lot.

"Bad news," the newbie wheezed, putting his hands on his knees. "When I tried to save the evidence, I accidentally inserted the infected flash drive. The photograph. The original footage. Everything is gone!"

"Barry, you fucking imbecile," Aston cussed.

"Are you kidding?" Capelli shouted, looking at Aston. "Is he kidding?"

"He's really not that funny, so I doubt it."

"I'm sorry, sir." Barry said nervously, eyes on Capelli, who was at least twice his size.

"Yes, that's exactly what you are." Capelli put a giant finger to Barry's pimply face. "A *sorry* excuse for a cop."

"Hey!" Aston put himself between them. "He might be fresh, but he's as much of a cop as you or me." Nobody was allowed to talk that way to Barry…except Aston.

Capelli backed off, pulling on his hair, then calmed himself. "You know what, it's okay. We may not have the evidence to back it, but we've got three eyewitness cops that saw her face. We can bring her in for questioning and get a warrant. We'll get new, better evidence."

"W-hell," Aston said. "I never actually saw the photo, and it being a Beverly Hills heiress is improbable to begin with. We're going to come off as nutjobs if we try to peg a powerful vigilante on a tiny girl with a fancy purse."

"You know I never forget a face, Ridder. It was her!" Capelli yelled. "Barry saw the photo. Tell him, Barry."

"I don't know," Barry said, "now that I think about it, it could have been a lot of people."

Capelli's gaze bounced between them, landing on Aston's sweaty forehead.

"You did this." Capelli backed up and pointed, staring at Aston wide-eyed. "You erased the evidence. Moore isn't the one who's been messing with your head; it's her, the Serial Catcher, isn't it? You're *protecting* her."

Aston crossed his arms over his chest. Barry noticed and did the same.

"Fine." Capelli moved to the door. "I'll bring her in myself. More glory for me."

Aston put a hand to Capelli's chest. "Actually, you can't. You're on my ground, and you have no jurisdiction in Beverly Hills."

Behind his back, Aston waved at the two security guards, and they stepped up behind the doors. They weren't there as muscle but as authorial witnesses in case the out-of-towner broke the law and Capelli knew it.

He turned to Aston. "You know what, I thought you'd changed, but you haven't, you've lost your freakin' mind!" Capelli shook his head. "Do you realize what you're doing, Ridder? You're throwing away your chance at the career you've always wanted, the FB—fucking—I, and for what...some *chick*?!"

Capelli was right. Aston knew he was an idiot. He was sacrificing everything, the FBI, his morals, his beliefs, the friendship of his old partner...for a girl who was engaged to someone else. It was the wrong choice, one that would send him down a withering path. But for the first time ever, Aston cared for somebody else's life more than he cared for his own.

"Leave the premises, Detective," Aston said.

Capelli growled and grabbed Aston by the collar. Their eyes narrowed, Clint Eastwood and John Wayne facing off. Aston wasn't sure who was who.

Capelli glanced at the security guards and let go.

"I'm going to bring her down, and I'm taking you down with her." He walked away from them, backward. "This isn't over, Ridder."

Aston watched his old friend walk away. That's where

Capelli got it wrong; it was over. He had no evidence, and even if he managed to get a warrant outside of his own Thousand Oaks jurisdiction, there was nothing to find. Aston had emptied Sapphire's attic before he left and placed the collection in a location where he knew no one would ever go. Barry's bedroom.

"Thanks boys," Aston nodded to the security guards, who he had warned, suspecting Capelli wouldn't go for the accidental loss of evidence.

Barry glanced over at him as they moved through the hallway in silence. Aston knew he would feel shitty for stabbing his old partner in the back, just not *this* shitty.

Barry opened and closed his mouth as Aston sat down opposite of Sapphire's room and leaned his head against the wall, tired. "Spit it out, Barry."

"Thanks…" Barry said, sitting down, "for defending me, back there, I mean."

"It's what partners do."

"Partners?"

Aston ignored him, closing his eyes. Barry had proved he had Aston's back no matter what; it was the best quality you could ask for in a partner.

"I'm taking a nap so keep your eye glued to that door," Aston mumbled. "Trust me, if she gets the chance, she will run."

He couldn't bring himself to arrest the Serial Catcher, but he still needed to make sure Sapphire Dubois was safe. If he didn't stop her, he knew she'd head for the Golden Mirage.

"You got it, *partner*," Barry beamed, nudging him with his elbow.

"Now you're pushing it."

* * *

Sapphire sat up with a jolt.

Tubes and needles were sticking out of her hands leading to IVs standing tall next to the hospital bed. She pulled the foreign objects out of her body in panic.

The last thing she remembered was being in the forest, and

she had no idea how she ended up in the hospital. Maybe Father O'Riley got the text after all.

She looked at the clock on the wall. 5:00 p.m. She needed to head to the Golden Mirage *right now*. She hoped Paul never saw her face the day before so she could still lure him in. Had he seen her, she'd find away to take him down anyway.

"Sapphire." Dr. Wells shut the door behind him, looking down at his chart. "I've been seeing a lot more of you lately. How are you feeling?"

"I feel great! Grrreat," she emphasized, aware that she sounded like Tony the Tiger. She gave the Dubois family physician a big smile. "Can I go home now?"

"You lost a lot of blood, it looks like someone tried to eat your thumb, and you have a pretty serious concussion, so I'm going to say *no*. We need to do a CAT scan and what everybody wants to know, including the cop who brought you in is, *what the heck happened to you?*"

"Who's the cop?" She already knew. Her stupid phone had sent the text to the worst person imaginable.

"Ridder, I think his name was. Do you feel ready to speak to him?"

"Not yet. Is anyone else here for me?"

"I think I saw Charles before. I'll go see if I can find him."

"Grrreat."

Dr. Wells opened the door, and Sapphire glimpsed Aston in the hallway. He was sound asleep in a chair next to Officer Harry who was playing rock, paper, scissors with himself.

The door closed and she looked around the room realizing none of her clothes were there. She'd have to make her escape in a hospital gown and ill-fitting slippers. Worse yet, she didn't even have her Range Rover. It was probably waiting for her in the mountain town's auto shop, and she didn't have time to get it.

In the middle of climbing out the window, she heard the door smack shut.

"Sapphire!"

"Charles," she panted, amazed by her stepfather's stance. He took two steps toward her with the help of a cane.

"What are you doing?" His words were so clear it was as if he'd never had a stroke.

"Um," she said, still in the window frame. "I'm *really* late for my manicure."

"Sapphire," Charles said in a stern voice, "I spent seven years locked inside my own body watching you. In my more lucid moments I realized what you were doing, why every newspaper in the house had certain articles cut out of them."

Sapphire's body turned cold and her gut twisted.

"I…" her voice was thicker than molasses. "I don't know what you're talking about."

"Yes, you do, and it is important that you stop."

He *knew*. Charles knew. Sapphire stood frozen though she wanted to run. The sweet old man suddenly looked demon-like as he came closer,, a vicious poltergeist that knew her secret.

When Dr. Wells' voice appeared outside the door, Sapphire snapped out of it and control returned to her body.

"I'm sorry, Charles." She heaved her other leg over the ledge and jumped.

Two blocks down, she found a cab and got in. She had two things to figure out.

One: how to capture Paul Butler at the Golden Mirage once she found him.

Two: how to outrun the cab driver, whom she wouldn't be able to pay, in hospital slippers.

∙ ∙ ∙

With Misty's death at the forefront of her mind, Sapphire pushed open the doors to the Golden Mirage like an outlaw with nothing to lose.

Buddy and a couple of the girls stopped to stare at her. It could have been because she walked in with a face that said: don't mess with me. Or—the more likely reason—because she strolled in wearing a paper gown and slippers. Even Homeless Herbert, the guy whose "look" included dreads and a foil hat, had gawked at her like *she* was the weirdo.

Sapphire ignored them, sights straight ahead, as she marched to Giles's office and knocked.

"I said *no*, Chastity," Giles yelled, his voice hoarse. "Are you deaf *and* mute?"

"It's Sapphire." She opened the door and the fire in her gut went out.

Giles stared at the computer in front of him with red, puffy eyes. "Have you been in—what do you Americans say?—the slammer?"

"No."

"Then where the bloody hell were you last night?" he asked, eyes still on the computer.

"Food poisoning."

"Your last excuse was better."

"I'm still in my hospital gown."

Giles looked her up and down. "Well played. Off you go then."

"But…"

"If you're here about the two spots, I haven't decided yet. Between the police and Chastity running in and out asking to be put on the wall, I haven't had time. At least that's what I assume she was asking, can't understand a bloody thing that one says."

Sapphire studied him. "I didn't know her as well as you did, but I'll miss her too."

Grief entered Giles's expression. "You know why I kept Misty away from the top spots as long as I could?"

Sapphire shook her head.

"She was a brilliant dancer, and she should have been our star a long time ago, but every girl who made it to the top let it go to her head and became the nastiest bitch. Believe it or not, even Ginger was quite pleasant before I made her a star. Misty was so sweet—I didn't want her to change."

Sapphire sat down and it clicked. The death of the girls had nothing to do with their spot on the wall. It had to do with their personalities. Paul Butler did have a favorite type of girl. She had missed it. He liked girls with bad attitudes. Misty didn't fit the description, but maybe she had been an exception.

"So…I was talking to Paul Butler the other day and was wondering if you've seen him around?"

"Ah," Giles pondered. "Saw him in the early hours before his shift. I don't know if he's still around. That man comes and goes as he pleases."

"Doesn't he look funny that one with his…" she studied Giles's face. "Broow…blooond-ish…short…"

Giles stared at her. "Sapphire, I haven't got time for this. I have a dying club on my hands, so feel free to *sod off*."

Sapphire headed to the dressing room and changed into her costume. The girls were quiet, all mourning Misty.

"Does anyone know Paul?" Sapphire's voice cut through the silence.

Candy frowned, wiping her eyes. "I've worked here for three years, and trust me, there's no one named Paul." A few of the other girls shook their heads.

It didn't make sense. Sapphire left the dressing room, confused. Something didn't add up.

She stepped out into the club, studying the male workers. She was just about to strike up a conversation with a maintenance guy when a hand reached out from the supply closet and yanked her inside, closing the door.

Sapphire scrambled to find the man's fingers in the darkness, then twisted them until she heard a crack and a scream.

He let go, and Sapphire sent out a kick. His body crashed into the shelf and Sapphire grabbed the hanging light switch.

For a second she was blinded by the immediate burst of light.

"Oh, come on!" Sapphire yelled. She stared at the man struggling to get up from a pile of boxes, paper cups, and cleaning supplies. "Would you just give it up already? I mean jeez."

The cowboy frowned at her, rolling around in the mess, looking like a beached whale.

Sapphire rolled her eyes and was about to offer him a hand. "Wait, you're not secretly an employee here whose name is Paul, are you?"

"No. Jim."

"Didn't think so," Sapphire sighed. She pulled him up and saw something on the shelf behind him. Dread washed over her.

"Jim, if I were you, I'd go home."

"With you?"

"No."

"Worth a shot."

The cowboy moved to the door as Sapphire stared at the homemade device.

A bomb.

CHAPTER 21

Sapphire dripped with sweat as she clutched the microwave containing the bomb. She took her time moving toward the back door.

She was no bomb expert, but the contraption had two sides of different colored liquids and she knew if they mixed, the outcome wouldn't be pleasant. The microwave wouldn't help to lessen the explosion, but she couldn't exactly stroll out of the closet with a bomb in her hands. If Paul Butler saw her, he might blow them up right then and there.

A chemist indeed, Sapphire thought, taking another watchful step.

"Sapphire." Giles walked up along side of her with a pad in his hands. "I've been thinking about this number."

"Mhmm," Sapphire said between her teeth. "Little busy here, Giles."

"You know Aerosmith?"

"Not well, only met them once."

"What?"

"Nothing. Yes."

"Well, since you do better with lyrical songs, we'll play *Pink* and…why on earth are you carrying my old microwave?"

"Er…working out?"

Giles shook his head. "Just be ready in five and I'll let the DJ know. Cheers, love." He smacked her on the ass, launching her forward.

She didn't breathe again until she realized she wasn't blown to pieces.

"Giles!" she shouted after him. "I really need to know who Paul Butler is!"

Giles frowned. "Are you having a piss? Or do you truly have some sort of goldfish memory issue along with your left feet?"

"What does that mean?!" He was already gone.

Finally outside, Sapphire placed the bomb in the dumpster, grabbed the metal chains, and locked it. She jogged back inside, heading for the stage.

The DJ rushed past her, bumping into her as he hurried to the backstage entrance. "Sorry, Sapphire Two," he called over his shoulder.

"No problem…" Sapphire stopped as she realized she didn't know his name.

The DJ. He matched Maggie Butler's age description.

Sapphire hurried after him and stopped behind the curtain. He finished up the techno mix for Candy on the stage, smiling a bit to himself as the dancer went through her last moves.

Sapphire spotted Chastity marching urgently toward the bathroom. "Chastity, do you know the DJ's name?"

Chastity moved her mouth, but nothing came out. Satisfied by her effort, she continued to the bathroom.

"Good talk!" Sapphire yelled, frustrated.

"Please welcome Saaa-pphire!" the DJ shouted into the microphone. Aerosmith's *Pink* filled the room along with the intimate crowd's hollers.

The second her feet stepped onto the stage, Sapphire was hit with a strange feeling. It grew as she danced, scanning the club. Something was off.

The TV on top of the bar was pushed forward, as if something was behind it. The table in the very back had a *reserved* sign on it and the chairs had been pulled to the center. *No one* would reserve that table.

There were more bombs.

She had no idea how many, but she knew they were all over the place.

Sapphire turned around to face the DJ. There was no *later*. She needed to take him down right now. But what she saw confused her. The DJ was picking the dirt out of his fingernails. His face was not that of someone ecstatic to blow up a club.

Sapphire spun back to face the crowd. Her eyes landed on a man standing at the other end of the room. He was looking around with an odd exuberance as he grabbed his jacket. He was leaving, but his shift had *just* started.

She understood everything. The girls, just like Sapphire, knew Paul Butler by another name. Giles had nicknamed Paul, like he did the girls. It was the perfect name for a person whose unofficial job description is to be the insightful pal. *Buddy.*

The bartender was Paul Butler.

Sapphire wanted to shout out *"BOMB!"*, but she didn't know if Paul had control over the devices. Her eyes drew to the fire alarm.

"Oh my God!" she shouted, pointing out over the club at an unspecific area. "Fire!"

The customers' heads turned and Sapphire leapt and smashed her hand onto the fire alarm. A sea of sprinklers hissed in harmony, showering the crowd with water. The alarm blared and people got up.

Butler's face turned to dismay as he watched the girls and customers disappear one by one. His eyes locked on Sapphire; she was the only one stationary.

They stared at each other through the rain, and he seemed to realize she knew something.

Sapphire hopped off the stage and jumped from table to table, crushing left-behind beer bottles and vodka glasses as she made her way to the bar.

Paul scrambled in his pocket. He pulled out a small remote as he headed for the door.

Sapphire pushed off the last table and threw herself over the bar, pulling him down with her. They tumbled to the ground, and the remote flew out of Paul's hand. It landed by the tall beer fridge.

Sapphire crawled and snagged the remote. Butler grabbed at her legs. She raised her hand and threw the remote over the bar. It hit the floor on the other side with a soft crack.

Sapphire kicked away from him and grabbed the door to the beer fridge, slamming it into his head.

Paul roared, covering his skull. "Had I known you were this much of a bitch, I would have killed you before."

Sapphire grabbed the lemon knife off the cutting board and held it to him. Paul looked from her to the knife.

"Speaking of which, why Misty?" Sapphire asked, taking a sweep of the empty room. Nobody had seen her take him down. She could easily tie him up and leave him for the police to find. "She didn't fit with the others."

"She was onto me," he said, eye still on the knife. "She wasn't as fun as the others, but I still enjoyed it." He let out a satisfied smile.

Sapphire nodded at him. "Yeah, remember to keep smiling like that when you're in jail; it'll probably land you a boyfriend or two."

Paul's smile vanished. "I'd rather die than go to jail!"

"If you don't want to go to jail, don't kill. I don't know why that's so hard for you people to understand."

"Every single one of those bitches deserved what they got. I'd kill them again if I could!"

"Oh Paul," Sapphire sighed, shaking her head. "Paul, Paul, Pa—"

Somebody pushed Sapphire, and she banged into the counter, dropping the knife. She turned swiftly.

It was Chastity; she was climbing on top of Butler.

"Chastity, he's dangerous!"

"Could I have picked a worse time to take a dump?" Chastity said. Her shoulders were poised and her otherwise meek demeanor was nowhere to be found. Her eyes shifted to someone behind Sapphire.

"Ridder?" Chastity said.

"Ridder?" Sapphire turned to see Aston in the door.

"Wilson?" Aston replied.

"Chastity," Sapphire corrected.

"Wilson," Chastity confirmed.

"Sapphire," Sapphire said, but that didn't make sense, and they both looked at her.

"And thanks to the confession I just heard," Chastity said,

pulling Paul up, "you are under arrest by the LAPD for the murders of some of downtown's finest strippers."

"You're a cop?" Sapphire asked, although pretty obvious.

"Damnit!" came from the door.

Sapphire turned to see Homeless Herbert.

He took off his foil hat and wig and stomped them to the ground. "I always miss the good part."

"Call for backup, Jones," Chastity ordered him. "We got him."

Sapphire blinked at Chastity/Wilson, Buddy/Butler, and Homeless Herbert/Jones right before he left. All the name changes were confusing.

"Move, girl!" Chastity barked. Sapphire jumped out of their way. "Ridder, you got any cuffs? These damn ho-dresses leave no room to hide 'em."

"In my car," Aston said and turned to Sapphire. "You. Don't move a muscle."

Sapphire stared after them as they moved toward the door with Paul in custody. She felt like a star who'd been upstaged.

It made sense. The LAPD had gone undercover to lure him out instead of using mass enforcement, which would've scared him off. The reason Chastity begged Giles to be on the wall was the same as Sapphire's—to become the next target.

Though it had worked out for the best and she was grateful she hadn't exposed herself to the cops, Sapphire felt deflated. Then again, she always felt that inexplicable disappointed at the end of a case.

"I'll be damned, Wilson," Aston said as they headed for the door. "They sent *you* for an undercover strip job? You must've really pissed off Chief Wendell."

"Tell me about it," she sneered. "He told me to make sure to keep my mouth shut so I'd pass for a lady. Can you believe that shit, Ridder?"

"Well…"

Paul screamed out, and his body plummeted toward the floor. The cop's grip was broken by the unexpected weight, and his hands slipped out. Paul army crawled on the floor then reached his hand out and slammed it down on the remote.

Chastity was about to jump on top of him when the room lit up in blinking red lights. The two cops knew exactly what was happening, and Chastity headed for the door, abandoning Butler on the ground.

Aston reached out for Sapphire, his body shifting toward her as he yelled out. Before he could take a full step in Sapphire's direction, his former partner's body plowed protectively into him, pushing him toward the door.

Paul Butler laughed in desperation, and the Golden Mirage exploded in a ball of fire.

· · ·

The force of the explosion sent Aston and Wilson flying out the door and across the street.

Aston could tell by their faces that the people outside the Golden Mirage were screaming, but all he could hear was loud ringing. He tried to stand but had no control of his body, so he lay like a vegetable on the pavement, staring at the Golden Mirage.

He knew this would happen. Perhaps not *this*, but something along these lines. The moment Barry woke him up at the hospital and told him Sapphire had jumped out the window, Aston knew she was about to put herself in a bad situation. She just couldn't help it.

Aston tried to focus his strength on regaining power of his arm. His fingers twitched toward the fire, trying to reach for her.

The world around him turned black, and the last thing he took in was the crumbling roof of the burning building, the woman he loved still inside.

CHAPTER 22

In the middle of the meadow sat a shabby door with cracks and scratches. It was held by nothing—suspended in air. Sapphire stared at the knob. She knew she was supposed to open it, but she couldn't bring herself to do it.

Aston appeared at her side and joined her in the stare down.

"What's behind it?" Sapphire asked, afraid.

"The truth," he said, grabbing her hand. He twisted the handle and the door opened, a black mouth waiting to swallow them.

The door slammed shut behind them and locked. Sapphire pulled back at the sight of the crimson motel room, but Aston held a firm grip on her hand.

Inside, her mother was dancing with her father. Like ghosts, they floated across the floor. Sapphire saw her young self in the corner, playing with the red toy.

"I've already been here. I've seen this. Can we go?" She pulled on Aston.

"Sometimes, we have to look twice to see what we missed the first time."

She forced herself to look again.

"That's not my mother." Sapphire had never seen this woman before. "Is that what I'm supposed to see? He was cheating on my mom, dancing with someone else?"

Aston slid over to her other side. "I don't think they're dancing."

Sapphire frowned and looked back at them. Sapphire's father's hands were clasped around the woman's neck. There was fear in her eyes. Her body was limp, paralyzed.

"He's killing her," Sapphire gasped. "We have to

do something!"

"You can't change it."

The room morphed. Instead of the bizarre, crimson-themed room, it turned into a regular motel room. The bed and the walls were white, and the carpet, beige. Every item in the room was spattered with blood. The woman's white dress was soaking in it, and her stomach was riddled by knife wounds.

When he was finished with her, Sapphire's father threw the woman's body on the bed. A purple mark lined her neck and her dead eyes aimed at Sapphire and Aston.

"My father killed someone."

"Come on, Sapphire." Aston looked at her as if she should know better. "Are these the actions of a man who's only killed once?" He nodded to the bed. "Or the actions of a man who kills often?"

"He's a serial killer." Sapphire whispered, warm tears burning her eyes.

Her father's head cocked to the side.

"You're not supposed to be here!" He shouted, his voice filled with panic. He was looking at young Sapphire. "I told you to always stay in your room."

Sapphire turned to her young self and watched as she sat in tears. She wasn't holding a red toy in her hands, but a knife. One dripping with blood. Her face, clothes, and hands were covered in red streaks.

Sapphire's father marched up to the child and yanked her into the connecting bedroom.

Aston led Sapphire to the room and pushed the door open.

After scolding her, her father's legs gave out under him, and he held young Sapphire's hands in his.

"I'm sorry I got mad," he whispered, wiping her hands clean of blood with a napkin. "I thought if I was careful I could have both worlds, but it's obvious now that I can't." He scooped her up in his arms. "You have to forget me, Sapphire. Forget everything you saw tonight. You can never talk about it, never think about it. It *never happened*. Do you understand me? *Never*."

The door slammed closed, and Aston looked at Sapphire

still holding her hand. "He's the one you've been trying to catch."

Snap!

.   .   .

Sapphire opened her eyes to a firefighter snapping his fingers above her. A delayed *snap* followed, forcing her to blink.

"There she is," he said, his lips moving before the words reached her.

Sapphire turned her head, realizing that she was on the ground outside of what used to be the Golden Mirage. All around her, people watched as the firefighters doused the smoldering ruins.

"You must have been blown right into the beer fridge because that's where we found you," the firefighter said. "You're lucky, too. If you hadn't, we wouldn't be having this conversation."

Sapphire looked down. Her hair and clothes were soaked in beer. Tiny cuts spread out over her arms where the broken bottles had sliced her.

"Aston," Sapphire said, her voice hoarse and hurting. Her eyes searched for him, frantically.

"I'm sorry, ma'am. He didn't make it." He pointed to a body covered in a white sheet.

Sapphire stared at it, her world crumbling. This couldn't be happening. Aston couldn't be gone.

"We just found him. I carried him out myself."

Sapphire shook her head, refusing to hear it, then stopped. Right before the explosion Aston was in the doorway; there was no way he was inside. The pure force would have blown him to the sidewalk.

"No!" she yelled, her voice straining. "The cop!"

"Oh, the cop. He's fine. Both the cops are a little banged up, but fine."

"Oh thank God, it was only Paul." A relieved laugh bubbled out of her.

The firefighter frowned disapprovingly.

"May he rest in peace," she added, replacing the smile with fake bereavement.

Aston was safe. Sapphire exhaled and felt her sanity return.

"The paramedics already left with the cops," the firefighter continued. "But they're on their way back for you." He wrapped a gray blanket around her before starting to walk off. "So don't move!"

Sapphire was just about to get up when Giles sat down next to her. The Golden Mirage sign hung loosely from a neon light bulb and finally snapped, crashing to the ground.

"I'm sorry you lost your business."

"Don't be sorry," Giles said, upbeat. "I never would have wished for this to happen, but I have quite the insurance."

"You're opening back up?"

A smile spread on Giles's lips. "No. We were a dime a dozen here in L.A. When you danced the other night to *Big Spender* I thought to myself, where did all the good old-fashioned dinner-dancing burlesque places go? That's what I will do, with a modern twist, of course. Um, I would offer you a job, but..."

"Don't worry, Giles. My dancing days are over," Sapphire chuckled but ended up in a coughing fit.

"So what do you think?" Giles gazed up. "Big lights that say *Misty's House of Burlesque*?"

"She would have loved that." Sapphire smiled, then saw the news van pull up. "Giles, can you give me a ride to the bus station?"

Giles nodded and they headed for his car. Sapphire thought about the things that had floated up from her subconscious.

She understood everything.

Sapphire's father wasn't like her at all; he was her *opposite*. The reason he had watched the police reports about certain killings wasn't because he wanted to do something about it like Sapphire, but to make sure he was still undiscovered. The reason he collected articles was because they were about his victims. They were his trophies.

To most people, realizing your own father was a serial killer would be considered traumatic news. Sapphire wasn't most people.

To Sapphire, it was a beacon of light shining down on the daunting dark basement of her subconscious, a place she'd feared to go. The light bullied the darkness away until the basement and its creepy qualities looked harmless.

Everything was so clear in Sapphire's mind. For the first time, she understood herself. There was a reason she hunted serial killers. She had been searching for *him* all these years. Subconsciously, her father was the killer she'd hoped to find every time she trapped someone. That was why she felt that inexplicable disappointment when she'd closed a case, because it wasn't him. It was so simple and obvious now. She felt like she'd known it all along.

Sapphire felt strong. She felt invincible with the knowledge and sense of peace it brought.

Plus, Paul was dead, meaning the rest of the girls were safe. Everything she just went through was worth it.

She sat down in Giles's car and looked up at the blue sky. She hadn't felt this serene since…ever.

Sure, the wedding was only days away, but she *would* figure out a plan to stop it.

Everything was going to be fine.

*　*　*

Things were about to get worse for the Serial Catcher.

Richard Martin smiled as he watched her—IT—Sapphire Dubois, from the alley. The woman whose vicious laugh he'd devoted months to quiet was finally within his reach.

Not yet, he had to remind himself.

She sat in the passenger seat of a man's car outside of the burning strip club looking infuriatingly pleased with herself. Her look was the same as the one she'd held when she captured him.

He knew what the look meant now. After shadowing her for awhile, he finally understood her. That understanding brought him a new course.

Richard had wanted to slit her throat like he did all the other women. This was no longer the case.

She wasn't like them. She was special, in the worst way. Richard's past and future no longer held any importance to him; the only thing that mattered was the demise of Sapphire Dubois.

He wanted to take everything from her the way she had taken everything from him.

He wanted to make her soul rot inside her body, the way she had made his.

He wanted to destroy her and he knew *just* how to do it.

CHAPTER 23

"I do," said John Vanderpilt.

All eyes were on Sapphire, waiting for her to return the two words. It was expected. They'd all come to hear the exchange of those two little words.

I don't.

"I do," Sapphire heard herself say.

"I now pronounce you husband and wife," the minister proclaimed, smiling at the couple.

They turned to face the applauding crowd and Sapphire felt the color drain from her face.

John leaned toward her, whispering into her ear as they started walking. "How do you feel, Mrs. John Vanderpilt?"

It had happened. She was really married to John. She was a Vanderpilt.

Sapphire stopped in the middle of the aisle. Aston stood among the crowd, staring at her, his face full of panic and pain.

Sapphire screamed and shot up in the darkness.

She wasn't Mrs. John Vanderpilt. She was safe in her bed. She took a breath, trying to calm her erratic heartbeat. *It's okay,* she told herself, *it was only a dream.*

Her bedroom door burst open, letting in the light.

"Up and at 'em!" Eloise sang. "It's your wedding day!"

She shut the door and Sapphire fell to her pillow.

Let the games begin.

• • •

"Sapphire," Eloise said. "Have a scone. You look a bit faint."

The elaborate breakfast on the sun deck looked tempting,

but Sapphire needed to stick to the game plan. "No, I don't feel well."

This plan would only stall the wedding until she could come up with something better. For the plan to work, it had to be pulled at the last minute.

Chrissy glanced at Sapphire from across the table, not looking too swell herself, then went back to her mimosa.

"It's just cold feet," Eloise brushed off. "Completely normal."

"I'm serious," Sapphire said. "I need to go to the hospital. I think we need to postpone."

Eloise's face withered. "This is the wedding of the season. You think I'll have my career ruined because 'you don't feel well'?"

Wanna bet? Sapphire was just about to drop to the ground and fake her way to the emergency room when the deck's door slid open.

"I'm ba-aack," Vivienne Dubois chirped, removing her sunglasses in a dramatic gesture.

Great, Sapphire thought. Next to Charles, Vivienne was the last person she wanted to deal with.

Sapphire's stepfather abruptly went to New York two days earlier, and his absence was the best thing that could have happened. She didn't think Charles would call the cops on her, but there was a possibility he'd throw her out or contact the nearest psych ward.

Unfortunately, he was due back soon. She was half-expecting him to burst in with two orderlies and a straitjacket with her name on it.

"Welcome home—" Sapphire started, ready for the standard let's-hide-our-messed-up-relationship air kisses.

"Is that a mimosa?" Vivienne walked past Sapphire and yanked the glass from Chrissy, taking it down in one sweep. "Thanks. The *spa* I went to refused to serve cocktails."

Sapphire didn't know that she actually had hopes for her mother's recovery until she felt disappointment at her guzzling the mimosa.

She glared at her mother who gossiped in a hushed voice with Eloise. Vivienne hadn't even made it past step *one*, acceptance. She was still in such denial that she couldn't even say the word *rehab*.

"Hello, Vivienne."

Vivienne's smile vanished along with the color in her cheeks. The flute glass slipped out of her hand and smashed to the ground.

"Long time, no see," Charles said with a bite in his tone. He leaned against the door frame, his hand in his suit pocket.

He was still old but closer to looking like his younger brother Gary instead of the corpse he'd been.

"Ch-Charles," Vivienne said. "You…how…what happened?"

Charles glanced over at Sapphire. Her eyes shot away, unable to meet his gaze.

"I signed for the new medical treatment," Sapphire said.

"You diiid?" Vivienne tried to smile.

Sapphire held back a laugh. She wasn't happy to see her stepfather at this very moment, but she enjoyed seeing him rub his health in her mother's face. It was payback.

Raul, Vivienne's driver, entered the doorway next to Charles. The young man's hair was in disarray and there were traces of Vivienne's burgundy lipstick on his neck.

"Mrs. Dubois," Raul said, "I placed the bags in your closet; would you like me to unpack them as well?"

"Yes, that will be all," Vivienne mumbled, unable to take her eyes off Charles.

"Oh come now, Vivienne. Tip the boy," Charles smirked. "I'm sure he's gone beyond his job description to…*satisfy* you. They always do, don't they?"

Vivienne's cheeks went from pasty white to flaming red.

"Sapphire," Charles said, "can we talk?"

"I can't. We're on a tight schedule."

"You have five minutes, but here," Eloise said, pushing a glass of OJ on Sapphire. "Take some juice at least, you'll need the energy."

Sapphire took it and rose from her chair realizing she would have to face him sooner or later anyway. Plus, so far, no orderlies in sight.

"Why did you go to New York?" she asked as they entered the upstairs lounge.

"I had some business with my lawyer, but that's irrelevant right now," Charles said, starting to pace.

As she sat down on the couch the tension lay thick around them like overcharged electricity waiting to explode.

Her stepfather settled by the window, looking out. "Did you know my father had frequent affairs?"

Sapphire shook her head and sipped her juice.

"One of his mistresses got pregnant and died in child birth. My father insisted the child should be raised in our house. My mother was accustomed to his indiscretions but feared the gossip that came with an illegitimate child."

Sapphire frowned, confused. Was she, or was she not, getting put in the loony bin for hunting serial killers?

"Gary and I were already adults and my mother, in her sixties; she knew she couldn't pass the child off as her own. So we pretended he was a distant relative brought to live with us. His name was William Dubois. Only the family and our lawyers knew the truth. My father was too old to handle a toddler, so William and I grew close over the years." He smiled out the window, his eyes misty.

"What happened?"

Charles came to sit by her. "He was caught doing something atrocious. Murder. We, the family, decided to cover it up to save our name. Then we disowned him. My mother burned every photo, every item belonging to him. He was shunned and tossed to the street. I was heartbroken and confused that the brother I loved so much could do something so evil. To the rest of the community, he was just the relative who went back to where he came from. To us, it was like he'd never existed."

Her stepfather's head sank toward his chest.

"After five years of silence, William called and begged me to care for two people in his place: his wife and child. So I did."

His face turned, and Sapphire's eyes fixed on his profile. "And though they never knew William was my brother, I married the mother and took in their daughter."

Sapphire stared at him, trying to grasp everything. "But my father's name was Will Green."

"Yes, that was one of his aliases. His birth name was William Dubois. You're a Dubois by blood." He opened his suit jacket and pulled out the picture he tried to give her the week before. "The man is me and the boy your father. It's the only picture I salvaged from my mother's bonfire."

Sapphire took the picture.

"You're my...uncle?" she said, shocked. "My father was your brother?"

"Half-brother, technically." Charles's voice was filled with pain. "I know I kept you at a distance when you were a child." Charles's gray eyes glossed with tears. "But I was terrified you'd turn out like him and that I'd lose you the same way I lost him. I planned on telling you everything once you were old enough, but then I had my stroke."

"So he's alive, right?" The white Audi flittered through her mind. Maybe he was keeping tabs on them. "Do you know where he is?"

"I don't." Charles looked at her with concern. "Don't try to find him, Sapphire. He's not a good man."

"Okay." He didn't believe her. She wasn't sure *she* believed her either.

"You're walking a thin line out there, Sapphire." He tapped the photograph. "*Be careful*...to not step into your father's path."

"Don't worry, Charles. He and I are as opposite as it gets." She felt overwhelmed.

"Either way, I love you. I've loved you like a daughter since the day I took you in. Whenever you need me, I'll be here for you."

Charles embraced Sapphire. She sat in shock as everything processed, not hugging him back, not moving at all.

Sapphire expected straitjackets, not this. She tried to hold back the tears, but they came anyway.

Julia loved the side Sapphire had chosen to show her but knew nothing of her abnormal obsession. Charles *knew* who she was and still loved her. She'd never imagined that to be possible.

Though she didn't need one at her age, she felt like Charles had offered to become the one thing she never had: a father.

"Now your mother on the other hand," Charles pulled back. "I'm not sure what to do with."

Sapphire wiped her tears.

Charles smiled. "It'll be my honor to walk you down the aisle today."

The pressure returned to Sapphire's chest. "Charles, about the wedding…"

"Yes?"

"Tick tock," Eloise said from the doorway. "Your five minutes are up. Makeup and hair will be here soon."

"We'll talk after breakfast," Sapphire said.

Charles went to his office to avoid Vivienne. He said he'd gone to see Mr. Goldstein in New York; a divorce was probably around the corner.

Sapphire set down the empty OJ glass on the deck's table, about to resume her fake fainting. After the wedding got postponed, Charles could help her come up with a better, more permanent plan. If he could deal with her hunting serial killers, he could deal with her not wanting to marry a Vanderpilt.

Sapphire ran her tongue over her teeth. "This wasn't a screwdriver, was it? It has an aftertaste."

"Just orange juice," Eloise said. "Well, and a few bars of Xanax to help with the cold feet."

"Xanax?!"

"Oh, don't worry," Eloise grinned. "I overdosed you a little, in a couple seconds you won't even care."

Sapphire knew she should feel angry, but calmness washed over her. She wasn't worried or panicked about anything.

She enjoyed the sunshine, the birds, and the little freckles on her hand.

"Sapphire," Eloise called from a rose colored reality. "How would you feel if World War III was around the corner?"

"I'm okay with it," Sapphire shrugged.

"And how do you feel about the wedding?"

"I'm okay with it."

"Excellent." Eloise and Vivienne shared a smile.

She understood that Eloise told Vivienne about Sapphire's "cold feet" and that the two had strategized. But she didn't care that she was a pawn in their game. Or that the wedding was only hours away.

Wedding schmedding, she smiled. There were more important things. Like the little freckles on her hand.

      •   •   •

"I have to pee."

"Then pick a tree," Aston said, adjusting the binoculars toward the deck.

"You're supposed to take me to a bathroom," Dylan insisted.

With everything in his head, Aston left for the chief's BBQ early. He needed something to distract him.

The chief had answered the door, still in his underwear, grumpy as fuck. Apparently, it wasn't okay to show up for a 1 p.m. party before sunrise. Or the Andersons—excluding their hyperactive son—just weren't morning people. The chief sent Aston and Dylan out to buy more corn, despite a fridge full of it.

Aston somehow drove past the farmer's market and ended up amongst the brushwood of the foothill above the Dubois Mansion. Since he had *accidently* grabbed his binoculars from the car, he figured he might as well use them.

"Why are we here?" Dylan asked looking around. "Daddy told you to get corn. Is there corn here? Where's the corn?"

"Good question," Aston sighed into the binoculars. It wasn't the wedding; he knew Sapphire wouldn't go through with it. So why were they here? For Sapphire? The Serial Catcher? Neither? Both? Corn? Not a clue. "I suppose…I'm looking for some kind of answer."

"I have to pee," Dylan whined again, dancing from side to side.

Aston spotted Sapphire on the deck. It wasn't the face he'd expected on someone who didn't want to get married. A genuine smile rested on her lips. Her face, her demeanor, was radiating bliss.

Aston's chest twinged and his heart fell. It fell all the way down his shirt, tumbling against his body, then through his pants and out his leg. He stared down at his major organ pasted in the dirt.

He'd been wrong. Really. Fucking. Wrong.

She *wanted* to marry Vanderpilt. In some way she must love the guy. Not him, but *that* guy. It took awhile for Aston's mind to reboot.

"Alright, kid," he said, stabilizing his voice. "Let's get you to a bathroom."

"I'm okay now," Dylan shrugged and took the binoculars.

Aston looked down at the kid's pants. His car was about to smell a lot less pleasant. "How do you feel about small spaces like, let's say, car trunks?"

"You guys are looking at *girls*? Yuck." Dylan grimaced behind the binoculars. "Don't you know they have cooties?"

"Yes," Aston agreed, "and that's why you always want to wrap up your Johnson."

"Who's Johnson?"

Aston frowned. "Did you just say 'you guys?'"

"You and him."

Aston followed the boy's finger. There was a man at the bottom of the hill. He had his back to them, staring up at the mansion and playing with something in his hands.

The sun hit the item, and its glare was unmistakable.

A *knife*.

"Hi!" Dylan shouted, waving.

"Shhh." It was too late; the man took off into the brushwood. "Stop! BHPD!"

Aston ran until his foot plunged into a rabbit hole and his bad leg snapped. He tried to continue the chase, until he realized he left Dylan alone with a madman running around. He had to go back.

Had it been a month ago, Aston would have assumed the man was just some random maniac, and the knife wasn't meant for Sapphire. And still, he realized, the knife wasn't meant for Sapphire, but for the Serial Catcher.

For the second time, Aston realized he'd been really fucking wrong.

He thought that Sapphire as the Serial Catcher made it less essential to bring her in. In reality, it was urgent that he did.

He *had* to stop her.

Not because it was wrong or illegal. If he didn't, Sapphire Dubois would be dead.

When he was in the hospital and found out that Sapphire had been safely pulled out of the Golden Mirage, he'd convinced himself she was out of harm's way.

But Sapphire Dubois would *never* be out of harm's way.

As long as she was the Serial Catcher, she would always be in danger and would end up dead. The stranger with the knife proved it.

It wasn't a matter of if, but *when*.

Aston loved her, and he would do anything to keep her safe. Even it meant he had to put her in jail.

Aston grabbed Dylan's hand and hopped back to the car. It would be excruciating to stand by and watch her marry someone else this afternoon, but he had no choice.

If he didn't go to the wedding, the man whose objective it was to kill her might just succeed.

CHAPTER 24

Sapphire snapped out of the happy-illusion haze she'd lived in and she found herself at the open French doors, staring down at the white aisle that led up to the altar in the country club's botanical garden.

She was in her Vera Wang, and John was standing at the end of the aisle in a tux. A crowd of three hundred well-dressed guests sat on the chairs below the stone staircase.

Sapphire turned to Eloise who was fixing her veil.

"You drugged me!"

"Oh darn it." Eloise checked the time. "I hoped they would last another thirty minutes."

Sapphire reared back in panic.

"Oh well," Eloise continued, placing something in Chrissy's hand. "You'll be over it by the time you're in the limo and on your way to your honeymoon."

Sapphire watched her unwilling bridesmaid, Petunia, pass by Charles at the bottom of the stairs. He was waiting to escort Sapphire to her death, otherwise known as John Vanderpilt.

Eloise and Chrissy placed the veil over her face and Sapphire watched her chest blossom in angry red hives.

"Now remember," Eloise said. "Gliiiide down the aisle. Gliiiide." She scurried off in her puffy dress.

Chrissy, her Maid of Honor, looked as sick as Sapphire felt. She squeezed whatever Eloise had given her and stared at the altar. Sapphire followed her gaze and stopped at John.

This was Sapphire's ultimate face off.

The marriage represented everything she was supposed to be and did not want. Saying *"I do"* wasn't an option. But opening her mouth to say no to a *Vanderpilt* was like screaming, *"I'm a witch!"* during the Salem Witch Trials.

Chrissy walked out and smiled like a beauty queen. Sapphire was next.

Her mind scrambled backward in frenzy, searching for a memory.

"When you're on your deathbed, looking back at your life, what do you want to look back on? A life you lived for someone else? Or a life you lived for you?"

Paul Butler may have been a serial killer, but it didn't make him less right. Sapphire didn't want to be an old woman named Mrs. John Vanderpilt. She didn't want to lay on her deathbed and hate the life she looked back on.

Since John went down on his knee, Sapphire had convinced herself that all she needed was a good plan. But she didn't need a scheme. She needed help. In order to get that she had to do the thing that scared her more than any serial killer.

Speak the truth.

"Come back," Sapphire whispered and people turned.

"I can't. I'm already walking," Chrissy hissed behind her smile.

"Please," Sapphire begged, lifting her veil.

Chrissy sighed and walked backward up the stairs, nodding and smiling to the confused guests below.

Sapphire closed the French doors and shut the curtains.

"What?"

Sapphire swallowed her fear. "I can't do it, Chrissy. I don't love him!" The pressure in her chest eased. "In fact, I hate him a little… Okay, I hate him *a lot.*"

Sapphire felt the burning hives retreat from her body.

"But he's a *Vanderpilt,*" Chrissy said suspicious, like she was being Punk'd. "I mean, seriously, the only worse thing you could do is walk away from a Kraft or a Rockefeller."

"I know," Sapphire kept going. "I still hate him, and his family, and his stupid Porsche."

Here Comes the Bride started playing. Chrissy stared at her. Sapphire's fear of the follow-up questions surfaced. Why would Sapphire hate a Vanderpilt? Was she abnormal? Did she capture serial killers?

"Well, THANK GOD!" Chrissy erupted.

"What?"

"I slept with John!" she blurted out.

"On purpose?!"

"It was the night after the rehears-rehearsal dinner when we couldn't find you. We went to a club and got so high that we barely remembered it the morning after. I tried to tell myself that it meant nothing, but I couldn't stop thinking about him, Sapphire! And I hate myself for it." Chrissy shook her head. "I tried *everything* to get my mind off it: avoiding you guys, shopping...well, that's really it, but it was a lot of effort."

Sapphire beamed. This was perfect. The Holy Grail of scandals.

"Please Chrissy, take the blame for me. I'll go out there, pretend that I'm going to marry him, and then when the minister asks 'does anyone object?' you say that you guys slept together. You're a *Kraft*, the gossip won't even last a month."

Chrissy was pulled between wanting to help her friend and social humiliation.

"Chrissy, I wouldn't ask you to do this, but it's my only way out. Also, you kind of owe me one for sleeping with my fiancé...slut."

Chrissy rolled her eyes. "Fine, but please tell me none of this is because you slept with that guy again. I mean, you're not giving up billions to get serious with a *cop* instead, are you? 'Cause seriously, Saph...*ew*."

"Well, I did sleep with him again, but that's not why." Sapphire drew a breath. "Though trust me, if I could be with Aston, I would."

They held hands and took a breath together, then opened the doors.

They were faced by a stunned crowd. John stared at them in shock. Everyone gawked at them, especially Sapphire. Vivienne looked like she wanted to kill Sapphire...and herself. Julia's thumb motioned over to the large speakers.

Sapphire looked at Chrissy. "What did Eloise put in your

hand?" She already knew. Her own words bounced back to her.

"It's the mosquito microphone. I was supposed to attach it to your dress when you got to the altar." Chrissy looked around at the echo of her voice. "What is that annoying sound?"

The crowd had heard *everything*.

Sapphire's eyes landed on Mr. and Mrs. Vanderpilt who were searing with hatred. She'd humiliated them in front of Beverly Hills' most superb. From this day on, the powerful pair would blacklist Sapphire from high society.

Though the botanical garden was hauntingly silent, Sapphire knew what was happening. The crowd was pointing at her, shouting: *"Witch! Witch! Witch!"*

By Beverly Hills standards, Sapphire Dubois was dead, and she knew it.

Then someone stepped closer to the crowd. He watched Sapphire differently than everybody else.

Aston.

Sapphire was socially bleeding to death and his presence was healing.

A smile grew on her face as she looked down on him. She hoped he'd heard her words. He smiled back, and in that moment, Sapphire felt as though everything was going to be fine. She didn't care about how the other 300 guests were looking at her, only this one. She wanted to run to him but, of course, she couldn't.

Or…could she?

Yes, she was still the Serial Catcher, but did she even care anymore? Wasn't being without Aston ten times harder than the complication of being with him?

Sapphire took the first step toward him, but whoever had kept them all on pause pushed play and all hell broke loose.

"You bastard!" John yelled and attacked Aston, who seemed delighted to fight him. They broke into a battle, tossing each other over dining tables, the six foot wedding cake, and finally into the fountain.

Chrissy was sniffing cocaine. Eloise sat in the puddle of her puffy dress, crying hysterically. Petunia laughed every time

Aston dunked John's head in the fountain. The rest of the crowd divided themselves up by family association and started screaming at one another. Even the ancient ones got into it, jabbing walkers at each other.

Charles was nowhere to be found. He'd probably escaped the mayhem.

Sapphire's eyes landed on Angelica Moore, who was pushing through the crowd, looking up at her with sympathy. She came up the stairs and grabbed Sapphire's hand. "Let's get you away from here. You look like you're about to cry."

They moved inside the club, leaving the chaos behind them.

"Did you come with Aston?" Sapphire asked, a bit out of it.

"Oh, no," Angelica said, rubbing her eye. "I didn't even know he was going to be here. I came with a mutual friend."

They walked through the hallway leading up to the Cigar Lounge. Sapphire glanced at Angelica.

"I have a weird question. You don't own a white Audi, do you?"

"What?" Angelica laughed. "No, I don't own a white Audi."

"Okay," Sapphire said, brushing away the thought.

Angelica's smile dropped. "I borrowed it."

Sapphire saw the punch coming, but the dress's off-the-shoulder straps kept her arm down and she couldn't block it. Angelica clocked her then shoved her against the door, locking Sapphire's arms in a cop grip.

"You greedy whore," Angelica roared. "You were engaged, but you just had to go after Aston. I watched you seduce him against his will at his father's house. He's mine."

Gross. Aston's father *had* seen someone.

"That's not what I heard," Sapphire said and brought her knee up to push Angelica back. She jumped to the side, keeping Sapphire's arms locked.

"You don't understand Aston the way I do," Angelica said. "He doesn't mean to reject me. He's only lying to himself. When he makes love to me, his body tells the truth of how much he loves me."

Wow. Sapphire's eyes widened.

"I know exactly what you're thinking," Angelica said studying her face. "Aston is lucky to marry her."

"Actually, it was more along the lines of: 'yikes, somebody should be medicated'." Sapphire struggled to get out of the grip.

"I'm not crazy! I don't need those pills any…" Angelica's eye twitched out of control. "…more." She let go of Sapphire to rub it.

Sapphire went to grab her and the dress's straps ripped. Angelica caught her and locked Sapphire's arm around her neck. She kicked open the doors to the Cigar Lounge and shoved Sapphire inside.

She tumbled to the ground and turned to face the doorway.

"She's all yours," Angelica smiled, closing the door.

. . .

Richard Martin stood with his back to the door facing the antique clock on top of the fireplace, feeling right at home in the midst of the luxury he'd grown up around.

He watched the Serial Catcher in the mirror above the fireplace, scrambling to lift her dress and get up.

The woman Richard ran into at the bar was a cop. She knew who he was and assumed by his sketch that she knew who he wanted to kill. She was right.

The cop offered him a deal. She wouldn't arrest him if he got *her* out of the way. He wasn't sure what the cop's thing was, but it seemed to involve someone named Ashton or Astein, the guy she said she was marrying. The deal would appear to be a win-win, but there was something the cop should have known. Never trust a killer.

The Serial Catcher stood and stared at him as if she'd seen a ghost. In a sense, she had.

"Hello, Sapphire Dubois." Richard smiled, tasting her name. "Remember me?"

Her white dress spread out as she leaned her back against the door. She could've run, but she was unable to shy away from the challenge like he knew she would be.

"Yes. We've already played this game," she said. "And if I recall correctly, *you* lost."

"Broken." Richard tapped the standstill clock. "Isn't it funny? All these places consider themselves crème de la crème, butthere's always imperfection to be found." He turned to face her. "Here, I would say it's you; you're the imperfection."

He paced, respecting the invisible line she had drawn. "I grew up like this, too, you know. On Park Avenue, surrounded by ignorant human beings."

"How did you find me?" Her face was straight.

"Destiny." Richard grinned. She was falling into *his* trap this time.

"Can we speed this up? I have a failed wedding to go back to, so tell me what you want? My head on a platter, I'm presuming?"

"At first, yes. But I've come to realize differently." Richard reached behind the couch and pulled the old man up. Gagged and bound, he moaned from the wound on the side of his head where Richard hit him. "I'm taking something from you since you took *everything* from me. I want you to watch your father die." He pulled his knife out and held it to the old man's chest.

Her eyes drew to the old man but revealed no emotion. She looked back at Richard, almost amused.

"Except that's not my father. I can see how you were confused since we have the same last name. That's my mother's husband." Her voice was icy, disconnected. "If you grew up like this, then I'm sure you know that relationships between stepfathers and stepdaughters are nonexistent."

Doubt hit Richard. He looked between Sapphire Dubois and the man he held by knife. "You're lying."

She shrugged. "Go ahead if you want to, but I studied you. I know you only take satisfaction in killing young women. I'm right here, so come get me instead. Unless you're…sca-wed?"

She was mocking him and he couldn't stand it. She was right. Killing men made him feel disgusting. He wanted to take the knife away from the old man and go after her. But, he realized, it was exactly what she wanted and would destroy his plan.

He pushed the blade to the old man's chest, piercing the

skin. The old man screamed behind his gag and she launched two steps forward.

"NO!" Her hand shot up.

Richard smiled. The girl had just realized he'd called her bluff. The power shifted back to him.

"Ever since that night I've done nothing but think about you standing over me in that…that *pit*," he spat in resentment, "with that look on your face and that *laugh*."

"Let him go." Her nostrils flared in distress.

"When I finally found you, boy was I surprised to see where you came from. I understood everything better than you can because I've already been there."

"What are you talking about?"

"That night, I saw it. You looked down at me so smug. You thought you were better than me. But you're not. You're in denial. I saw the darkness, the black hole you're trying to fill. It reached through your eyes. After months of analyzing you, I finally understood it. You're just like me."

"I'm nothing like you." Her face reddened. "I'm not a killer."

"Maybe not yet, but you will be. Just like me, you feel alive, as if you can finally breathe when you hunt, when you track. It's only then that your life has purpose."

"I'm not like you," she said, but her eyes told him different. "Let him go."

"You feel it right now, don't you?" Richard urged. "I see it in your eyes, the sickness rising within you, urging you to kill me, telling you how *good* it would feel."

She looked guilty.

"The day you evolve, you'll understand that you're supposed to give in," Richard continued. "You were born to do it."

"I know right from wrong. I'll never be like you."

"We'll see." Richard kept his eyes on her and smiled.

He drove the knife into the old man's chest and a muffled cry escaped him. With pleasure, Richard watched her heart shatter as he twisted the knife.

He let go and the old man fell face first to the floor,

gasping in pain.

Richard let the knife remain in the chest just like he'd planned. He backed off, waiting for the next piece to fall into place. He felt no fear.

The time had come. Finally, he would silence Sapphire Dubois.

* * *

Sapphire screamed as Charles's body hit the floor. Blood was gushing out of the slash in his chest and every muscle in his face spasmed from pain.

After that, everything happened fast, but to Sapphire, every second was an eternity.

She ran to him and removed the gag. She put the skirt of her dress on the wound to apply pressure around the knife. The blood was spitting out.

"I'm sorry," she cried.

Charles gasped for air and placed a red hand on her cheek. His eyes were filled with regret and panic. His thoughts were clear. He just started living again and wasn't ready to die. He wanted to stay, to hold onto life.

"I need you," Sapphire whispered, her voice breaking.

Charles's eyes welled with tears and his lip quivered as Sapphire held his gaze. His face drained of color and the pool of blood underneath him grew.

His hand fell to the floor. His strained breath ceased. His eyes remained open, but Charles's soul was gone.

Sapphire cried out as a thick pain tore through her chest. The grief ripped through her, leaving agony in its trail. She screamed to release the sorrow from her body, but like a parasite, it had found its new host.

She heard a laugh.

It was the laugh of the man who killed Charles.

Sapphire's grief was swallowed by a more powerful emotion. A hot anger grew stronger, feeding on the sorrow. It took over and Sapphire fell under its command. She wrapped her fingers around the knife's handle.

Somewhere in her shattered mind, Sapphire heard a door open, but it didn't register. All that mattered was Richard Martin's laugh.

Sapphire pulled the knife out of Charles's chest and rose to her feet.

"You killed him," she said in a strange deep voice she didn't recognize.

"No," Richard Martin said, "you killed him."

Sapphire launched at him. She grabbed him by the neck and drove the knife into his gut.

For a while there wasn't a sound. Not even their breathing. The room stood still. Even the dust particles froze in alarm over the event that had taken place.

When their eyes met, Sapphire understood what he had done. Even though he'd soon be dead, Richard Martin looked fulfilled, satisfied to his very core.

This was his plan all along. He made her into one of *them*.

The knife turned to shame and burned her hand. Sapphire threw it to the floor and backed up in shock. She felt like she'd left her body and now returned to find it covered in blood.

Richard fell to his knees and then to the floor. He remained still.

Sapphire turned to see Vivienne and Petunia standing by the side entrance in shock.

"Dear God, Sapphire," Vivienne gasped in denial. "You've completely *ruined* your Vera Wang!"

Sapphire couldn't get a word out. She remembered the sound of the door. Petunia and Vivienne entered at the exact moment when Sapphire pulled the knife out of Charles. To them, it looked like she killed them both.

"Sapphire," Vivienne said with a traumatized hollowness, "I think I need to go back to *rehab*...Raul!"

She left and Sapphire's eyes shot to her cousin. Petunia's expression drained of shock and filled with glee.

An evil, satisfied version of glee. She turned her heel and ran out. Sapphire knew exactly what her cousin was going to do.

"What the fuck!"

He had replaced Petunia in the doorway, the man Sapphire so badly wanted to be with, a witness to what she had done.

"Aston?" Sapphire whispered. There was no way she could explain it all.

Her world had changed forever in a few short moments. There was only one familiar thought that made sense.

Run!

*   *   *

Before Sapphire made the move he saw it in her eyes. He'd seen this look on so many guilty criminals before they ran.

The floor flooded with blood and she was covered in it. She had been involved in whatever went down.

"Don't—" Aston started.

Sapphire turned, opened the doors, and ran.

"Shit." He took off after her.

Aston chased her through the hallway where the guests had gathered to take back their wedding gifts.

"Move!" he yelled. The crowd stood frozen and watched the bride bolt past them in a blood-soaked dress.

Some people screamed, others fainted. Aston pushed through the crowd trying to get to her. "Sapphire!"

Her wedding dress slowed her down and Aston caught up. He was just about to tackle her when someone grabbed him.

"No. No. No. It wasn't supposed to happen this way!" Officer Moore's fingers dug into his arms.

"Move! I don't have time for this!"

"How are we supposed to get married if you keep acting like this?!"

"Marri—*What!?*"

Moore pointed to her hand. The missing piece of Aston's Dodgers shirt had been tied around her finger to look like a ring. Officer Fatso's words echoed in his mind.

"Ridder, congrats, I just heard!"

Laura, the receptionist, had told him he'd said. Moore's friend.

Aston saw Sapphire shove the doors open. He tore Officer Moore off him and ran.

"Aston!" Officer Moore yelled as he reached the doors.

Aston wasn't sure what made him turn. It could have been instinct or the sound of a Smith and Wesson being cocked.

"What are you doing?" Aston asked, staring at the gun in Moore's hand.

"I warned you." Moore's eye twitched. Her face burned with hatred and her body shook with jealousy. "I told you to be careful with her, so you wouldn't get hurt."

"Moore…" Aston tried to calm her.

"*Angelica*," she corrected and pulled the trigger.

CHAPTER 25

Sapphire was going 100 miles an hour down the 405.

Her eyes strayed to the mirror again, expecting to see Aston's car, and his tag-along cops. The only people chasing her were angry drivers trying to catch up to give her the finger for cutting them off.

When she burst out of the country club she'd spotted the limo meant to take her and John to the airport and their honeymoon. The windows were down, the keys in the ignition, and Sapphire didn't think twice before she took it. She sped away from Beverly Hills without direction.

Sapphire grabbed her phone again.

"Call Father O'Riley!" He was the only one not connected to her Beverly Hills life. Maybe she could hide there.

"Father O'Riley is out of the coverage area."

"He's not! Search yellow pages, match, and call Father O'Riley *home*."

"The number has been disconnected."

Sapphire yelled and tossed her phone to the spacious back seat.

It didn't matter, she realized. She needed to get out of California all together. She needed to get as far away from Beverly Hills as possible.

A gap opened up ahead and she floored it, trying to see through the side mirror. She'd ridden in plenty of limos but had never driven one. The rearview mirror was useless and hard to navigate.

She pulled to change the lane. A car came out of nowhere, crashing into her side, taking her side mirror. Sapphire swerved too hard for her speed, and the steering wheel spun on its own, sending her into a loop. A truck smashed into the rear, pushing her to the shoulder.

Sapphire held onto the wheel as the limo came to a stop. Shock took over and she stayed motionless. She couldn't move. Her hands were fused to the wheel.

She was breaking. She could feel the tears coming. She tried to breathe, to keep it together, but no air reached her lungs, all she managed were short gasps. She let her head fall down to the wheel as the light headedness grew.

"Oh my God. Oh my God. Oh my God." The negative mantra spilled out of her. She had never felt more alone.

The man she wanted to be with was probably about to put her in jail for murder. Charles was dead and the sorrow of never seeing him again was excruciating. She's trade anything for a chance to see him one more time. She wanted to hold him tightly and beg for his forgiveness.

Because of Petunia, everybody would think Sapphire killed him, even her own mother. In a sense, Sapphire had killed him. She hadn't held the knife, but it was her actions that drove somebody else to do it.

Sapphire cried, her lungs wheezing. She had nobody. No money. No answers.

The wall she'd built to keep Beverly Hills and the serial killers separated had collapsed. There wasn't a way to put it back together. She couldn't return home, and she had nowhere else to go. This was Sapphire's apocalypse.

She raised her tear-filled eyes to the rearview mirror, looking at the destroyed figure in the reflection. Her eyes drew to the champagne bottle in the back. It had been meant for her and John to celebrate with.

Her eyes refocused and saw it.

The message was so clear that it seemed as though it was surrounded by a divine aura.

Her way out.

• • •

Aston knew he was bleeding to death on an operating table in the E.R. He also knew he was under anesthesia but he could hear everything. He even heard them drop the bullet into the metal bowl, a bullet that Aston had coming. It was karma for all his women over the years. He'd always figured something like this would happen one day.

"Blood pressure's dropping," a stressed female voice announced.

His mind was present where his body was located, but some part of him traveled back to the wedding, the moment Sapphire stood on top of the staircase and smiled down at him.

"If I could be with Aston, I would." Her voice sang through the speakers.

At that moment, she hadn't been the Serial Catcher. None of the baggage that kept them apart existed. It felt like they would walk out of there together, not worried about the obstacles that would come.

"We're losing him," the female said, this time with urgency. A dragged-out beep from a machine followed.

Losing him? He wasn't going anywhere. Aston had shit to do. The important kind.

When Sapphire headed out those doors, he knew she wasn't just running to escape the heat of the moment. It was...it was...

"Clear!" a male voice yelled.

Yes, it was clear, she would keep running.

"He's gone," the female voice said. "Doctor, let him go. He's dead."

Dead? Fuck that.

Aston didn't have time to be dead. He had to wake up, walk out of that hospital, and find her. He didn't care what he had to do or where he had to go. He would search the whole freaking planet if he had to, and he wouldn't stop until he reached the World's End.

"Clear!" The male voice was defiant.

If Aston did reach the World's End, Sapphire would be standing there, waiting for him with a mischievous smile.

"What took you so long?" she'd say.

He'd swear at her for making him walk all the way to the World's End. Then he'd take her and never let go.

Aston Ridder had never followed orders, and he wasn't about start now. He simply refused to be dead.

The machine's sound changed again. "Doctor, we've got a pulse."

* * *

Sapphire pushed past the crowd scrambling to get to baggage claim. She'd stolen a sundress from someone's outside clothing line and washed up in a restroom at a gas station. The people hustling by her would never have guessed that less than twelve hours ago she'd looked like a cross between Carrie and Mrs. Havisham.

When she saw her and John's pre-prepped passports and honeymoon tickets next to the champagne bucket, she knew it wasn't only the right choice, but her only option.

The long plane ride had been horrible. There was nothing to do but think. It was like squeezing months of mourning into just one night. She felt sick from it now and her body had gone numb to filter the pain.

Sapphire headed for the exit as she turned her phone back on. She slowed up until the cart transferring luggage to Dubai was close enough, then slipped it into someone's duffle bag.

"Good riddance," she mumbled. In case Aston figured out a way to trace her phone, it would lead him to the Middle East.

She was in no rush, yet she hurried out through the revolving doors and up to the railing across the airport.

The alien city spread out in front of her, blanketed in early morning darkness. Sapphire closed her eyes feeling the heavy sorrow rip her apart again. She could never change what had happened, no matter how much she wished; Charles would never come back. He, along with the only life she'd ever known, lay in destruction behind her, a wasteland after an atomic bomb.

The thought of never seeing Aston again cut through her chest like a razor.

Aside from losing Charles and the other bad *thing* that happened in that room, it was hard for her to take that Aston had witnessed Sapphire at the worst moment of her life.

She clutched the railing. This dark unfamiliar place below her, where she knew nothing and no one, was now her life. When she woke up the next morning it wouldn't be to Julia's phone call, Vivienne's voice, Chrissy's friendship, Aston's piercing blue eyes, or—worst of all—Charles's lopsided smile. She *had* to accept it, no matter how much it hurt.

"Um, Ex-cew-say…" an older man with his back to her asked a cab driver. His hat, Hawaiian shirt and shorts, made his American nationality obvious.

The cab driver took off, ignoring the man.

"Aw, come on," the old man said, turning.

"Oh my God…" Sapphire gasped. She blinked, unable to believe her eyes. It was really him. She had never been so happy to see anyone in her life.

"Sapphire?"

She lunged at Father O'Riley and hugged him. She held on as she laughed in relief. Then all the panic, fear, and regret surfaced.

"Wait, are you laughing or crying?" he asked, patting her back.

"Both." Sapphire let go to wipe her tears. "HOW are you even here?!"

"Because of you," Father O'Riley said. "Remember when you said, I wasn't happy where I was and I should leave?"

"That was sarcasm."

"I know, but it made sense. I'd been struggling with my faith ever since the…you know…"

"Boning," Sapphire nodded.

He gave her his look of disapproval. It felt nice, familiar.

"Anyway, I sent a request to Vatican City, thinking, what better place to reaffirm my faith than the Catholic capital?" His eyes sparkled.

"You're going to Rome? Then what are you doing *here*?"

"I haven't been in this part of the world since I was a kid

so I've been traveling for a bit. I just came from Berlin. This is my last stop. I wanted to have some fun before I lock myself up with the monsignors. They're not the most chipper bunch, you know."

Sapphire's phone had been right. Father O'Riley had been out of the calling area. *Way* out.

"Why didn't you say goodbye?"

"If it makes you feel better, I just took off, didn't even bother telling my brother." He studied her. "What are *you* doing here?"

As Sapphire told him everything—the good, the bad, the ugly—they watched the city below starting to rouse.

"So that's it," she finished, feeling a lump clog her throat. "My life is gone. It's...dead."

Father O'Riley rubbed his chin, eyes on the rising sun. "Sure, that's one way of looking at it."

"Are you *kidding*? What other way would there possibly be of looking at it?"

He got that look. He was going preachy on her.

"You see, Sapphire, when the Blessed Virgin Mary went to—"

"No."

"When God said—"

"No."

He sighed. "I'm trying to tell you about rebirth."

Father O'Riley's wise eyes beamed with calmness. "Ever since I've known you, you've lived two lives. The life you were born into and the life you chose. Despite the terrible circumstances, it was the life you never wanted that you lost."

Sapphire gazed out over the city glowing in the sunrise, realizing he was right. Never again would she have to sit through an event and pretend to be someone she wasn't. Never again would she have to think: *Run!*

This time, Sapphire *did* run.

"Do I agree with the danger you put yourself in? No," Father O'Riley said. "But I know how much it means to you, and this is your chance to go be whoever it is you want to be."

Sapphire looked at the Eiffel Tower and the ancient French

metropolis around its feet, seeing it in a different light.

Paris was a city of adventure; a place roaring with opportunity for people to come and start anew. The years past dropped off her like weights, leaving only one.

Aston.

Sapphire had a strong feeling that he would cross her path again. He wouldn't give up on her; he never had before. Nothing would stop him. Not Dubai. Not the ocean separating them. On the logical side of her brain, the thought made her want to run faster. On the emotional side, the thought brought bliss.

Aston *would* find her. Until that day, she would do something she'd been dying to do. She hadn't even realized how badly her insides had been screaming for it until now. Sapphire was going to live for *her*. Nobody else.

The pain inside her wasn't gone, but gaining a freedom she'd never had before was remarkably curative.

"Sapphire, come on!"

Father O'Riley had grabbed his luggage and was waving at her from inside a trolley.

Sapphire ran as the cart started rolling, then grabbed the side bar and jumped aboard. She got two seats as Father O'Riley paid their fees.

She noticed a woman finishing the newspaper about to throw it in the trash.

"*Excuse-moi*!" Sapphire said. "*Tu as fini?*"

"*Oh, mais oui.*" The woman passed the newspaper, waving at her to keep it.

"*Merci bien*," Sapphire smiled, then turned to face a stunned Father O'Riley.

"You speak French?"

"No one graduates Winchester Private Academy without being at least semi-fluent," Sapphire said, flipping through *Le Parisien*. "Well, except Chrissy."

Her eyes landed on an article and didn't stray.

"Good, then you can navigate us," he said and sat down. "I've got three days before the Vatican expects me. Let's start with the Loo-ver...Loafer..."

Father O'Riley's continuous butchering of The Louvre became one with the background noise as she felt the familiar rush. Her senses sharpened and mind focused. Everything around her vanished; everything but the article.

Sapphire Dubois smiled, knowing the hunt had begun.

EPILOGUE

William Dubois stared at the woman whom he'd taken from the Beverly Hills Country Club. She knew she was going to die and she couldn't do anything about it.

Her body was paralyzed, but her mind was alert. It had taken him years to develop the concoction from hemlock, a plant with immobilizing toxins.

He turned up the music from the motel's radio and grabbed his knife. William smiled at the panic in her eyes, happy he'd taken her.

He'd watched the country club through the gates, hating the fact that he admired the building. He'd spent the last two-and-a-half decades away from luxury, living off nothing but odd jobs to pay for his crappy motel rooms, which had rats under the floors and dead hookers in the walls. They were *his* dead hookers, but still.

Watching the people of Beverly Hills always filled him with disdain. He enjoyed catching glimpses of his daughter and ex-wife, but he couldn't wait to get on the road and have this place that had forsaken him at his back.

He returned every so often to check on them. It wasn't until his daughter turned twenty that he noticed her extracurricular activities. She, his little Sapphire, captured serial killers. *His* people. She'd grown up to become his polar opposite; his enemy.

Was it a coincidence? Probably not.

When he left Sapphire and Viv all those years ago, he wanted nothing more than for his daughter to be raised far away from his world. Away from the place where knives, blood, and darkness rose so high in the sky that it was hard to see the sun some days. Yet there she was, diving in headfirst.

He just happened to show up to the country club on Sapphire's wedding day. Except, from what he could tell, she never got married. She'd rushed out of the doors and drove past him in the limo, unaware that her father was watching her.

He didn't blame her for splitting on the groom. The Vanderpilts, though extremely wealthy, were terrible people. Not terrible like William, but terrible nonetheless.

He thought about following her then a guest screamed Charles was dead. It was his brother, the one who had sacrificed a life with a family of his own to care for William's.

Had he the capability, William would have wept. He always liked Charles the most, even when he joined the rest of the family in kicking William out for stabbing the maid.

What would happen to his ex-wife and Sapphire? Who would take care of them now that Charles was gone?

Him? Not a chance in hell.

He felt something akin to—what he assumed was—love for them, but he had proven to himself years ago that he was a killer, and a killer only. A father and a husband he would never be.

He watched as the young woman with golden curls came out in tears. The Vanderpilt Sapphire was supposed to marry was hugging her to his shoulder. Comforting her as she bawled the way humans did when they got so very emotional.

William felt the dig in his stomach. The Hunger wanted her.

She cried harder, and he recognized her. It was Christina Kraft. He couldn't kill Sapphire's best friend...could he?

The Hunger egged him on and explained how easily Sapphire could get a new friend.

"No." William tried to hold his ground. He didn't want to cause his daughter more sorrow. She'd just lost Charles.

The Hunger muttered, then stayed silent.

William was just about to jump in his car and leave California when he saw her. She was working her way toward the gates by foot, dialing her phone.

"Take her," The Hunger demanded. *"Feed me."*

He couldn't wait to get out of Beverly Hills, but The Hunger grew too strong and overpowered him. He got in his car and parked around the bend of the country club's stonewall.

He could hear her talking on her phone as he waited, hoping she'd tide him over until he got out of L.A. County.

"You won't believe what happened at the Vanderpilt wedding…" she said into her phone. "A cop got arrested for shooting another cop, and two people got stabbed to death!" She turned the bend and William readied himself. "Guess who stabbed them!"

He put his hand on the door handle, watching her through the tainted glass.

"Sapphire Dubois!"

William froze, missing his cue.

"The cops are looking for her right now."

He opened the door and got out.

"My account is going to blow up the minute I tweet this: Heiress Sapphire Dubois wanted for murder!"

"Excuse me?" He prepared his most charming smile.

She turned, took one look at him, and melted. "I…I'll call you back." She hung up and blushed.

They all blushed. He had that effect on women. In his profession it helped.

"So sorry to bother you, but my car won't start and my phone's out of battery." He kept the smile on. "Do you mind terribly if I use yours?"

"N-no, go ahead," she giggled and hurried up to him.

He looked at her as if she was the only person in the world and her breaths grew heavier.

"Beautiful, they suit you." He nodded to her ugly earrings. "Do you mind?"

She let out a nervous laugh and moved her hair away so he could touch her ear.

William put the needle in her neck. Within a few seconds the hemlock had turned her body into stone, allowing him to toss her in the trunk.

He drove her to the cut-rate Motel 6 off the interstate and

used one of his fake driver's licenses to get a room. He got the woman and all her accessories inside, still feeling the adrenaline her words created.

He'd failed to see the truth in Sapphire all these years. The apple hadn't fallen far from the tree after all. It was surprisingly exhilarating. William had never thought he could have both worlds, but if his daughter was like him, he could have it all.

He kept the woman alive over night, refilling her with hemlock, preserving her until The Hunger was screaming for her. The way it did now.

Her terrified eyes stared at William as he raised the knife over her stomach and stabbed her. Again and again, he plunged his knife into her, meticulously choosing his spots so that she wouldn't die prematurely. He had to finish her off by strangling. The Hunger loved the two-for-one, always had.

He pulled back, out of breath, patting his hair in place.

"Hrrr," came from her frozen lips. Her face stayed smooth, but he knew she was in excruciating pain.

He dragged her off the bed and held her up by the throat, pushing in on her jugular. He watched the panic rise in her eyes and something amazing happened.

Within her, he saw all of them.

Her expensive hairdo, accessories, and dress screamed of the people who'd abandoned him. He pushed harder, feeling his anger grow, then ease as the life drained from her. To think he'd avoided the Beverly Hills people all these years.

She took her last breath, and William shoved her dead body back onto the bed. He picked through her thick Louis Vuitton wallet.

"Great. I was running low on cash, so thank you…" William studied her ID. "Eloise."

Eloise Parker. 2053 N. Beverly Glen, Beverly Hills, California, 90210.

The perfect lair.

William's direction had changed and his new future played out for him.

He wouldn't leave until his daughter had joined his world.

He would take Sapphire under his wing and show her everything she needed to know about The Hunger that ran through her veins.

William Dubois smiled. The prodigal son had returned. His revenge was just beginning.

ACKNOWLEDGMENTS

First of all, I'd like to thank that warm night in April of 1986. Without it, my parents might've never felt frisky, I would never have been born, and would never have gotten the opportunity to thank all these wonderful people.

I, like a fool, forgot to do acknowledgements for the first book in the Sapphire Dubois Thriller Series, so please consider the following to be for both *Stalking Sapphire* and *Silencing Sapphire*.

Had I not started with the inappropriate story of my own conception, I would've started by thanking the person who changed my life forever and made all this possible. To my dear agent, Elizabeth Kracht, who has gone above and beyond her job description with me and Sapphire. Liz, when I think of a strong, modern woman, I think of you. You're a role model and I look up to you immensely. I'm well aware that many authors claim their agents to be the best. Obviously, they only think so because they've never encountered the complete package of kindness and force that is Miss Kracht. I, undoubtedly, have the best agent in the world.

Thank you to Mary Cummings, my freakishly talented editor at Diversion Books. Mary, I've never come across a person who understands story and character as well, and as *fast* as you do. I often find myself wishing I could keep you around for the whole of the writing process, but, apparently, kidnapping is illegal.

Thank you to the marketing and publicity manager at Diversion Books, Angela Craft, also known by her superhero name: the social media savior. Many of the amazing things that have happened, pre and post-publication, are because of you. Thank you for always answering my questions and for rescuing me when I don't have a clue what I'm doing.

Thank you ALL at Diversion Books, the kindest and coolest publishing house in New York. A special, giant thanks to Sarah Masterson Hally!

Thank you to my husband, Chadley, who read, read again, and read the manuscripts some more. You're my rock, my best friend, and my life, without your support and creativity none of this would've happened.

To my parents, Ylva and Mats, who moved mountains to send me halfway across the world so I could chase my crazy dream: Thank you for *never once* telling me to give up, be responsible, and get a real job. *Tack*!

To my sister, Linda, aside from that one time you tricked me into eating horse food, you have always been the best big sister. Thank you for reading and loving my stories—especially the bad ones—and for cheering me up after rejections.

Big thanks to my husband's family, the whole Thompson clan. Faye and Bruce, you've fed us, sheltered us, and pulled us out of way too many binds. Skylar, my fabulous niece, your input on Stalking Sapphire made a world of difference.

Thank you, *tack*, to my third grade teacher in Sweden, Kerstin Truedsson for telling a nine-year-old she should be an author; your words stuck. Thanks to my grandparents, *Mormor, Morfar, Farmor, Farfar*. I have a feeling you're supporting me from The Great Beyond. Thanks to ALL my bosses and coworkers—especially the lovely girls at Binion's—for you encouraging words and for putting up with my general peculiarness.

Lastly, thank YOU dear reader! Whether you just picked up the sequel or came back after reading *Stalking Sapphire*, I'm so glad you did. I wish I knew your name so I could thank you personally but, until I gain psychic powers, just know I'm eternally grateful that you chose to come along on Sapphire's adventures.